BAD DATE

A Jane Yeats Mystery

Liz Brady

Second Story Press

National Library of Canada Cataloguing in Publication Data

Brady, Elizabeth
Bad date : a Jane Yeats mystery

ISBN 1-896764-38-X

I. Title.

PS8553.R24B32 2001   C813'.54   C2001-930731-4
PR9199.3.B72B32 2001

Copyright © 2001 by Liz Brady

Edited by Charis Wahl
Copy Edited by Laura McCurdy
Cover ©2001 and Book Design by Stephanie Martin

Printed and bound in Canada

*Second Story Press gratefully acknowledges the assistance of the
Ontario Arts Council and the Canada Council for the Arts
for our publishing program.
We acknowledge the financial support of the Government of Canada
through the Book Publishing Industry Development Program
(BPIDP) for our publishing activities.*

Published by
SECOND STORY PRESS
720 Bathurst Street, Suite 301
Toronto, Ontario
M5S 2R4
www.secondstorypress.on.ca

This book is for Patrick, ghost buster and super hero ...

> Children know the grace of God
> Better than most of us. They see the world
> The way morning brings it back to them,
> New and born and fresh and wonderful ...
> — ARCHIBALD MACLEISH
> "J.B."

ACKNOWLEDGEMENTS

THE MATERIALS QUOTED in Chapters 21 and 23 originally appeared on the Web site, "DOWNTOWN VANCOUVER-eastside" (www.missingpeople.net), created by Wayne Leng and dedicated to the memory of his friend, Sarah deVries, and to all the other missing and murdered Downtown Eastside women. I have altered these materials as my narrative demanded. Wayne Leng's devotion to Sarah exemplifies the tenacity of love and righteousness.

I am grateful to Charis Wahl for superlative efforts to fight my prose misdemeanours (her generosity and wit are rich parentheses enclosing her editorial craft); to Margie Wolfe, my publisher, for surviving with grace an industry under pressure; and to the Ontario Arts Council, Writers' Reserve program, for a grant that enabled me to finish this book.

For friendship and support, I am deeply indebted to Bob Brandeis, Lisa Brandeis, Lena Iannaci, Lucy Robinson, Wendy and Gerry Rogalski, Lea Rossiter, Shelagh and Dave Wilkinson. You are my bridge over troubled waters.

AUTHOR'S NOTE

For the past seventeen years I have lived in Toronto's Little Italy, the only place in my peripatetic existence I have come to know as "home." The characters in this novel described as residents or business people are fictitious and bear no factual relation to real persons in my neighbourhood.

If I make the lashes dark
And the eyes more bright
And the lips more scarlet,
Or ask if all be right
From mirror after mirror,
No vanity's displayed:
I'm looking for the face I had
Before the world was made.
— W. B. YEATS
"A Woman Young and Old"

Chapter 1

EARLY THIS MORNING my next-door neighbour got dispatched to glory. Her shrieks surely penetrated our common wall. Had I not been pole-axed by debauchery, I might have dialled 911 and saved Tina's life.

A less bibulous person might label my profound slumber a 'blackout.' My conscience settled on 'prolonged narcolepsy.'

Having gone to bed with chestnut hair and awakened with white, I had dragged my bones straight to the shower — along with my dog, Max, whose black coat was also caked with plaster dust. The renovator had walked out when my bank account hit $208.07, leaving my row house with a concept as unresolved as a transsexual in mid-alteration.

Clean hair still dripping, I was brewing a revivifying pot of Continental Dark as Max, pedigreed hound of Hell, stopped shaking the water from his fur and set up an unholy wail in response to pounding on my front door. Through the frosted glass I recognized the snowy hair and broad, black-draped shoulders of the beatific Nina, the elderly widow who lives in the house south of mine.

At that ungodly hour I hadn't yet come to voice. To discourage conversation, I opened the door only a crack.

"*Madonna, Madonna,*" she wailed. Definitely the wrong door.

She tried again. *"Polizia, polizia,"* flinging an ample arm in the direction of my garden.

All summer long she'd complained about the goldenrod, in my view a fetching background for her rose bushes. Sure, choose sun-up on Sunday to threaten me with the weed police. I looked towards the offenders. Then I grabbed the phone and screamed at the 911 dispatcher, "There's a dead body in my weeds!"

Designated crime scenes happen on *DaVinci's Inquest*, not in my front yard. Yet plastic barrier ribbon garlanded my fence, fluttering the yellow warning: 'POLICE LINE — DO NOT CROSS.' The first cops on the scene had quickly secured the site (roughly the size of a dog kennel), and rerouted traffic around my short block. The coroner declared the victim dead. The Ident team were searching outside the tape.

I'd been ordered to remain inside, where I nursed a case of shock, in addition to the usual hangover. In lieu of a drink, I offered up a variation of one of the lovely prayers to Saint Dympna — for fortitude:

Courageous St. Dympna, in your kindness help me to imitate your example in all matters relating to the police, and gain for me fortitude to bear with the misfortunes I meet at their hands and at those of other assholes, and strength to overcome my weakness in wanting to strangle them all. Amen.

Untroubled, Max circled his blanket, flopped down in a relaxed fetal curl, and began to snore.

Detective Lou Sandford stood with his back to the room, observing the ritual in progress beyond my fly-specked window. A technician was taking photos. The dazzling flash momentarily backlit Sandford's mammoth body, which blocked both the daylight and the cruel interrogation of my property.

"How did you become aware of the deceased's presence?" he asked, without turning to face me.

"My next-door neighbour, Nina Moretti, banged on my door. When I saw what was making her hysterical, I called 911."

I reached for a cigarette.

"Can you identify the victim?" Now he was scrutinizing my face.

"You mean go out there and actually look at it?"

"I mean, did you recognize the victim *before* you called Emergency?"

"No way. I just took a quick glance. She was naked, so white ... so dead. When I saw the flowers, I panicked. It didn't even occur to me to check if she needed help."

Sandford walked to the door. "Please follow behind me in my steps. We want as little of the scene disturbed as possible — rain's already washed away a lot of the evidence. Take a good look and tell me if you can identify the body."

I trailed him in numb compliance.

Two detectives were knocking on doors across the street. A third was studying the sidewalk in front of the house north of mine so intently he might have been hunting for dandruff. Another was writing or drawing in his notepad, as the photographer paused to let me view the body without the distraction of his flash gun. Standing on the narrow concrete walkway leading to my house, I glanced over the wrought iron fence, scrunching up my eyes the way I did as a kid during horror matinées at the local cinema.

The corpse looked no more terrifying than a Modigliani nude in serious distress. Gradually I relaxed my eyelids, fully taking in the first dead person I'd ever seen outside a coffin.

Tina Paglia appeared to have been dumped like so much

garbage. Just yesterday her big bleached hair, bold makeup, sprayed-on miniskirt and fuck-me stiletto heels had advertised her in-no-way-respectable but in-your-face vulgarity. This morning she was smaller than I remembered, her wan form almost shrinking into the damp soil. I wished for a blanket to cover her.

Her limbs were flung out in the careless abandon of a nude sunbather, crushing the huge hosta on which she'd landed. A slug slithered into a nostril. A few stray maple leaves were held in the pool of congealing blood around her throat. The dark roots near her scalp now were closer in hue to the wet hair beside her face. Dried blood veiled her blue-tinged features. A fine scar from below one blank eye to her chin line. Left arm pocked by track marks. A pouchy slackness about the belly. Legs carelessly shaven, a few razor nicks, a missed patch of hair above the right ankle.

Her mouth sprouted a handful of black-eyed Susans.

Shock drove my mouth into auto-drive. "That's my next-door neighbour, Tina Paglia. She lives in the second-floor apartment," I said, gesturing at her windows to the north. "The ground floor apartment is empty. They moved out after Tina moved in, about a month ago."

Sandford looked undisturbed by the ghastly spectacle. Maybe violent death becomes as routine as donuts. "Had you gotten to know her?"

"Yeah, sort of ... better than I wanted to. The way she lived made me crazy. Non-stop noise, twenty-four hours a day. TV, music, screaming, sex, more sex. Weekly fights with her dealer, daily fights with her boyfriend. Clients after midnight. I heard it all through the party wall. There's no brick between us." Nerves drove me to babble.

"Her lifestyle must have made you crazy. Like, did you

bang on the wall, speak to her about it, complain to her landlord?"

"All of the above." That I might be a suspect hadn't yet entered my muddled brain. "Someone down the street complained to you guys about her Friday night. The beat cop there was the first one to answer the call, along with his partner, a woman. I think his name's Macintosh." I glanced towards the street, where a coven of spectators had forsaken 8:00 a.m. Mass at St. Francis of Assisi to watch the crime-scene team — and me. "Hey, can we go back inside? I feel like I'm on *Jerry Springer*."

My interrogator summoned Constable Macintosh into the house. "Hi, Jane," he greeted me, with guileless spontaneity.

"Macintosh, am I right in assuming that you also recognize the victim?" barked his superior, reclaiming the sociable young cop's attention from my nipples, alert with embarrassment under my T-shirt.

"Sure, she's well known to us. Tina Paglia. Worked the Parkdale track for years. Druggie. Lots of busts. Done a few stretches at the Metro West Detention Centre. We've been keeping an eye on her lately because she's been trying to work College Street. The local residents' association is on our case."

Sandford's sour expression hinted that residents' associations gave him as big a pain in the ass as hookers. "So what was the complaint against her Friday night?"

"Quasimodo, her dealer, also known to us, had been bashing at her front door, flinging stones at the upper windows, and shouting at her to let him in. The neighbours got fed up listening to the uproar. We figured that she owed him some money or maybe screwed him on a deal and he showed up to settle the score. Turned out that she'd 'borrowed' his mountain bike. Anyway, when we questioned them, both parties lied about what was going down. We let them off with a warning."

Sandford raised a caterpillar eyebrow.

"She wasn't communicating for any purpose other than being obscene, and he wasn't in possession. It was a busy night."

"How did you meet Ms. Yeats here?"

"She came out shortly after I arrived and warned me to play it cool with Paglia. Told me that she'd been freaking out a lot lately, acting real paranoid, and maybe we shouldn't hassle her any more than necessary if we didn't want the situation to escalate." He essayed a nervous smile in my direction.

Sandford's icy stare dropped the ambient temperature ten degrees. Had I the misfortune to be one of his minions, I'd wear Depends to work. "I'll get back to you later, Macintosh."

During their exchange, my wits began to work cautionary riffs, but Sandford didn't miss a beat. "Let's get back to your reaction to Paglia's lifestyle. What happened when you complained to her about the noise?"

I tried a vaguely authoritative tone. "I'll spare you the details — at least until I have a chance to talk to a lawyer — or Ernie Sivcoski."

"Why Sivcoski?"

Ernie and I go way back to the time before I met Pete, the now-dead love of my life. We'd gone out a few times, mostly to jazz clubs, but our relationship had never grown wings. He joined the force in the late '70s, moving through the ranks from beat cop to drug squad, to homicide. Recently promoted to Detective Sergeant, one of six on the Squad, he heads up a team of eight detectives.

Ernie has a fine heart and he is a damn good homicide

detective. But he spends too many of his working hours dealing with women like Tina Paglia to adjust in his off-hours to women who walk a straighter path. He reads us the way he scans a whore's rap sheet: broads are born into sin, not much of it original. Last year our relationship really got put to the test when he hauled me in for questioning about what turned out to be a suicide. Since then, we'd met over beer only once, unable to get past his resentment — that I had shoved my way into a murder investigation — or mine, that he had treated me so shabbily.

"We're friends, old friends," I informed Sandford. "I'm sure he'll tell you to look somewhere else for your prime suspect," I lied. "In the meantime, I'll admit that Tina and I exchanged words — nasty, vulgar words. We had a couple of arguments, okay, but it never came to blows." Only because I'd deflected a garden hoe before it rearranged my face.

"A few neighbours can give you a full description of our fights, I'm sure. They advanced on our yards like Tyson was in the ring. Like they have now." Very soon after moving here, I discovered that life on Shannon Street is a fishbowl. Bottom feeders get the highest ratings.

"Where were you last night, Miss Yeats?" he persisted, dumb as a goat. His refusal to acknowledge my request for a lawyer or Ernie was pushing me off the ledge of conversational decorum upon which I so tenuously crouched.

"Call me 'Jane' or 'Yeats.' My brain doesn't respond to 'Miss,'" I snapped. "I was at The Last Temptation — my mother's boyfriend's restaurant — until closing time. Etta threw a pre-opening party for all her regulars who didn't want to wait 'til she officially reopens her bar next Saturday. I'm sure any one of at least a hundred drunks can confirm that sorry fact. I came straight home and went to bed. Still haven't left the house. Only my dog can swear to that, though."

Max obligingly barked. Uppity Woman and WonderDog failed to deter Sandford from his quest. "Our officers are interviewing your neighbours. Might any of them have seen you come home?"

"At least one would be happy to screw up my account if you gave him half a chance," I retorted. "Mario Pepino, a.k.a. Pinocchio, the guy who owns the sandwich shop two doors up and the house between it and me. We're mortal enemies, ever since I complained to the Health Board about his stable of pet rats. And we had a fight when I replaced the rotted-out back fence along the line where his real estate meets mine. He's Tina's landlord, so I also bitched to him about her shenanigans more than once." Definitely I'd moved into what Etta labels 'cutting off my nose to spite my face.'

"Lady, I asked if any of your neighbours might *confirm* your story," he said wearily. He hadn't taken a shine to me and that was fine. I wanted to terminate this relationship as quickly as possible.

"Most of the people out around three a.m. are drunks from the Dundalk Tavern. They usually just throw up, stagger into their cars and race off. So I don't know if anybody actually saw me arrive home. But Mrs. Moretti next door probably heard me come in. The walls are paper-thin and my dog always barks a greeting."

Only plaster and lathe separates Nina's bedroom from mine. That's how I know she's an insomniac. With extraordinarily persistent flatulence. But she's unlikely to co-operate in a police investigation — unless it involves some desecration of her roses. My inner liar urged me not to add that I had tripped on the hall carpet, then knocked over a lamp in the bedroom.

The phone rang twice before my answering machine kicked in: "If I didn't know better I'd say you was avoiding me. Think I haven't figured out that you set your machine to answer so fast 'cause you wouldn't pick it up if you was sitting on the goddamn thing?"

Trust my mother for a burst of comic relief. I decided to respond to the infernal machine before Sandford collected more evidence of my non-traditional kinship with She-Who-Birthed-Me.

"Hi, Mom. Sorry I couldn't get to the phone faster, but I'm in the midst of being interviewed by a homicide detective." That should give her pause.

"I thought you said you was going straight home last night. Put the bugger on the line and I'll tell him you was too drunk to kill anybody until this morning. Or is he there because you picked him up on the way home?"

"What would I do without you to console me in the bad times? Listen up, Mom: there's a dead body in my front yard."

"Like I didn't warn you about that neighbourhood? You'd be safer living in Bosnia." She paused to suck on a Cameo. "So who's the stiff?"

"The victim is the hooker next door. And no, I didn't kill her — if that was your next question."

She hacked for ten seconds. "I wouldn't of blamed you if you had bumped her off. So look on the bright side, maybe you'll get a nicer neighbour now. Anyways, I gotta go. Nikos and me are going out dancing later and I need to do my hair and nails. I'll call you first thing tomorrow, eh?"

She banged down the phone.

Chapter 2

"ERNIE, AM I GLAD TO SEE YOU." My greeting radiated a lot more warmth than normal circumstances would elicit.

Before I could close the door, a vehicle screeching to a sudden halt drew Ernie's attention. Peering over his shoulder, I saw Mario Pepino, a.k.a. Pinocchio, fresh from the market, hurriedly exit his ancient station wagon packed with somewhat-fresh produce.

Ernie seemed to recognize Ratmeister, whose practice of dispensing free sandwiches to the boys in blue made San Giovanni's a routine pit stop. Pepino took in the scene, his wild eyes coming to rest on the corpse. Ernie told Constable Macintosh to escort him as far as the sidewalk in front of my house.

"Mother of God, it's my tenant," he shouted, crossing himself. Then he spotted me behind Ernie. "Good work, sir. Already you caught the person who done this horrible thing."

"I'll be talking to you later, Mr. Pepino. Then you can tell me why you assume Ms. Yeats here killed your tenant. In the meantime, I'm afraid you'll have to go back to the other side of the tape until we're done here."

"So who's gonna make my famous sauce with my store closed?"

Ernie closed the door on Pepino's business problems,

and his eyes absorbed the interior of my domain.

"Looks like you really screwed up this time."

How could I ever have found this man attractive? He looks like Fabio with a flattop. "Are you referring to my house or the corpse?"

"Tell me the difference."

Looking up at my two-storey worker's row house for the first time last summer, my mother had remarked, "And I worked my fingers to the bone so you could buy a house worse than what I was born in?" If Etta had worked any part of her anatomy to the bone, it wasn't her fingers.

The block on which my hovel alarmingly leaned to the south drew forth more unsolicited maternal candour. "Within a couple of steps, you got a cheesy bar, a pizza parlour, and an Eye-talian sandwich shop. You'll love this place. Never have to leave the street — that is if you can make yourself understood in English."

When you're talking houses, the horizontal lines should run parallel to the foundation. Over the century prior to my tenancy, 6 Shannon Street had diverged. $75,000 worth of structural "corrections" later, my contractor assured me that I wouldn't wake up to find the roof sharing my bed. Last week I confessed that my money had run out. So did he, leaving me inhabiting a semi-gutted shell scarcely more accommodating than an empty wine barrel.

A smart-ass might jest that this place is like me: cheap, distressed and frayed at the seams. Detective Sergeant Sivcoski is a smart-ass.

His wisecrack hit a nerve. "Ernie, if you're going to give me that shit you can leave. You can't even charge me with littering, for God's sake."

"In case it escaped your notice, I'm here on a murder

investigation — at your *personal* request. This castle of yours is a crime site and one of your neighbours has pegged you as the prime suspect. So you'll just have to tolerate my presence."

I was on the verge of tears, a rare and pathetic spectacle Ernie has never witnessed. Alpha males usually transform me into Xena, Warrior Princess.

His face and tone softened. "Look, let's cut the hostility, Jane. Of course I wouldn't put serious money on you being the perp. Just tell me anything you think might be relevant and we can let you get on with your life."

While I composed myself and my response, Ernie tiptoed through to my kitchen-to-be, pausing to study the image I'd taped to the window over the sink. It depicts a crowned maiden with a sword and the devil on a chain. She's praying on a cloud surrounded by a group of lunatics bound with golden chains.

"Never would have taken you for a pious woman." Some of us have graduated to irony, but Ernie remains mired in sarcasm.

"That is Dympna, an Irish virgin and patron saint of the mentally ill. Her father chopped off her head when she refused to sleep with him."

"Sounds like your kind of girl. So what's the scoop on your dead neighbour?"

I drew a deep breath. "I'm sorry for jumping on you. This whole scene has got me more irritable than PMS. Here's what you need to know. The victim you've identified ... right?"

"Yeah," he confirmed. "Already we've got two crime scenes to process. The coroner thinks she was killed somewhere else — like in her own apartment. Your garden is just the dump site. So what do you know that I need to hear?"

I gave him a thumbnail profile of Paglia's lifestyle.

"Here's a shortlist of people she had serious conflict with since she moved in last month: her boyfriend, Hammer Hopkins; her dealer, Quasimodo; and me, Jane Yeats, pain-in-the-butt.

"Beginning with Hammer. He doesn't seem to live there, just drops by a lot to hassle her. Occasionally stays overnight. I'm sure he's not her pimp because he mostly kvetches about what a junkie slut she is and that if she doesn't give up the life and the crack she'll never get her kids out of care. She always responds with the same mantra — *fuck off ... I don't love you anymore, Hammer ... get out of my life, but before you do would you check the dirty laundry to see if my blow is in there? ... can't remember where I stashed it.*"

Ernie nodded. "Sounds like a sitcom gone way wrong. Did it ever get violent between them?"

"All the time — but with a wrinkle. From what I heard through the walls, or through the window if I was in the back garden, Hammer would threaten to flush the junk if he could find it, then the thumping would start. But it sounded like she was hitting him."

"How would your feminist friends handle that scenario, Ms. Steinem?"

"That's not a question, Ernie," I retorted, "and it's unwarranted. I've never suggested that women have a corner on virtue — or self-restraint. Hell, man, even a pacifist like me can be driven to violence."

Too late it occurred to me that maybe this was not the best time to raise the fact that he'd hauled me into the station last year after I'd executed some delicate embroidery work with a broken wine bottle on the neck of the jerk who'd jeopardized Etta's life. Hell, if anybody has a right to kill my mother, it's me.

I consoled myself with a reminder that my haul from

that investigation became the down payment on my house.

Ernie threw up his hands in mock innocence. "Hey, just ask anyone who works in correctional services or substance abuse programs who they'd sooner deal with. Even the women would choose male offenders."

Recalling why I'd terminated our social relationship, I lit another Rothmans. "Ernie, you and I have been around this particular block so many times the pavement has worn thin. Can I get back to my statement?"

I inhaled a lung-scorching drag. "That's all I can tell you about Paglia and Hammer. He always sounded genuinely distressed that she didn't seem to give a shit about her kids being with Children's Aid. She always sounded pissed that he kept getting in the way of her career and her crack."

Another deep drag on my cigarette. Today I didn't even bother renewing my daily vow to quit my twenty-year habit. "Now, Quasimodo is another story. Hammer has his redeeming qualities, but Quasimodo is the Satan-spawn that kept her too jazzed even to remember where she stashed her supply, let alone begin to think about turning her life around. Macintosh said you guys know the dirtball."

Ernie was still pondering the entrails of what I call 'home.' "Oh, yeah. If we had more resources, Quasimodo would be doing a long stretch. Started off about ten years ago, feeding weed to school kids, graduated to dealing crack and cocaine from some of the sleazier College Street bars. Lately he's been doing the entrepreneurial thing, breaking in a few young girls he's got so doped up they'll do a blow job for ten bucks, a straight lay without a rubber for an extra five."

He looked out the window to check on the progress of the crime-scene guys. "You hear about how he got that scar on his face? When he was in his teens, he used to run with some of the thugs in the neighbourhood. A rival gang member carved up his face in retaliation for some drug double-cross. To show his defiance, Quasimodo got the friggin' scar tattooed — in red." Ernie shook his head at the reflection of his own flawless face.

"Is Quasimodo a nickname?"

"Nope. It's a legitimate Sicilian surname — and nobody dares to call Rocco 'The Hunchback,' either."

"Lately Tina'd been extending her territory," I offered. "I'd often see her working the corner of College and Shannon, kitty-corner from Canicatti's."

The Can is a neighbourhood institution, a venerably greasy Italian spoon that celebrated its thirtieth anniversary in August. In search of a new local since my move to Little Italy, I've been test-driving the indigenous watering holes. Although the Can dispenses the cheapest draft on the College Street strip and boasts a huge, sun-drenched patio, I'd scratched it off my list. One trip to the Ladies' left me with two options: bring my own chamber pot or get catheterized prior to every visit.

"But I didn't get the sense that Quasimodo was her pimp. She was such an ornery, independent woman, I don't think she'd let any guy control her biz. And I honestly can't see how a pimp could derive any serious income from her. She was really wrecked, Ernie, and the poor woman was no Sunshine Girl to begin with. A lot of tricks must have hit the gas pedal when they saw her eyes. They were bulging with rage."

My reflection must have caught Ernie off-guard. "Makes you wonder what was done to the woman to make her that angry and that fucked up, eh, Jane?"

Chapter 3

"YOU WANT TO KNOW something, Ernie — strictly off the record? Until I had to look at her wasted, dead body this morning, I never once bothered about what might have driven her into that pathetic life. I was way too busy obsessing about how much aggro she brought into mine.

"Moving right along ... I've already told Sandford about the scene outside here Friday night when some neighbours called in a complaint about Quasimodo trying to settle some bitch he had with Paglia. All I can guess about what provoked him is that yesterday morning Hammer showed up to bark at her for getting the cops involved. She told him that Quasimodo was freaked because she ripped him off for something — I didn't hear what. Then they got into another big argument that ended with him threatening to punch out her lights and her screaming, 'go for it, asshole, I can't see them anyway.'"

Ernie looked earnest. "Jane, with all you've heard and seen over the past few weeks, which one of those model citizens is the likelier suspect?"

"Not much to choose between them. I'd say Quasimodo, but that's because I find him such a loathsome, pernicious piece of work. Maybe the maggot decided to work her over for screwing him on a deal and got carried away. Maybe he wasted her as a warning to other smart-ass junkies on his turf.

On the other hand, maybe Hammer finally reached his boiling point. God knows, she could have provoked Mahatma Gandhi to murder."

Ernie leaned back on my overstuffed sofa, stretched his legs along the plaster-dust-embedded carpet, and drew his arms behind his head. Experience has taught me that Ernie shifts into pseudo-relaxation mode prior to launching an attack.

"Gandhi provoked to kill is a bit of a stretch, Jane. *But you?*" The shithead actually yawned.

I considered commanding Max to sever Ernie's jugular. "Get real, man. You know that I've had real reason to kill — and that I passed." I had settled for terrorizing my victim until he peed his silk boxers.

Ernie's eyes lasered into my skull. "Sure, he just killed himself shortly after you worked him over. At this moment I need to hear everything about your fights with Paglia. Your neighbours will supply any significant details you leave out."

"OK, here it is. Short, truthful and sordid. There were three confrontations. All took place on the street. Each one started with me complaining about the intolerable noise. Now, we're not talking normal noise here, Ernie. We're talking major-decibel, eardrum-shattering noise from the TV, the bed and her mouth. The TV and the bed are right smack up against our party wall.

"I can recite every word that's emanated from her favourite trash-talk shows and the Home Shopping Channel. The cable guy hooked her up even before the furniture was delivered.

"The noise coming from her bed sometimes came through the wall with a TV accompaniment, sometimes *a cappella*. Oh! OH! Yes. YES. Oooohhhh. To sex-starved ears, the music of human copulation is not hummable." I stupidly made eye contact with my interrogator.

Ernie's leer sang out loud and clear: *If you had a real man [like me] in your life, darlin', you'd be humming right along.* He took a foolish stab at psychoanalysis. "Jane, maybe you were kind of, well, *hypersensitive* to sex sounds."

"Let me guess, Sigmund," I retorted. "'If this broad got well laid on a regular basis, she wouldn't be jealous of the neighbours.' Maybe you should talk to the pervs in the morality squad who bug bordellos. The sound made by sex between people who have a relationship is not the same as the sound of commercial sex, Ernie. All those weird toys and scenarios I bet you and the missus aren't into."

I didn't bother to suppress my grin when my own personal homicide cop squirmed, reddened from the scalp down and recrossed his thick legs. Ernie could model for a GQ ad. Hair so slick, watch so Movado, shoes so Gucci, and threads so Hugo Boss I'd be speculating about how he supplemented his salary had I ever doubted his integrity.

I continued with an innocent smile. "I've become something of an expert on the acoustics of bonking. And the sourest note — the one that separates real sex from the kind you pay for — is a hooker's voice cooing every manner of encouragement and admiration to a pathetic little willie that's afflicted with stage fright."

Ernie shrugged laconically. "So wrap up this learned disquisition on noise, would you? Am I the only one in the room who's lost track of where it's heading?"

Given my hangover-wracked brain, I thought I hadn't been doing too badly.

For the second time this morning, my front door resonated to a flat-handed thumping. Macintosh shoved his cute face around the door to apologize for the intrusion. "I couldn't stop her, sir."

Nina Moretti pushed Macintosh aside with her right hand, while her left steadied a large bowl wrapped in an irreproachably white tea towel.

In her wake trailed the beguiling scent of Shannon Street — a mélange of simmering tomato sauce, exhaust fumes, spilled garbage from cat-shredded bags, and dog shit.

Nina bulldozed her bulky way to my kitchen counter, leaving a non-plussed Ernie muttering, *sotto voce*, "Madam, this is a crime scene."

Could he be so far removed from Little-Italy reality to think she would honour his admonition even if she'd understood it? The lady hails from Calabria — hears, sees and speaks no evil.

From Nina's standpoint, only two people currently occupied my house. Neither was a cop. *"Pasta e fagioli,"* she declared, resolutely setting the bowl down on my counter. With a magician's flourish, from nowhere she produced a demi-tasse. *"E espresso."* This offering she identified with undue emphasis.

She barged on out as though Ernie were invisible. *"Madonna."* What was her world coming to, when a nude body could drop out of the sky during the short-wave broadcast of the *rosario* from the Vatican?

Prior to Tina's death, I had felt strangely book-ended between sanctity and sin. On the south, Mother Teresa; on the north, Mary Magdalene.

Now only saintliness remained my neighbour, maintaining a perpetual vigil behind her curtains, witnessing the neighbourhood comings-and-goings like they were a soap opera. Thank God she sleeps while I prowl.

Belatedly, Ernie attempted a save-face. "So — TV noise. Sex noise. Paglia's fighting-with-boyfriend-and-dealer noise. Pushed beyond Superwoman endurance, you go all pro-active. What happened?"

My stomach retaliated with a bass growl. I leapt for the bowl, bypassing Ernie's probable hunger. A quick, eye-watering gulp of Nina's *espresso* confirmed my analysis: 80% brandy.

My thinking swiftly became crystal clear. "The first time, I introduced myself, then politely asked if she could reduce the volume a bit. I even explained that, as a writer, I was having trouble concentrating on my work. She told me that writing wasn't real work and if I found it too noisy, I could move. The second time I asked less politely. She told me to fuck off and die. So then I spoke to Pepino, who rents her the dump. Whether or not he spoke to her, I don't know. It made no difference to the noise level.

"Then, on Friday, I got more aggressive. After the cops left, I told her I'd complain to the Noise Board. She stuck her face in mine and spat, 'If you ever bitch to anyone again — me, my landlord or the friggin' authorities — I'll fucking cut you.' I retaliated by screaming, 'Don't threaten me, slut.' That's when she grabbed a hoe that was resting against the fence, but I'm stronger than she is. All day Saturday she actually cranked up the noise. But Friday night was the last time I actually saw her."

Ernie shifted his buff frame on my sofa. "Thanks, Jane. I don't consider noise rage sufficient motive for murder — even given your Celtic temper. And factoring in the likelihood that you were shit-faced last night, I don't see you dumping the victim in your own garden. The team has already established that Paglia was murdered in her flat. So all I really need to know is what you heard through the wall after you got home in the middle of the night."

This next bit was embarrassing. "If Paglia had stepped on a land mine last night, I wouldn't have heard the explosion, Ernie. I went up to bed as soon as I got home and immediately fell into a very deep sleep."

"You passed out?"

As I finished off my breakfast, I prepared to parry his impertinence. "No, I did not. I know to cut myself off in time." The line separating fact and fiction can be stretched no finer.

Suddenly a banshee set to wailing outside. I beat Ernie to the window.

Hammer Hopkins had shown up just in time to see two forensics guys bagging his girlfriend's body.

Chapter 4

SILVER MARACLE bestrides the corner of College and Shannon like a colossus, six feet high and rising, pushing three hundred pounds. A thick braid falls down her back. Her black eyes, set in a broad, high-cheekboned face, scan the street. Today she is wearing her work uniform — blue denim overalls and an acrylic-smeared T-shirt under a purple leather jacket.

For years we've been close friends, each disconcerted by her own career success, but not a whit surprised by the other's. Until I bought the house, we'd been inmates of an old roughly-converted cough-lozenge factory in the west end, her studio a floor above mine. It was Silver who first came upon my habitat the day it was trashed, who encouraged me to walk away from the devastation into a fresh space. Though we're poles apart in so many particulars, some powerful undercurrent of shared values and cranky temperaments always bridges race, culture and work. She's an artist and I like that. She wishes I'd remain a writer because she likes knowing that I am safely in front of my computer, not on the streets, shit-disturbing, drinking and otherwise endangering myself. She never complains about my Harley, though, loves my dog and seems to think that my mother is normal.

Today we were meeting for a late lunch on my invitation. I'd passed the Monday following the discovery of Paglia's body totally unproductively, neurotically abandoning one project after another, too preoccupied to focus. Added to the shock of the murder was my financial distress. Money and I have never been intimate, but lately we've become totally estranged.

To finish work on the house, make the mortgage payments, cover the utilities and keep Max and me in groceries, I'm obliged to contrive a source of income. Last year, stoned with my success on the Durand case, I briefly contemplated getting my PI's licence, but I don't believe in licences for activities you can perform without them — like practising psychotherapy on my mother. (Guns are my one exception, begetting the very kind of crap they are thought to eliminate.) Besides, I can't imagine performing the class of services advertised by licenced private investigators, like 'Babysitter Performance Analysis using covert CCTV systems' and 'Spousal/Significant Other Loyalty Tests.'

No longer can I avoid the writing that should be on the wall. Since graduating from university, I've supported myself with my scribbling. In Canada, this is no small achievement.

My unplanned career trajectory had nudged me from crime-books columnist to crime reporter to true-crime writer. An investigative series on corruption in the Toronto police force netted me a national newspaper award. My first book, about a prominent murder case, hit the best-seller list. I followed it up with a winner on stock-exchange fraud and insider trading. A third book, on the history and operations of the Toronto Police Department Homicide Squad, grew into a contract for scripting a TV documentary. I won some enemies in high places, a couple of friends on the police force, and two more awards.

So what's stopping me from building on that?

Last year I happily passed on writing the book of my career — much to my agent's displeasure. For the first time, I'd thrown myself into investigating a case, instead of researching it from a safe distance. In reality, true crime is the shit that goes down unmediated by folks like me. It's way different than letting your eyeballs do the walking through Truman Capote or Ann Rule. Investigating white-collar crime, my area of expertise, brought me into brutal contact with a class of individuals whose behaviour haunts me still. To write it up would have entailed revisiting scenes I wish I hadn't walked through the first time. To earn royalties on doing so seems only one step up from paying a convicted killer for his memoirs.

Words are my business. Shaping them into true-crime narratives brings me closer to comprehending some of the deviant behaviours that screw up our social contract. Not that my books end on a grace note, with order restored to a fractured community — we've wandered too far off the moral compass. But what the criminal justice system can't deliver, a writer can document and lament.

To be honest, the biggest obstacle to starting a new book is my fear that I've encased myself in a protective cocoon of words in the three years since Pete's death. Maybe writing shields me from feeling.

As I can always count on Silver to give me an original take on any topic we chew over, maybe spewing about Tina's murder will give me enough clarity to beat my fear and kick-start a return to writing.

As I reached the corner, my friend was winding up an encounter with a Native woman I recognized as one of the regulars at Sistering, a nearby drop-in centre for women.

"What's up?" I asked.

She shrugged eloquently. "Same old, same old. Soon as I

show my face I get hit on, eh? Girlfriend there told me to give her five bucks. When I knocked my donation down to a toonie on account of her bad manners, she says, 'So if you won't give me no decent money, maybe we can trade boots.'" Silver glanced down at her fire-engine-red snakeskin marvels that Etta would sacrifice a boyfriend for. "In her dreams."

I held open the door to Canicatti's, which she chose over the more upscale cafés, trattorias and bars that dot the College Street strip. They offer a menu of sex, pasta, drugs, pasta and rock 'n roll. Some American magazine described College and Shannon as the "intersection where white counterculture meets hip ethnicity." Figuring she lost out on both counts, Silver refused to eat anywhere in the vicinity that served presentation rather than food.

"Won't eat in any joint that's into purple garnishes and perverting spaghetti but can't fry burgers right. When the Creator lowered us to Turtle Island, there was peas, beans, berries and grains — no radicchio, no arugula, and only three species of pasta. The other stuff was all created by mad white geneticists working for the CIA."

Silver is a Mohawk. Only a much bigger fool than I would rush in to ask where burgers fit into the Creator's culinary legacy.

Sunlight shafting through the front windows does not stretch into the recesses of the Can. Gloom is kinder to the chipped faux-marble tables, faux-leather padded chairs and mustard walls generously streaked with nicotine and grease. Huge black ceiling fans fail to extract the smoke — *Apocalypse Now* without the Wagner.

Silver stood studying an autographed photo gallery of nearly-famous-all-over-Toronto celebs who dined here and lived. As we sat down, the King was belting out "Jailhouse

Rock" from a super deluxe Hyperbeam Laser Disc jukebox loud enough to set the ketchup bottles table-dancing. On the wall beside us, archival photos of city streets competed for space with framed birthday greetings from local politicians.

Lena, who has been serving tables since that momentous day the Can opened thirty years ago, schlepped an unhurried path to us on red rubber flip-flops. She made a lifeless pass at the crumb-strewn table with a smelly rag. "Ya need a menu?"

"I need a burger, fries and a large Coke." Silver can trade bad manners with the best of them.

"Same for me, but substitute a pint of Upper Canada Maple Brown for the Coke, please."

Silver turned from sourly regarding a straggle of dusty plastic ivy atop the napkin holder. "Isn't it a bit early to be drinking — even for you?"

Silver doesn't drink. Says Indians can't metabolize booze. Always appends that the Irish can't either.

My turn to shrug. "After what I went through Sunday, it's remarkable that I haven't moved into a brewery. Add to that I'm broke."

My sob-story left her underwhelmed. "Thank you for sharing, but you are only temporarily broke, a condition a whole lot of folks would envy. And why are you taking the murder so hard? I thought you hated the broad. You look like shit, by the way."

I parried, "So how's your work going, Silver? New show taking shape?" Her last show generated a media buzz other artists would eat paint for. Since then, she'd dropped a few hints that she was painting up a far more menacing storm.

"If I needed to talk about my work, I would have asked you to lunch. And if chattering about my obsessions worked for me, I'd be a writer. Let's just say that the show will probably be closed before it opens."

I knew better than to pursue the subject. "Um, what was it you asked me?"

"You're way too young to be losing your short-term memory. Maybe the beer's dissolving your grey cells. What I asked you was, *Why the hell are you taking this murder so hard?*"

So much for cunning diversionary tactics. I gazed at her with barely suppressed incredulity. "Last month when my furnace croaked, I thought I'd seen the last of everything bad that could conceivably happen to 6 Shannon Street. Finding a dead body in your garden is not a normal occurrence, Silver."

She rolled her eyes. "I've never known your life to be blighted by *normal* occurrences. Is it the fact that she got herself murdered? Or that the homicide boys hassled you? For sure it can't be because they destroyed your landscaping searching for evidence."

Lena plunked down our beverages. "Burgers ya have to wait for. Cook's gone to the toilet."

Beer is my favourite comfort food. I appreciatively drank down a couple of inches. Nice, but not world-class if Guinness is your benchmark.

Firm as a judge's gavel, I set down my mug. "My initial shock was a normal human reaction to seeing a naked corpse in one's yard. I've only ever seen dead people after they've been tarted up and placed in a $3,000 recycling box. The remnants of a sudden, violent death are not a pretty sight."

"Really? Never happens on the rez."

The girl had a point. "Sorry."

Silver grunted acceptance of my apology.

"But when I realized that Paglia probably was killed just a few metres from where I sleep, that scared me. Even when part of the roof caved in, remember? I still felt safe inside my house." My drinking hand shook as I raised my glass.

"You're probably safer now than you were before, what with cops swarming all over the street." She took a too generous swig of Coke and burped. Her jet eyes probed mine. "You are a tough woman, Jane. And usually too fearless. So what is this reaction? Some delayed fallout from getting your studio trashed last year? Something else entirely? Tell me what's really upsetting you."

I paused while Lena expertly slid our plates across the table. Both came to rest precisely under our chins.

"You should tell the cook about Metamucil. Three spoonfuls a day will keep him on schedule," Silver solemnly advised the waitress, who flip-flopped away without comment.

I tried to describe the one feeling I never anticipated in the wake of Paglia's demise — guilt. Since Paglia had moved in with her noise track, I'd regaled my acquaintances with ribald stories about "the hooker next door" — her working life, detailed descriptions of her slutty clothes, clown makeup, Nashville hair, fights with Hammer and Quasimodo, white-trash TV viewing habits. Her drug habit made me doubly contemptuous. And when we fought, every shaming word I threw at her oozed righteous indignation — from some self-created moral high ground. What a joke. Probably the only thing that keeps me from promiscuity is sexual timidity, reinforced by long-lingering grief over Pete. I stared at my near-empty beer glass. Nor was I a stranger to substance abuse. Mine just gets better press than what you have to inject or snort. It's legal.

That I had slept through Paglia's swan song, incapable of rallying an intervention that might have saved her life, I did not mention.

Silver shoved aside her empty plate. "Cook can't shit for beans but he sure knows how to flip a burger. Fries were a bit soggy, though." She scowled. "Do you have to light up before you've finished chewing?"

I ignored her latest health bulletin.

Silver ignored me. "When you start doing a Born-Again impersonation around any alleged sin, I know something's gone haywire. What is it about a girl being a hooker that makes you crazy?"

Startled, I gulped down the remainder of my beer while signalling Lena to rush me another. "Oh please, Silver, even you wouldn't want your daughter in the biz." I couldn't be bothered arguing this one through.

"I've never devoted much time to thinking about my non-existent daughter's career. But a few friends of mine who moved to Toronto from the rez are working the Dundas and Sherbourne track. Doesn't take a lot of brains to figure out why they ended up there. Does take some self-discipline, though, to consider them still members of the human race. Hell, I liked them when we were growing up and nothing about them has changed enough to make me care for them any less. Who am I to judge? Why the hell should it get up your nose? Maybe you should invest your anger in homelessness or poverty or addiction or racism or homophobia ... "

I rarely saw my friend get so worked up. "Maybe we should just drop the subject, eh?" Perhaps a brief time-out while I emptied my bladder would lighten us up.

While on the can, for distraction I read the magenta flyer taped to the inside of the cubicle door.

DRAWING A LIFE THAT MATTERS!!!™
LET GWENDOLYN DE QUINCEY GUIDE YOU THROUGH A
DRAWING MEDITATION OF YOUR LIFE,

AS YOU WOULD LIKE IT TO BE IN:
SPIRITUALITY   LEARNING   LIVELIHOOD
COMMUNITY & RELATIONSHIP   SOCIAL JUSTICE
YOU WILL CREATE AN ORIGINAL WORK OF ART
NO DRAWING EXPERIENCE PAST KINDERGARTEN REQUIRED

I unstuck it, hoping Silver might be amused.

Amusement was not on the agenda. "Look, Jane, you need to take a serious look at where all that moral baggage comes from."

I totally lost patience. "Hey, I'm a feminist. You think I haven't anguished over it? That bloody conference on women and violence those sex workers took over? — nothing they said changed my thinking. And don't give me that crap about 'prostitution is just another job.' No self-respecting woman sets up shop as a sperm bank."

Silver's eyes raged a warning. "Issues of white feminism and self-respect aside, let me try this one on you. Have you never wondered how this particular Indian woman helped put herself through art college?" She jabbed a thumb at her chest.

"Don't bullshit me."

"If I'd brought my eagle feather, I'd be holding it now. In third year I got so broke I couldn't pay my rent or buy Kraft Dinner — forget art supplies. So I answered an ad in the back pages of NOW magazine and got a stint as a dominatrix. First time my size favoured me in the job market. It's not like I could have been a lap dancer, right?"

"Tell me this is a joke." I felt sick.

Without a trace of defensiveness, she gave each word equal weight. "What else was I going to do? Work at a McJob for six months, leaving me no time to paint ... or twitch a whip for a few weeks and pay a year's rent? The experience was good, too. I learned a trick or two I still use in private practice," she cackled. "Don't see any lineups outside your back door."

"FUCK YOU, SILVER. FUCK YOU."

I rose to my feet, snatched my jacket from the back of my chair, and fled the Can before she could see my tears.

I had walked in with a dear friend and run away from a woman I didn't recognize.

Chapter 5

"FREEDOM'S JUST ANOTHER word for nothin' left to lose," complained Janis Joplin.

Yeah, right. Look where terminal freedom got you, blues-wailing woman. Same six feet under as Paglia, I fumed.

My brain couldn't process Silver's assault on my unexamined take on prostitution. Heavily relapsed into my ritual for sanity-saving — manual labour 'til you drop — I dipped my putty knife into a bucket of rapidly-drying joint compound, slapped a wad against the drywall joint, and smoothed it as best I could. Bubbles formed and popped merry as champagne, excess compound oozed lava-like from the narrow space between the two sections of drywall.

I stepped back to survey my handiwork. The wall was a crazy quilt. Before necessity forced me to become my own renovator, I'd underestimated the skills of experienced artisans. Maybe I could paint the pronounced seams in a sharply contrasting colour. Folks might mistake the result for a postmodern refutation of Martha Stewart.

As I focused on reducing the damage I'd inflicted on my kitchen wall, an unsolicited voice louder than Joplin's clamored for attention. *Maybe, just maybe, Silver had a point.*

I flung my putty knife at the floor. Next application I'd abandon it for a cake-decorating bag.

Silver's righteous rage, which had felt like rancor, was

obliging me to take inventory of my ethics storeroom — not a pretty sight at the best of times.

This was not the best of times.

I put Max on his leash. We'd romp to his heart's delight through Trinity Bellwoods Park.

The real estate agent who'd showed me the house last June exhausted every deceitful euphemism to describe the "handyman's special" I was about to mortgage my soul for. The rabbit warren of tiny dark rooms offered a wonderful opportunity to explore an "open concept." The gouged, curling-at-the-edges lime linoleum concealed "real hardwood floors." Standing at the kitchen sink, she conjured a lovely walk-out deck overlooking a "pocket" garden in place of the four empty wine barrels, rusted mattress spring and roofless tool shed. The unfinished, low-ceilinged basement possessed "income potential." *Was she thinking hydroponic marijuana or chinchilla cages?* The nearby sandwich shop, pizzeria and tavern exuded "quaint ethnicity," not noise, litter and traffic congestion.

But she had overlooked the house's only selling feature, apart from affordability. This I discovered walking down to Dundas Street — a huge park sloping three blocks wide and four deep towards the lake. Scooped from the centre of this huge, irregular rectangle of well-tended grass and ancient trees was a valley, its perimeter rimmed by an asphalt track. This was Max country.

So excited was I about introducing him to Trinity Bellwoods Park our first morning in our handyman's special, I pulled on a track suit, poured my coffee into an insulated mug and headed straight out the door. Well before we crossed heavily-trafficked Dundas, Max so strained at the lead that he cut off his air supply, his nose twitching ecstatically at decades of accumulated doggy scents. This being Toronto, a city sink-ing under the weight of its by-laws, a sign soon intruded into the view: "Dogs allowed unleashed in park before 10:00 a.m. and after 7:00 p.m."

I was able to keep Max more or less in sight as he hared straight down into the valley and proceeded to leak a few drops on almost every tree he encountered.

Max is a border collie. He can't resist the blood-pull to herd anything with a pulse, and our introduction to the park soon erupted in snarling, barking and shouting. Behind a low brick building with a Parks Department sign on its front wall, I saw my housemate warily pacing around a mound of old clothes ringed by bulging plastic bags, his ears flattened, fangs bared.

Terrified by Max, who held him trapped as a fox, a man huddled inside the mound, crouched on his knees, his blackened hands slapping away imaginary enemies threatening his chest. "We really are scared, aren't we? They know that you are seeing them. Don't tell them. We don't want any trouble. We don't mean any harm." A renewed staccato of slaps into the innocent air.

I got Max under control and snapped on his lead, securing it around a small tree trunk a good distance away. By the time I retraced my steps to apologize to the poor man, he was scurrying about collecting a clutch of crammed LCBO bags into a large garbage bag. Liquor-store bags are a favourite with homeless people. They're durable.

He was a large guy, although not much meat clung to his broad frame. Probably only in his late twenties, but his pocked and ruddy face appeared to have weathered at least another decade. Big black beard prematurely shot with white. A large growth, angrily red around the edges, swelled the right side of his forehead. Dishevelled hair hung in oily dreads over his shoulders. Two lower front teeth gone south. Red T-shirt printed with a diminutive spaniel and DR. BALLARD'S PUPPY CHOW over a black sweatshirt, hot pink polyester track pants. Sockless feet in huge mismatched running shoes, one with a lace, undone.

Grimacing, he anxiously interrogated his belongings as he finished packing them up. "Are they giving you those looks again? They don't know we had a dog once. We wear a puppy on our T-shirt. Can't they see? We are not the enemy. We might ... no, we can't. They told us we can't ever again ... "

Instinct instructed me not to move one inch closer. If my home were a public park, I'd need a generous allotment of territory. If only Max could observe human boundaries as faithfully as he does the canine variety.

"I'm sorry my dog frightened you, sir. He is not vicious — just too curious. We're leaving now, we'll not bother you any more if you want to stay here," I offered, backing away. "Is there anything I can do for you ... ?"

He didn't look up, signalled nothing to indicate that my words had registered. But his agitation seemed to drop a notch. "Yes they're going away. No trouble. No harm. Then they changed the drugs. Things got worse for us after that, didn't they? Isn't that too bad?"

Still tethered to his lead, I led Max through the old stone archway at the south end of the park. His raggedy tail was between his legs — mutt for *I truly am ashamed of my aggressive antics.* We made our way back home through an intricate maze of one-way residential streets bordering the park.

As I opened my front door that morning, the imperfect fact of my crooked little house hit me with the sudden rush of a gift of grace ...

Today as I walked Max along the asphalt path ringing

the perimeter of the valley, I scrutinized the area for recent signs of the homeless man's tenancy, surprised by my disappointment at his absence.

That old lapsed-Catholic tic again — needing to do penance, where often none was due.

Just as we reached home, Ernie Sivcoski's car pulled up. I politely invited him in, intending to make him very uncomfortable. When Ernie bent to pat his head, Max snarled a canine rendering of *Don't patronize me.*

"To what stroke of good fortune do I owe this visit? Did the forensics incriminate me?" I snarkily inquired, without offering him something to drink.

In spite of the attention he'd lavished on his appearance, Ernie looked discouraged and far less aggressive than usual. "No, I just wanted to update you ... for old times' sake. I know you took Paglia's death pretty hard."

He must have forgotten to take his nasty pill this morning. "That's decent of you."

"That sudden burst of rain early Sunday morning washed away or contaminated the evidence from your garden. Ditto the path from her front door to the point where she was tossed over the fence. We've confirmed that she was murdered inside her apartment. There was lots of blood, all of it hers. Plenty of trace evidence — hairs, fingerprints, fibres, semen on the sheets. Given her occupation, that's no surprise. Both Hammer Hopkins and Quasimodo regularly visited Paglia, so anything we might track back to them is worth squat."

"What about that footprint impression I saw one of your team working on?"

He shook his head ruefully. "It was a good one. That big plant of yours shielded it from the rain. We even matched it to a shoe — glued to the right foot of an old drunk who staggered into the station Monday morning to ask how the lady in your garden was doing. Told us he spotted her body on his way down to a hostel on Dundas. He stopped outside your house to relieve himself through the fence. The silly bugger figured Paglia must have passed out. Said he left her some daisies to cheer her up when she came to. Didn't remember picking them or sticking them in her mouth, nor did he think it remarkable that she was naked. Couldn't tell that Paglia was dead and mistook her open mouth for a vase. Guess the Aqua Velva dissolved his grey cells."

Lifting a weapon from Etta's arsenal, I went for him while he was too depressed to maintain his defences. "But you must have followed up on Hammer and Quasimodo anyway? God knows, Ernie, they sounded motivated enough to kill when they fought with Paglia."

"Hammer had to be sedated after he saw us bagging her. Maybe he's a good actor, maybe his grief was genuine. By the time he got coherent, he was able to come up with the names of four guys he swears can vouch for his whereabouts. All four are about as reliable as jailhouse rats, so we're trying to find slightly less-criminal types who might have seen Hammer at the after-hours club he claims to have been in. Quasimodo dropped out of sight. That scar makes him so easy to spot, he's probably gone into deep hiding."

To soften him up a bit more, I offered him a beer, stale Digestive cookies even. Reaching behind the imported hops, I snagged him a Blue. "Ernie, other Toronto hookers have been murdered in the past couple of years. Could Paglia's murder be linked?"

He shook his square head. "Nah. Totally separate. The few we've solved, the killers are out of circulation. The fifteen or so still on the books look like random stranger kills. The victims were all street prostitutes who got killed on the job. There's no hard evidence pointing to a serial killer, in spite of what a lot of prostitutes believe. Why go speculating when we've got two perfectly good suspects here?"

Ernie's mind is as sharp as his threads. Maybe he was doing a smoke-and-mirrors thing to avert my journalistic thinking from a notion the police were withholding from the public — "Fear of serial killers haunts Toronto sex trade." Several forces came under intense criticism for bungling the Bernardo investigation. If homicide investigators are currently tracking a serial killer, they must be keen on dodging media scrutiny.

"Has all the data on those homicides been fed into VICLAS?" Call me tenacious.

Set up by the RCMP and also used by the OPP, the Violent Crime Linkage Analysis System quickly tags correspondences between crimes of a violent, predatory serial nature. The underlying premise is that repeat offenders exhibit distinctive characteristics and patterns.

Like all systems, VICLAS functions better in theory than practice. Every scrap of paperwork for every relevant crime must be gathered at police detachments across the country and downloaded into the central database. Investigators then concentrate on those cases they have the best chances of solving.

Ernie's words were laced with incredulity. "VICLAS? Give me a break. Our budget's so bloody tight we're sending new recruits into dangerous situations alone. You wonder why we're shooting more suspects and just plain crazy people in the last couple of years? We got men out there so scared they'll pull their Glocks on a rat. We've cold-cased so many hooker kills the files could pack a small library. When a girl shows up dead, we do the routine legwork. If we run out of leads, we call it quits. We have to back off the cases that are going nowhere."

"And that doesn't bother you?"

He fortified himself with a long swig of beer. "Of course it bothers me, but ... remember Alison Parrott — the young athlete who went to meet some guy claiming to be a newspaper photographer ... couple of kids found her body a few days later? That's the kind of crime we've been feeding into VICLAS. We also dug into all the old blood and semen samples to run DNA checks. And it paid off — a murder conviction, albeit thirteen years later. Putting the hooker files on the back burner doesn't draw much negative press. Most people figure violence is part of a whore's job description. Only other whores bitch about it, mostly because they're scared for their own sorry asses."

So much for God seeing the little sparrow fall.

After asking if I'd managed to recall anything that might be relevant to Paglia's murder, Ernie rose to leave. "I'd appreciate it if you'd keep an eye peeled for Quasimodo, eh? Sooner or later, something will drive him out of his cave."

I watched him lower his bulk into the car. A good cop, doing his routine legwork. Then he'll file Tina away.

Chapter 6

ETTA SUMMONED ME to check out the restoration before her Grand Ole Opening Nite. She'd shrouded the 'new look' in such secrecy you'd suspect she was designing a nuclear facility. And I was to be her honoured first viewer. Papal audiences are not to be missed. Before dropping in at Sweet Dreams, I decided to take my bike for a spin through Rosedale.

Heading east along Bloor Street, then north up the Rosedale Ravine, I effortlessly zipped my way in and out of traffic, then wove past gracious single-family (plus nanny and housekeeper) dwellings with gardens maintained way better than I am. I was hoping my inadequate muffler was disturbing the natives. Maybe my nose was out of joint. Hell, these mansions changed hands for a few million bucks.

Only recently have I been feeling totally in command of this machine. I've got a Zen thing about needing my bike to be as responsive as my nerves and muscles, a heavy metal extension of my intentions. For five years I'd been married to a reconditioned Harley-Davidson FLST Heritage. Then, late one dark and stormy night, a couple of young guys on a tear "borrowed" my bike for a joy-ride.

Every day since, I've wished that I had just walked home, reported it missing the next day and devoutly prayed for its eventual recovery:

Dear St. Dympna, come to our aid in our need, and pray to God for us that he may see fit to restore Harley to our bereft arms. Amen.

About two hours after the theft, an alert cop on Highway 401 spotted the celebrants raising hell with the Highway Traffic Act. Sure enough, the cop initiated one of those high-speed chases that ends abruptly and predictably, as my bike met a concrete wall at 150 km an hour. Both kids were killed instantly.

I considered replacing the Harley with the bike of my dreams, a stunning red Ducati 851 Sport, the 'Ferrari' of motorcycles. The last hand-built bike in the world, in a limited edition, with a computerized fuel injection system. But the price tag would have eaten up my down payment on the house. Much as I love fine bikes, I've never seen one I can live in.

When Hank, Harley devotee and my mechanic, phoned to say he had a deal for me, bike-deprivation drove me straight to his shop. What awaited me wasn't love at first sight, but it was a Harley-Davidson XLH883 Sportster. Ten years old, cherry red, with the trademark 45 V-twin layout, but fitted out with a better engine, five-speed gearbox, and alloy where iron used to be. The price was more than fair, Hank had reconditioned it himself, but I knew that this baby appealed to the nostalgia market, urban riders and commuters who wouldn't have considered wrestling with a true Hog.

I silently noted that the Sportster weighed in at about a hundred pounds less than Harley, promising my right knee joint (never properly healed after some thugs laid a good beating on me) a respite when I braked to a stop. And I did favour its lean profile, which would allow me to park it in the front hall. My house doesn't have a garage. Etta says that's because it is one.

Driving it home, I fretted that no one would take me seriously on this machine. Balls are a state of mind, I consoled myself. The Sportster handled well, though, and Hank had sworn over a case of Blue that it could hit 165 km an hour. But the first XL model, produced forty-one years ago, was a whole lot more handsome.

My brief spin through Rosedale did not blow away my black cloud of guilt over Tina Paglia's death, exacerbated by yesterday's fight with Silver.

And something else nagged me. Etta tirelessly reminds me that the stove stopped being my favourite toy only after I set a chubby young palm atop a glowing element. "Always had to find out for yourself, dear."

Whether Ernie's assurances that no link existed between Tina's murder and the sex workers who'd disappeared or been murdered was a diversionary ploy or a genuine reflection of his thinking didn't matter. I had to find out for myself. A.S.A.P.

Nothing's changed, Mom. Nothing's changed.

On the Danforth just east of Broadview I braked Harley outside Sweet Dreams. The exterior looked no different than it had prior to the Big Burn. The red brick facade had been cleansed of the smoke stains, though, and the four main-floor windows replaced. Above the entrance, the large hot-pink neon sign still flickered SWEET DREAMS, the stem of the "T" still capped with a Stetson. Etta must have used the insurance loot to tart up the interior.

Thanks to Toronto's superb fire fighters, the adjoining buildings suffered only smoke damage. I hoped Etta had paid for cleaning up The Last Temptation, the Greek restaurant next door. Nikos, the proprietor, was her latest erotic conquest — to my knowledge, which she hadn't updated since their "honeymoon" trip to Greece. Monogamy is not one of Mom's strong points. A cruise ship probably offered far too many irresistible side dishes for her to curb her appetite this side of the main course.

She must have heard me pull up. "I'm A Stranger in My Home," a duet Kitty Wells cut with Red Foley sometime near the beginning of the Cold War, greeted me. Etta likes to set a mood with a well-chosen country classic. I've always suspected she knows it gives her a strategic edge, even before she starts talking at you.

The panorama that greeted me was so déjà vu that I needed a few minutes to assimilate what my mother had spent a few hundred grand not doing. In Sweet Dreams' first incarnation, Etta had recreated Miss Kitty's Long Branch saloon. The fire had incinerated it to a crisp.

My current survey confirmed that I'd fallen deep into a *Star Trek* time-warp. Every item in the old bar had risen phoenix-style from the ashes. Her autographed photos and posters of legendary country music stars plastered to the barn board walls alongside beat-up guitars and fiddles, the wagon-wheel light fixtures, the chrome and Formica ... even her sacred relic, Hank Williams' ten-gallon hat in which, she claims, he died. It's certainly big enough. They all looked brighter, though, purged of their historic nicotine discoloration.

"Revivify, don't renovate," Etta explained. "So my decorator reconstructed the whole place from the photographs in my scrapbook, while I perched on his shoulders making sure he got every last little detail right."

She was dressed on schedule. If it's Tuesday, it must be the orange satin shirt, stretch jeans and matching tooled cowboy boots. Diminutive but stacked, wantonly coiffed, a geriatric Dolly Parton.

I strained to stifle my incredulity. "Mom, this place was screaming out for a total face-lift, a change of identity."

"Mine don't need a lift and my bar didn't neither. What's the matter, you don't like it?" she snapped.

I tried to meet her eyes, but a barrier of mauve eye shadow obstructed my view. "Well, I just thought you'd ... update it." I was testing perilously thin ice.

She poked a long scarlet acrylic nail at me. "Let's not start pretending you've got any taste, dear. Your house looks like it took a land mine."

Time to search for the bright side. "I guess the new washrooms will be putting me out of a job." No more midnight emergency trips across the city to repair her plumbing. I glanced over at the Plexiglas shrine. "Now, that can't be the original Hank Williams hat."

She relaxed into a shameless cackle. "I got it same place I bought the original — at the Hadassah Bazaar. Had a rider on my policy to cover its replacement value. Insurance guy was stupid as he was cute. Actually coughed up two grand for the relic. So pull up a chair and I'll tell you my plans for Grand Ole Opening Nite."

"First, may I draw a draft?"

"You'll just have to draw yourself a picture of one. Taps are shut because the gauge on the CO_2 canister needs adjusting. But I can phone and ask Nikos to bring over a glass of *ouzo*, if you want." Etta's boyfriend makes his own, like the real thing isn't toxic enough.

"Thanks, but I'm driving." Before she could snap, "Never knew that to stop you before," I asked after Nikos.

She fidgeted with a curl before confessing. "Actually, I'm getting a bit bored with him, dear. And I do worry about his wife finding out, you know."

"Never knew that to stop you before, Mom."

She emitted another cackle. "You haven't seen the broad. She could lift my jukebox above her shoulders without breaking a sweat. Have you heard from that Michael of yours?" she deflected. "You was crazy not to move out west with him — not that I wouldn't have missed you, of course," she added, belatedly.

One of my big reasons for remaining in Toronto is that I can't imagine daily life without Etta, even if she does drive me nuts. But I wasn't about to tell her that. Neither of us is into schmaltz.

"No, Michael hasn't called me and I don't expect him to. He really had his heart set on some rustic log cabin on one of the Gulf islands."

Last year, I drew Michael Diamond into my life because I needed his expertise as a tax lawyer. On my behalf he jeopardized his career — and his freedom, if you need to get technical — by pilfering corporate files and subjecting them to some serious forensic accounting. Together we verified that a pillar of the old business Establishment was money laundering for the Mob.

I also drew Michael into bed, thinking I was but yielding to the call of my wild hormones. Then lust deepened into caring — and fear. The scars from Pete's sudden death had begun to fade, but letting another man get too close just exposed me to fresh pain. I couldn't do it.

Etta vigorously shook her head without disturbing a hair, another triumph for hair spray that sets like concrete. "You're a fool. Ever since Pete died, you avoided men like you was a lesbian, then when you finally landed one you let him slip away like there's a hundred class guys in every bar."

"I guess I didn't inherit your genes for the man thing." I tried to sound disconsolate.

"For the *sex* thing, you mean. You've never had a normal amount of men in your bed — not all at the same time, although it might do you good."

"Etta, now that you've turned yet another conversation to sex, there's something I want to ask you." Fidgeting with my cigarette pack, I briefly reconsidered her *ouzo* offer. "How do you feel about prostitution?"

"You thinking of looking for a new job, dear?"

"Damn it, I'm serious. Since that hooker — I mean, since Tina next door got murdered, I've been feeling pretty shitty about how I spoke to her and about her — like I was going for the Terminal Disrespect award. When I tried to talk about it with Silver today, we wound up having our first fight."

Her face grew grave. "Silver is a nice girl, even if she is an artist and doesn't appreciate men. And I know my daughter. You came off sounding like one of them sexophobic preachers, eh? Well, you know a thing or two about how I feel about sex, so why shouldn't some poor girl earn a living doing it?"

"'Some *poor* girl.' Do you mean the only thing that separates 'us' from 'them' is money?"

Etta banged her hand on the Formica. Fretfully examined her fingernails for signs of damage. "That sure as hell is a big part of it. Never knew any pro who did it for fun. I mean, most of the johns gotta be wankers or weirdos, paying for shenanigans their wives wouldn't do. The rest of us women owe hookers a huge favour."

I knew how to catch her up. "So you wouldn't have any problem if I started hooking?"

She hooted. "*You* are the one who'd have the problem, girl. First, you'd need to trade in your Doc Martens for stiletto heels. And that hair — not that it ain't pretty hair, but it always looks like you've been sleeping next to a helicopter. And forget working the stroll on a Harley. You'd attract all the queers, them thinking you was in drag. Finally, the way you carry on about sex, you'd think your body was a temple. So you better stick to writing, although how you practice it, it's probably as dangerous as prostitution."

Philosophy comes easily to Etta, even if her readings of the ethical branch are unconventional. Definitely I should have known better than to turn her way for a sermon on the evils of lust.

There was more. "You read the papers. You must have seen that full-page ad last month what got paid for by that family-values asshole — you know, Reverend what's-his-name?"

Etta never forgets a name. Feigned amnesia is her favoured device for mentally exterminating people she loathes. "You mean Ralph Herbert. He's just trying to shield the nation from 'bathhouse morality,' Etta. Give the guy a break."

"W-e-l-l" — her deftly protracted enunciation made that small word a rhetorical guillotine. "What next, Jane? You gonna picket gay funerals with that other Reverend asshole — the one with the GOD HATES FAGS signs? They get their rocks off trashing normal people's harmless pleasures. And high-falutin' as you might get, my dear, it's not like they'd approve of the likes of you. Them zealots are poison."

Etta couldn't fence-sit if her sex life depended on it. I had to hug the old girl. "Thanks, Mom. I've got a lot to think about."

"First time you ever let on your mother had a brain as big as her boobs." She raced in to take advantage of my vulnerability. "Apart from baby-sitting the bar and fixing the toilets, I never tell you to do nothing. But this is an order: go apologize to Silver. Friends like her ain't exactly falling out of the trees."

Chapter 7

THE FOLLOWING MORNING I assembled all my gear to begin painting the kitchen. The living and dining area was still in ruins, clots of ancient plaster clinging to exposed lath, but I forged ahead, in the hope that wrestling one small area into submission might drive the rest to surrender.

I had one long wall covered with a coat of Peach Blush latex when I conceded that no amount of paint could smooth its carbuncled surface. Turning to my cutlery drawer for inspiration, I selected utensils for which I'd never found any use, and randomly applied them to the fresh layer of drywall compound I'd slathered over the Peach Blush. An hour later my wall looked intentionally textured. I even signed my masterwork with a snail fork.

An energetic voice on the radio snagged my ear. "Our country music fans will remember the terrible fire that nearly destroyed Sweet Dreams, the city's best-known juke joint," burbled Shelagh Rogers, host of CBC Radio One's *This Morning*. "Well, you'll be delighted to hear that the owner, Etta Yeats, will be back in business this coming Saturday night. She's hosting a Grand Ole Opening to celebrate the occasion and she's come into the studio to talk about it. Good morning, Ms. Yeats."

My mother cleared her throat straight into the microphone. "Call me Etta, dear. And a 'good morning' to you, too.

I can't smoke in here, eh?" Her mike picked up the defiant click of a Bic.

"Etta, you must have been devastated by that fire. Sweet Dreams was a Mecca for country music lovers."

"Still is. I am not the sort of woman to let a gas bomb get her down. Even before those sexy boys from the Fire Department left, I swore I'd have my bar up and running again soon as I could."

Setting aside the matter of one's legs ending before the other's begin, Mom calls to mind Tina Turner, another tough woman who survived a conflagration and moved on to light all her own fires.

"But there must have been a downside to that experience, Etta."

"Well, the loss of poor Hank Williams' hat was a bad blow, I do admit, Shelagh. It was a gift from his son, who phoned all the way from Montgomery, Alabama in 1961, when Hank was posthumously inducted into the Country Music Hall of Fame — back when you was in diapers, dear. You see, the archivist discovered some of his old love letters …"

Rogers leapt innocent as a newborn into Etta's strategic pause. "You mean, you and Hank Williams were lovers?"

"Let's just say I mighta been on his mind when he recorded 'Hey, Good Lookin',"' replied Our Lady of the Sound Bite.

Hey, it could have been television.

Now I understood why Etta hadn't said a word to me yesterday about her scheduled radio appearance. She was hoping I wouldn't hear the rosary of lies she'd strung to create free publicity for her big event. When Hank Williams died in 1953, Etta was girlishly resident in a Catholic boarding school in Dublin.

"Your press release promises a whopping good evening,"

Shelagh obligingly enthused. "I see here that some very big names will be on hand to help you celebrate."

Etta giggled coyly. "Let's just say that Garth Brooks and I were on the phone recently. And I wouldn't be a bit surprised if k.d. lang dropped by after her show here in town. My stage will be packed with the best singers and bands in the country and we're recording the whole shindig. Everybody's welcome. Beer's ten bucks a pitcher, food's free. So come on out, folks."

Etta's offer of free food will hardly impact her bottom line. Her cook should be imprisoned for crimes against the palate.

The merry host wrapped up the interview by cueing to "Hey, Good Lookin'."

Throughout Etta's shameless performance, I had been aiming my hair dryer at the damp wall.

I cleaned up, while Shelagh Rogers attempted to mediate a heated discussion between three guests on street prostitution. One, a representative from a residents' association, used Paglia's murder to remind decent citizens that street prostitution is a nasty blight on our otherwise comely cityscape. He spoke on behalf of decent folk weary of raking used condoms from their lawns, decent men angry that their wives and daughters get hit on when they walk to the corner store for a loaf of bread, and decent parents terrified their toddlers might pick up a tainted needle. He alluded only briefly to the sex trade's negative impact on property values.

The second panelist, a sociology prof, presented two theories of prostitution — functionalism and feminism. Neither perspective seemed to offer much in the way of a remedy, but I suppose they kept students off the streets writing term papers.

It was Rosemary Miller, a social worker who heads up

Prostitutes' Recovery Outreach Services (PROS), who went straight to the heart of the problem. "It takes something more powerful than legislation, social services, and drug treatment programs to persuade a prostitute to get off the streets. I like to remind our clients that he who befriended Mary Magdalene — history's most famous sex worker — is there to save any girl who wants to leave the trade."

Guess the CBC didn't think to invite a sex worker. I switched to a hard rock station.

My mind meandered back to Ernie's last visit. Tina Paglia's slaying probably was an isolated incident — still, checking out the other murders might be productive. But a serious change in my attitude was called for. Since the discovery of Tina's body, I'd been reacting from my gut, mired in knee-jerk reflexes I didn't even know I owned, mouthing bullshit and bigotry that left my two favourite people shaking their heads in disapproval.

I brushed aside the notion of sifting through the emotional detritus that had landed me on this patch of ignorant ground. My faith in therapy is as shallow as my belief that Jesus loves me. Prostitution is an issue I need to *think* my way through.

Tina's body dropping in my front yard had created such ripples that at this moment were spiralling inward to a sudden realization: my brain was labouring under the pains that signal the birth of a new book idea. Ernie admitted that throwing a lot of expensive resources at unsolved hooker murders wasn't a police priority. So ... what the police lacked in resources and motivation, I bloody well had. "Fifteen or so" unsolved hooker murders, he'd said, almost twice as many missing prostitutes ...

Writing is thinking in action. The best person to hit on for the information I needed to determine if my idea had legs was Sam Brewer, veteran crime reporter for *The Toronto Post*. We'd been colleagues back when I did the crime-books column for the paper, and often used to drink together on Friday nights. He'd lost his wife to breast cancer shortly before Pete was killed. Although we haven't seen much of one another since his recent remarriage, we keep in touch by phone, hungrily exchanging information, rumours and speculation about the city's more remarkable crimes.

Crime reporters share some occupational characteristics with cops. Daily exposure to the worst we humans can do to one another leads them to view the species through decidedly jaded eyes. It's hard to get past the black humour. Sam works hard to see life in the round, but that's a tough assignment. One morning he may be interviewing the victim of a violent crime. That afternoon he's schmoozing a pimp who preys on runaway kids.

Sam owes me a mammoth favour. Last year I gave him all the documentation he needed to write the big-breaking story of his career. My motive had been to force a police investigation into the wheelings and dealings of the nation's most powerful corporate baron. All I asked for in return was Sam's promise to pass my archive on to Ernie Sivcoski, after he'd written up the story for the *Post*. Acting on my non-negotiable instructions, Sam claimed to be the recipient of an anonymous brown envelope. It didn't matter if Ernie believed him — as a reporter Sam hadn't been obliged to disclose his source.

That story so enhanced Sam's stock that he got a raise and a book contract on the strength of it. Tonight I planned to make him cough up in spades.

Chapter 8

I KNEW THAT SAM had recently worked his deep contacts within the police department to extract the cold case files on unsolved homicides from a detective who owed him many favours. Yet so swiftly did Sam plead a prior engagement when I invited him and his new wife to meet me for dinner, that I nearly hung up.

My postlapsarian scheme had run like this: Sam owed me, but what I was about to ask of him far exceeded his debt. To make up the deficit, I needed a serious inducement. Lechery was out, him being in love and newly-wed. So I opted for gluttony and insobriety. My VISA card had taken to belching whenever merchants slid it through their authorization check. Only the $146.31 in my bank account separated me from tits-up.

Go for bust, dear. Etta's voice had echoed generations of besotted Irish elders in the face of impending poverty. *Go out with a bang.* God would take care of the damages.

Bribeless now, my tongue ran haywire. "I have a favour to ask. Kind of a big one."

"I can't remember the last time a writer asked me for a small one," he chuckled.

Taking his laughter for encouragement, I plunged in. "You know that my neighbour got murdered on the weekend. Well, I want to do something to make her death matter. Maybe if I could read the documents on the unsolved hooker slayings I'd get a sense of the big picture. Maybe when I read through them, I'll find a case that looks solvable. Maybe if I can interview some old witnesses, dig up a few new ones, raise fresh questions — force the police into an investigative review. But, Sam, without those files I'll probably never know if Tina Paglia was killed by someone she knew or by a stranger with a hate-on for hookers — maybe a bad date."

Sam didn't ask why the case had so piqued my curiosity. We both make a living researching items most people forget about when they recycle the morning paper.

Any reservations he may have had were swept aside when I stammered my way through my guilt about Paglia's murder, including the bit about being too hammered to have tuned in to her swan song.

He volunteered to photocopy everything relevant to my investigation and drop it off the following morning.

When I gushed gratitude, he interrupted, "Hey, Louise and I are a damn sight closer to paying off our mortgage because of you."

Etta, there is a God.

St. Francis' bell lobbed nine grenades into the firmament as I opened the door Thursday morning. There stood Sam Brewer, holding a heavy cardboard file box with my copy of the morning paper on top.

I approvingly noted that Louise hadn't made a fashion make-over a condition of their partnership. The Hush Puppies were new, but Sam's worn trousers still held the pleated impression of his bony knees. I recognized the elbow patches on his Aran cardigan, but the garment had been steamed back into something less than a shroud for a drowned fisherman.

"Sam, I've missed you."

"Me, too," he blushed. "Hey, this is a beautiful little place you've got here."

Sam Brewer comes from a different planet than Ernie Sivcoski. This makes him easy to love.

When I expressed my disappointment that we'd not been able to meet for dinner with Louise, he coughed nervously. "Actually, I've been trying to shield Louise from my work. I know it frightens her. She's led a pretty sheltered life — the woman's a children's librarian, for God's sake."

"*Shield Louise from the likes of me* is what you're really saying, Sam."

Setting his file box on the floor, he plunked himself down on the sofa. "More from the darker side of myself. When we first started seeing each other, I was covering the Bernardo trial. Month after bloody month, sitting in that courtroom, listening to tapes and testimony from hell."

As if to exorcise the memories, he shook his head. "I don't know what was worse — the shell-shocked expressions on the faces of those poor girls' families or Karla Homolka's indifference. Ditto her husband's. As if none of the ... horror had been inscribed on the killers' psyches. How could that be?" His weary face broadcast a childlike perplexity.

"A quarter of a century into crime reporting and I came close to a total crack-up. Not burnout — breakdown. None of us wants to believe that the likes of Hannibal Lector exist outside the movies, but they do. And there's something that totally unprepares you for a homegrown freak. We're the nice folks who gave the world Anne of Green Gables and noble Mounties.

"You know, when I first got into this business I was naive enough to believe that if I just paid enough attention, maybe I could figure out what makes such twisted shits perform such unspeakable acts. Thirty years down the road and all I know is that *it makes them feel good.* Mother of God, I have to find something else to do." He put his face in his hands.

I didn't want to hear this. I've always clung to the notion that if Sam could survive with his compassion intact, so could I. "What are you saying?"

Detecting the quaver in my question, he put his hands around mine. "Crime reporting is my life, but too many years of staring freaks in the face has worn me down, Jane. By the time I got through the trial, all I was left wanting to do was retire and build a normal life with Louise."

I stifled all my objections. "Sounds like a good plan — and congratulations to both of you, Sam, whatever you decide. If it's any consolation, you'll leave an impressive mark on our field. Maybe Canadian crime reporting won't sink as low as it has south of the border."

"Thank you. I needed to hear that."

I jumped up. "Let me make us a coffee."

As I brewed up some Continental Dark, he interrupted my cheerful banter about the costume I planned to wear for Etta's Grand Ole Opening. "Jane, I can tell that you haven't heard the news."

He placed the *Post* on the kitchen counter, headline facing me.

Another Prostitute Found Slain:
Body sprawled in Jarvis Street parking lot

A prostitute who moved to Toronto five weeks ago was found murdered yesterday. A resident of a downtown apartment building spotted the body of Karen Clarke, 24, lying in a wind-blown gravel parking lot off Jarvis Street at about 7:15 a.m.

Dozens of apartments in four buildings overlook the lot where hookers and johns conduct business on the east side of Jarvis near Carlton Street.

Last week, after the discovery of Tina Paglia's body in a residential garden on Shannon Street, police asked sex workers to come forward with reports of violent attacks. A special task force is looking into possible links between the murders of a number of strangled hookers.

Homicide Detective Ian Bufwack said it's too early to determine if Clarke's death has any connection with the other murders. An autopsy will be performed today.

Police taped off an area of about 50 square metres in front of a chain link fence where garbage gathered at the east side of the lot.

Clarke wore a synthetic fur coat, white high-heeled boots and a mini skirt. A Canadian citizen of Chinese origin, she came here from British Columbia and stayed downtown with a friend. She had been working as a prostitute in the Church and Gerrard area.

Her friend, who requested anonymity, said that Clarke was in Toronto to visit her father, who is hospitalized with lung cancer. She planned to return to her husband and three children as soon as she had earned enough money for her fare.

Clarke is the sixteenth prostitute murdered in Toronto since 1996. There have been no arrests.

I sadly looked up at my buddy. "Sam, all these articles read like they came from the same journalistic cookie cutter. Only the victims' names change."

"You're right, but a good investigative writer like you can't ignore any of the details. And you know why most of them are there, tawdry as they sound. The police are hoping that someone will remember seeing Clarke last night, maybe come forward with some helpful information. This time they might. One hooker murder is chance, two maybe a coincidence ... but sixteen?"

"Isn't it a bit of a stretch that so many prostitutes were

killed — by a different person? And the murders are happening closer together. So where are the words 'serial killer?'"

Sam grunted. "You know tabloids use those words, Jane, not the police and not any respectable paper. As well as terrifying every woman who finds herself on the street at night, it wouldn't look good for the task force, would it?"

I shook my head in frustration. "Screw their image. Every woman in the city *should* be terrified. Think about how many women got raped that summer by one guy — same description, same M.O. — while the cops told women in his target area zero about the danger. Only *after* a victim sued the police department did they seem to get it. Had they warned residents — instead of using them as bait — women could have taken extra precautions." My voice was tight with barely contained fury.

Sam didn't say anything. He knows my rants escalate when I get interrupted.

"And what has this totally ineffectual task force done? Why the hell shouldn't it get some bad press? Sounds to me like it was created just so the media can refer to its existence every time a prostitute is murdered so it'll look as if the cops are pouring resources into these killings."

Sam gestured towards the file box. "I wouldn't wager on it, but you might be more sympathetic when you read through these files. I get the sense that, at least in the past six months, they've thrown as many officers into the investigations as their emaciated budget permits."

"Forgive my cynicism, Sam, you know the attitude: *Another dead hooker. Yawn.* But a home invasion in Rosedale — shit, they're ready to bring in the army! They posted a reward for that missing property months before the one for the hookers.

"And what about the off-duty officers who force prostitutes into sex by threatening them with arrest if they won't go down on them — a perk for being on the morality squad, I hear. Flash your badge and grab a freebie."

"You're right. It happens."

The whole subject had scraped a nerve already inflamed by guilt. "Sounds like rape to me ... and remember the two cops who stopped a hooker's car on Queen Street, then drove her to an underground garage, where they took turns raping her in the front seat of the cruiser? She committed suicide before the hearing ended."

Sam shook his head in resignation. "Jane, I'm not a cop and you're not a hooker. *We're writers.* That means we should at least strive for objectivity. For every officer who's gone bad, you'll find many more who haven't. That much I know from covering the crime beat. If we were thrust into the kinds of situations we pay cops to resolve, God knows how we'd behave."

"Okay, Sam. You're right; but god damn it, women don't cruise the streets like randy goats looking for a lay."

Sam raised his hands, palms towards me, to fend off a verbal *tsunami.* "Jane, Jane, before you hop aboard one of your hobbyhorses, hear this. Two homicide cops dropped into my office a couple of months ago. Been on the force for more than half their lives, good cops who just want to catch the bad guys. They came to see me because they'd gotten so frustrated investigating that double murder of the two pros found in a Regent Park stairwell. Along with three other detectives, they conducted more than a hundred witness interviews and still hadn't cracked the case. In desperation, they asked if I'd write a 'human interest' piece to try to persuade anyone who had any information to come forward."

"I remember that article, Sam. You managed to flesh out the victims as individuals, with lives beyond their work. Everything else I read about the case boiled them down to being 'crack whores' — as though whoring and drugs constituted their entire identity."

"Thanks. I interviewed the mother of one of the victims. She kept asking where she'd gone wrong, all the while hugging this photo of her daughter, back when she was a high-school cheerleader. I wish my article had helped out, or even pushed the inquiry a step forward. It didn't, but the police have now offered a $100,000 reward in that case and at least one of the others."

He glanced around, then grinned. "Don't get angry if I suggest that $100,000 would get this house a lot closer to *Architectural Digest.*"

"However did you guess my secret ambition? Actually, I'd be delighted just to rid this dump of roaches 'n rodents."

"All kidding aside, those files could form the basis of a terrific book, Jane. I know the Durand case soured you on writing white-collar crime. So why don't you set your investigative sights east of Bay Street — on the strolls?"

"You think I'd have a snowball's chance in hell of digging out some information the cops have missed? I mean, five experienced homicide detectives working the double murder for almost a year, interviewing all those witnesses?"

He gave me the encouragement I craved. "Those two cops said they knew in their gut the murders were solvable. Somebody out there knows who did it or is holding onto some important information. Because the police have exhausted their resources doesn't mean someone outside the force can't find that person — especially someone ... special."

"Isn't 'special' what anxious mothers call their kids when they can't pass kindergarten?"

My effort to dissuade him from analyzing me proved futile. "Your hostility about authority — hell, even about *respectability* ... somehow you've turned a temperamental disability into a plus, certainly in your career. People who don't trust cops — prostitutes are a fine example — would probably open up to you. You walk a different street than most of us. So do they."

He looked like maybe he was anticipating a slap across the face.

I gave only a fleeting thought to the unpleasant possibility that my talent for alienation was spilling over into my personal life.

"Hmph. For a self-styled rebel, I carry around a lot of knee-jerk moralizing. I have to do some serious work on my head before I can expect to gain the confidence of any smart whore."

"That surprises me. Your outrage around cops who abuse prostitutes sure sounded genuine."

"Don't flatter me. You know I give good outrage. It's one thing for a feminist to speak her politics, quite another for her to walk the talk. If there's a book in this, I need to get closer to the streets, Sam."

"As a sop to your conscience and maybe to suck a big enough advance from your publisher to finish your renovations. Watch your butt, woman. People who associate with criminals rarely open up to outsiders. They don't want to wind up dead. Meantime, good luck with those files."

Sam glanced at his watch and jumped up. "Oops ... got to run. Louise and I have a lunch date. Phone if I can clarify anything you find in there. Phone anyways."

As I walked him to the door, he added an afterthought: "Oh, I tossed in the files on the pros who are just missing, too. You might want to have a look at them."

How do you thank a colleague for trusting you enough that he doesn't even ask that you never reveal how confidential police files strayed into your possession?

Chapter 9

"FOR MOST PEOPLE IN this tight-assed city, Tina Paglia is just another dead whore. Civilians think that getting the shit beat out of you — even getting murdered — is in our job description. *No way, my friends, no fucking way.* We've come here tonight to tell Toronto that we are going to keep speaking up, shouting up and acting up for our rights."

Moses could not have delivered the Ten Commandments more fervently. The speaker was Antonia Romanoff, spokesperson for SWAT, the Sex Workers Alliance of Toronto.

On this chilly Thursday night, about seventy people had marched from the corner of Dundas and Sherbourne, the city's most notorious track, to Allan Gardens a few blocks north. The Gardens, a huge public square with a beautifully restored greenhouse, is a hangout for drug dealers and consumers. Gay guys do the nasty. Homeless people crash here when the hostels are overcrowded. Multi-functional, Allan Gardens is a year-round breeding ground for orchids and outcasts. Follow the cobblestone paths, admire the flowers, the fountains, the fragrant lushness ... and smell the desperation.

Tonight, an impromptu flower-laden memorial. Lighting candles for another dead cohort and fanning the firestorm of controversy and rebellion that had ignited the prostitutes' rights groups. I didn't envy the cops, having to walk a perilous tightrope between them and the residents' associations and the religious right, equally outraged at their very existence.

A small anti-vigil was taking place behind the shelter of some huge old trees, well removed from the main site. One power-suited woman clutched a sign: "The Lord has struck again." Other signs condemned prostitution as immoral and blamed whores for AIDS. Some handed out pamphlets — pro-life and anti-everything else.

Defiantly resplendent in full-length mink slung over provocative street drag, Romanoff raised her voice above the noise of the crowd. "We are here tonight to affirm that our human rights are just as important as everyone else's. No one has been arrested in Tina's murder. So we can add hers to the already frightening number of unsolved hooker slayings. We make easy targets — it's easy to kill us and easy to get away with it. Tonight I'm asking you to do something you normally wouldn't even think about. The police are urging us to come forward with unreported violent sexual assaults. Until now we've been circulating private bad date sheets among ourselves.

"Even though our relationship with the police is hardly a friendly one ... " Romanoff paused while the crowd growled. "... I think it's time that we start reporting what we know. I'm suggesting this because our lives are in serious danger. Next vigil, one more of us won't be here."

Again she paused when a few dissenting murmurs competed for attention. "You all know the word on the street — there's a serial killer out there. He's already picked off more than a dozen of us. Even the police think so. They've pulled together a task force to look into the murders that seem to be linked. They're working on a reward poster featuring photographs of the disappeared women.

"So far they're saying they have nothing to indicate that

Tina's slaying is connected to any of the others. All that means is that there's more than one murderous lunatic stalking the strolls. So give the cops all the help you can. But if they give you any shit, phone me."

In another life, Romanoff could have been a circuit-riding preacher. "Never has Toronto witnessed such a level of violence against sex workers — especially those of us who work the streets. If *nice* girls were getting beaten, raped and murdered at the same rate, the public outcry would be deafening. So tell me: *why the hell isn't the shit hitting every fan in every government office and police station in the city?* I'll tell you why: *because we're prostitutes.*"

Another chorus of affirmation.

She stared solemnly at the flowers. "That kind of crap is totally unacceptable. We have the same right as other workers to do our jobs in safety. Violence should not come with the territory. Too many people are sitting back and passing judgement while we die. Let's fight for the right to work free of fear, free of violence, free of hatred."

She pumped both arms into the air. "Fight back. Fight back." The crowd picked up her chant.

The final speaker was a friend of Tina's, a defeated-looking woman with stringy hair and a bad complexion. Apparently the trade had been less kind to her than to Romanoff. She spoke softly, the uncertainty in her voice diminishing with each word. "Tina Paglia was a human being. She deserved respect and dignity, which she sure as hell never got none of when she was alive. Sure she was a junkie, but she tried to get clean. Sure she was a hooker, but that was her job. Let's all remember her as a woman with a name and a face, not just a label and a price. And to the folks who were close to her, we're real sorry for your loss."

I followed her glance towards the back of the crowd. A man in a hooded sweatshirt was staring at the frosted ground, shoulders tightly hunched, hands tucked into his jeans pockets. Although I couldn't make out his face, I sensed he might be Hammer Hopkins. I inched my way closer gradually, not wanting to frighten him off.

Once I could confirm it was Hammer, I positioned myself so I could readily follow him when the crowd broke up. I'm very good at tailing people, a skill I picked up in grade eight when I took to tracking Sister Immaculata, whose mission it was to persistently humiliate me in math class. Although she never did enter a bar, bordello or even a Bingo parlour on my watch (I'd been fervently praying for some blackmail dirt), I escaped detection whiling away many hours that might otherwise have been misspent over a math textbook.

The din of yelling, whistling and clapping lasted for almost three minutes. As it died down, Hammer walked north towards Carlton.

This neighbourhood makes me very nervous, especially at night.

Chapter 10

HE TURNED INTO THE FIRST BAR on the block, the Back Street Bar and Grill, a dingy watering hole. I waited outside for a couple of minutes to give him time to settle in with some suds. Then I ventured in, hoping to unobtrusively nurse a beer where only the dimmest light fell, while I figured out how to approach Hammer.

The bartender, evidently a veteran of the World Wrestling Federation, spared me the trouble. "If you've come in here to hustle, honey, forget it. The street's lousy with cops tonight and I don't want no trouble. If I lose my booze licence, the fucking residents' association will make sure I never see it again."

So Etta was wrong about me needing to invest in a new wardrobe to get taken for a whore.

One sodden wit turned around on his bar stool to give me the once-over, ending at my Doc Martens. "Hey guys, we should take up a collection. If this broad don't invest in some new shoes, she's gonna have to start repairing motorcycles for a living."

His observation, closer to the mark than he knew, drew a growl of appreciative guffaws. Just as I was contemplating walking very slowly backwards towards the entrance, another poet came to voice. "For Christ's sake, Gus, pour the broad a beer." Hammer glared at me from the far end of the bar. He picked up his bottle and came over.

"Why don't we go sit at that table?" he asked, not making it sound much like an invitation. "Like, I figure you must have followed me in here, eh?"

He led us deep into the darkness, snug jeans hugging his skinny frame and terminating a good four fingers above the ankles of his white sports socks. Once seated, he looked at me, his gaunt face framed by the sweatshirt hood reminding me of a medieval monk who had barely survived bubonic plague. "So, you happy now she's dead? All you ever did was bitch at her."

Remorse was probably not the route to go. "Living next door to Tina was not a pleasant experience, Hammer. Besides, from what I could hear through the walls, you spent a whole lot more time bitching at her than I ever did." I could deck him if he took offence — provided he wasn't carrying.

To my amazement, his eyes welled with tears. The bartender gave him an unsympathetic look as he slammed down another Blue.

"I was only trying to make Tina get her life together. Joke, eh? You don't have a fuckin' clue what her fuckin' life was really like. I got her that apartment, you know."

He took a deep swig, some beer dribbling down his sweatshirt. He wiped his mouth on a cuff. "Before, she spent the whole summer sleeping in parks or in jail. So I got to thinking — maybe if she had her own place it would be easier for her to get clean. Shit, a couple of weeks ago, she was off the stuff for four straight days. I even started believing maybe we could get the kids back."

Sudden anger enlivened his dead eyes. "Yeah, yeah. I know what you're thinking: better for the kids this way. Would've been better for her if someone had offed her old man, for sure. Bastard abused her from when she was just a kid. The first time she left home, she was only seven. When she was twelve, some asshole judge called her a 'habitual runner.' She started hooking at fourteen. Last July she got busted for possession of stolen property — a fuckin' microwave I picked up for her. It was her 100th conviction. Some kinda record, eh? She couldn't trust nobody after what she been through, see, not even me."

He sounded desperate for a sympathetic ear, and evidently I'd been arbitrarily chosen. Could be he had no one else. Guessing that he wanted me to hear out his sodden reminiscences, I tried to lead us into how his woman might have met her end.

"Hammer, you said you figured I was glad Tina was dead. But you are very wrong on that count. You see, I feel very guilty about how I treated her ... so I've sworn to do everything to help find her killer." The declaration popped out of my mouth without checking my brain for clearance.

Guilt is the emotional equivalent of a kidney stone. Atonement can dissolve it, but I've always left making amends to religious penitents and AA disciples. Yet seeing Tina's naked body, forsaken as a dead alley cat, brought on a need for absolution. She was not a model citizen, I had demonstrated my disapproval of her, and she had been killed — while I slumbered.

Hammer peered at me, curiously. "There's talk about you in the neighbourhood, you know — that you got some heavy crime thing. Is that true?"

"It's true."

"I ain't surprised. You don't look like a normal broad." Chuckling at his unintentional compliment, I remarked, "My mother says the same thing."

"Yeah, well, you drive that bike like you know what you're doing."

"Hey, I wear what it takes to ride a Harley — from the driver's seat."

He squirmed as if a mouse was nesting in his crotch. Those jeans sure didn't leave his balls any room to boogie. "Tina always figured you for a dyke, eh?"

Where my hormones lead me is nobody's business but my own. Many moons ago, I realized that defending my sex life is a big energy drain. Maybe I'm like a lot of whores in that regard.

"So who cares? For sure not me. I don't wanna sleep with you."

I took this disappointment in stride. "Hammer, help me here. Have you got any idea who might have killed Tina?" No way was I going to intimate that he struck me as a likely candidate.

"That fucker Quasimodo." He extinguished his cigarette into a dented tin ashtray with enough vigour to put out a small brush fire. "He supplied her with the goddamn crack and he was always trying to push her back onto the street so she could buy more junk from him. But he wasn't her pimp, eh? Not like them other chicks. Tina wouldn't work for no man. She earned her money all by herself and she was keeping every friggin' penny. But sooner or later almost all of it went into his fuckin' wallet anyways."

He slammed down his glass so hard Gus shot him a warning glance. "There ain't nobody in this whole butthole of a city I hate more than that prick. I swear to God, when I find that little bag of shit, I'm gonna waste him. Even if he didn't actually kill Tina, the way I see it, he's responsible for her being dead."

"How bad was her habit?"

"She'd go on these binges, eh? Sometimes she would booze a lot when she was using, to chill when she got all hyper and paranoid. Them last three days she spent smoking crack and swigging tequila. Her runs sometimes lasted for four, five days, 'til she had no more drugs. She could smoke a small fortune during a binge. Afterwards, she'd crash, all whacked out, starving to death and depressed, swearing she'd never pick up again. If she got real paranoid, she'd drink some more. But she always went back to chasing the dragon. Like, if you coulda seen her when she crashed, you'd see why she'd do fuckin' anything — she was desperate. I'd show up, she'd be crawling around the floor looking for pebbles to smoke. Finally she'd give up and head back to the stroll."

I encouraged him to dig deeper. "So why would Quasimodo want to kill Tina? Sounds like she was one of his best customers."

"Yeah, well, there's only one other asshole who wanted her dead." He scratched his scalp under the hood. "See, Tina got beat up real bad last year. One night she's working Queen Street, this guy pulls her into a laneway. He puts a shoelace around her neck and a bag over her head, duct-tapes her hands behind her back. Holds a knife to her throat ... and ..." The scratching intensified.

"And what, Hammer?"

His eyes stayed stuck to the floor. "And r-r-r-rapes her." Then he challenged me with full eye contact. "A joke, eh — a hooker getting raped?"

"Rape is rape and it's never a joke."

His scowl relaxed a few lines. "Anyways, two cops caught the bastard climbing a fence. They got him to confess to sexual assault with a weapon and threatening death."

Hammer's word-hoard was enhanced in the familiar territory of police charges. "So they persuade Tina to testify against him. Threatened to pull her in again for communicating. I told her it was a real bad idea but she done it anyways. So I figure maybe he got let out with one of them weekend passes like he got when he raped her. Killed her to shut her up, right? But then I find out them shrinks at the Whitby nut bin suspended his passes after what he done to her the first time."

"So that leaves Quasimodo."

"Him and her go back a long ways. A while before I met her, they lived together for a couple a months. Nothin' to do with sex, they both just needed a roof. Once last week, when she was crazy for some more smoke, she told me she could blackmail Quasimodo into *giving* her enough shit to keep her up for the rest of her life. She weren't thinking too clear, eh? It would have been a whole lot cheaper for him to whack her. I mean, making it look like she OD'd would have been a piece of cake. Or he could have picked her up, gone to some parking lot or back to her apartment by promising to fix her up, then ... slit her throat. Cops'd blame that serial killer all the girls are talking about. You heard Antonia tonight." He extinguished another butt.

Remembering the cops at her door, I ventured, "Hammer, do you know what Quasimodo was hassling her about last Friday night? The man was very pissed off."

"Oh yeah. When she hit on him for a vial, he told her his price had gone up — just to make her crazy. It worked. She rode off on his $5,000 mountain bike while he was doing a deal. Wheeled it into the hallway of her apartment. Now, Quasimodo gives a much bigger shit about that bike than about his own mother. So Tina got a real charge outta watching him go ballistic when it went missing."

Diligent as a clock cuckoo, Gus reappeared with two more Blue. We both declined his suggestion that we order some burgers. We'd be safer ordering *cucaracha* stew. Before he had time to get offended, Gus hurried off to break up a fight gaining steam near the back door.

I picked up the broken thread. "So were Quasimodo and his beloved bike reunited?"

"Sure, but only after Tina slashed the tires and scraped up the paint real good. Cut the brake cables, too. She was some piece of work, my girl." He gave me a sad, proud smile.

He lit the filter end of his umpteenth Export 'A', confirming that the beer was not his first of the day. *Who could blame the poor bugger?* But before he married the linoleum, there was something I wanted to clear up — his possible implication in Tina's death.

That mine-field I approached stealthily as a leopard with an ailing antelope on the menu. "Hammer, you've got to be kicking yourself in the butt for not being at Tina's place when she got attacked. What kept you away, man? You usually showed up Saturday nights."

"Me and a buddy was doing a b-and-e up on Summerhill Gardens Saturday night."

People are forever sidling up to me in bars to tell me shit they hide from God. Obligingly I grant absolution, forgive damn near every slack-ass I ever meet. Except myself.

My face must have registered surprise, though, which he misinterpreted as disapproval. "Hey, Tina hooked, I steal. That's how we get by," he explained. "Anyways, Salvatore — that's my buddy — must have dropped his fuckin' wallet at the job. Not the brightest bulb on the porch. Anyways, after I seen them hauling Tina's body off to the morgue Sunday morning, I headed for Sal's place to chill. Cops showed up."

He snapped the disabled filter from his cigarette and lit the remnant. "I just got outta jail this afternoon, right? Cops kept me because the dirtbag lawyer I got through Legal Aid screwed up my paperwork. Next week I gotta be back in court."

Seems we've all got a bone to pick with the justice system.

I'd ask Ernie to confirm Hammer's story, although I was sure it would check out. I was down to one known suspect — Quasimodo, whose coincidental disappearance looked like guilt to me.

Chapter 11

WHEN I ARRIVED BACK HOME close to midnight, Max was waiting at the door with his hind legs crossed. Five minutes later, he yelped at the streetcar shelter on the north edge of Trinity Bellwoods Park. A huge GAP ad obscured the interior. Peeking in from the entrance, I spotted a hodgepodge of lumped fabrics under the aluminum bench. A length of emaciated hairy leg lay exposed between an oversize running shoe and a slice of hot pink polyester.

It was cold enough that city officials had issued an extreme-cold-weather alert. I wanted to make sure he hadn't passed out. I knocked gently on the wall. "Good evening, sir. Do you remember us? The lady with the rude dog. His name is Max and he is on his lead. No danger to you this evening."

"Repeat."

A simple request. "I'm the lady with rude dog. Named Max. No danger to you tonight."

"We heard you the first time. I'm not deaf. Repeat — MY NAME IS REPEAT."

"Oh, sorry ... Repeat. My name is Jane."

"The dog is Max. His mother is Jane." This time he didn't shout. "Tarzan is not at home." He giggled.

"Um ... we haven't seen you for a while, Repeat. Have you been away?"

He struggled to his feet, reaching into his pocket for a

cigarette. "Yes — and no. I went to the church for supper. All Souls. Too many body lice. Slept a few nights on a pew. Then came back here. Sometimes sleep here when it goes real cold. Won't go into those other shelters. You get robbed when you're sleeping." Lighting a crumpled cigarette, he inhaled deeply.

"I'm glad you're OK, Repeat. Can I get you anything ... a sandwich, maybe a coffee?"

"Coffee would be very nice. Yes we do love coffee. Double-double, please." He blew three perfect smoke rings and monitored their demise. "Tonight they are signalling the Delta code. Lock your doors."

When I returned from the donut shop, he had gone back to bed. I placed the Styrofoam cup on the bench under which his head rested, then slowly backed away.

A hand jerked out from the bundle of clothing to grasp the cup.

"Good-bye, Max and Jane," was Repeat's muffled farewell. "Lock your doors. Secure your windows. Batten the hatches. Danger is afoot."

Chapter 12

THE YOUNG AND THE FRENETIC party 'til dawn on the College Street strip. From funky, candle-lit martini bars to 1:00 a.m. drag shows, the street rocks. Yet St. Francis of Assisi Church, a neo-Gothic grey rebuttal of the late twentieth century, remains the true heart of Little Italy. Built in 1914, it anchors the nearby corner of Grace and Mansfield. The original Irish congregation was gradually replaced by Italians who immigrated here in the early fifties to join the post-war construction boom.

The leaden tolling of its bell has marked the passage of five of my elderly neighbours within a month. Rugged men who fled Calabria to build a more hopeful future for their young wives and kids-to-be, now pensioned off into tending their gardens, grape vines and modest homes. Their prosperous offspring have moved to the suburbs. Most of their grandchildren cannot speak Italian.

St. Francis marks Holy Week with its annual Good Friday procession, which draws far bigger crowds than the Santa Claus parade. Donkeys, centurions, and the usual suspects re-enact the stations of the cross to the lugubrious accompaniment of church marching bands.

Now that Christmas looms, hymns blare forth from woolly speakers over an outdoor sound-and-light crèche extravaganza, through which the denizens of Disney's Animal Kingdom run amok, dinos to rhinos.

Shortly before ten Friday morning I enter the church to hear the Requiem Mass for Tina Paglia. The clutch of mourners is dwarfed by the magnitude of the church. At the front, a sprinkling of elderly neighbourhood ladies who never miss a funeral; a few rows back, half a dozen women whose hairdos and attire hint that they are work colleagues of the deceased. The pall bearers are funeral-home guys. I figure two other guys for undercover cops, checking out the scene in the hope that life might emulate TV and someone suspicious show his face.

Hammer and Quasimodo have taken a rain check. There is no one who might be family.

Apparently the Sex Workers Alliance collected the $2,000 needed for her modest, closed coffin and funeral arrangements.

During the "Ave Maria," birdsong reverberates high up in the rafters. "Father Antonio's canaries," whispers a black-shrouded crone beside me in the back pew.

Assisted by a septuagenarian priest, Father Antonio conducts the Mass and delivers the briefest of eulogies in Italian. Given all those Biblical injunctions against whores, he must have selected his words of final remembrance very cautiously.

Last night's secular observance, the vigil, had conferred a gritty, visceral sense of the streets Tina had walked to her death. But this ritual gives her a sweet dignity markedly absent from her life.

Home again, I plunged into some background reading prior to poring over Sam's cold-case files.

I first reached for my clippings file, where I'd tucked my favourite year-end list — the one detailing city homicides. I'm a crime-stats junkie. When some guy at a sports bar tries his luck with, "You know how many strikeouts Sandy Koufax pitched for the Dodgers in 1965?" I can swiftly volley back, "No, but in that year Nannie Doss died in prison while serving a life sentence for killing four husbands by slipping rat poison into their stewed prunes. She claimed she was searching for the perfect mate." Maybe this is why I go home alone.

Over the past decade, Toronto's homicide rate has declined from a high of eighty-nine in 1991 to this year's low of fifty-two — exactly one a week. It doesn't get much lower in any North American city with a population of over two-and-a-half million. This fact is not lost on American tourists, who warmly congratulate us for maintaining such a safe, litter-free city. It's like winning the Immaculate Underwear award.

Seventy-one percent of the most recent crop of victims were male, one of whom slipped his mortal coil just a block north of my house. Whether or not he should appear in the stats at all remains dubious, the 91-year-old victim having succumbed to a heart attack in the midst of a punch-up with his drunken 85-year-old tenant.

I digested the stats pertinent to female victims. Fifteen in the past year, domestic violence accounting for most of them. If Toronto women can avoid irate partners, we needn't fear for our lives — *unless we are street prostitutes.*

Of the fifteen female victims, five were known prostitutes. Now, that's a wildly disproportionate number.

So, how many Toronto prostitutes have been slain over, say, the past decade — and how many of those cases remain unsolved? I was stunned. Thirty victims: ten arrests, eight convictions. Two of the convicted men had killed at least five hookers between them. That leaves nineteen unsolved, their perpetrators still on the streets. So, the homicide rate is declining, and hooker slayings are escalating. Fifteen in the past three years, six in the past twelve months, two in the past two weeks.

Who was killing these women? Whackos with a homicidal tic about women who sell sex? The escalating body count could mean that at least one was on a spree, driven to take greater risks, make mistakes, establish a pattern.

So, was there any discernible pattern?

The cold-case files confirmed that I was on a wild-goose chase. Loathe as I was to admit it, Ernie and his homicide colleagues had solid grounds for shifting their investigations. What street hookers do is go off to isolated locations with strangers. Since so many working girls are runaways, transients and druggies, their disappearances often go unremarked — making it often impossible to reconstruct the circumstances. Some aren't even reported missing for months, sometimes years.

I carefully returned all the papers to their files, shuffled them into chronological order, and placed them in the carton. A file lurking at the bottom caught my eye. Unlike the other neat computer-printed labels, this one was hand-written. "Missing persons — hookers?"

At some point — perhaps during a slack period when he was trolling for story ideas — Sam had gone through the missing-persons files for the last two years and pulled out those that identified the disappeared as 'prostitute.'

How could so many women go missing in such a short space of time — and attract so little notice? Silver was right. Mom was right. Time to cast a cold eye on my moral baggage, which made me complicit in rendering their lives invisible, even before they vanished.

I drew up a crude chart. Twenty-four rows, one for each woman. Columns for age, race, appearance (height, weight, hair colour), last known address, strolls, hangouts, known acquaintances, police record, drug/alcohol addiction, date reported missing, location last seen, person reporting disappearance ...

In the midst of my flurry of note-taking, a notion began to gel. There is a book here — Sam could see that — but a book about what? Absence? Twenty-four women whose collective biography could be summarized in a generic paragraph? Why let that stop me?

My phantom book had no thesis and promised no conclusion. It had to be predicated upon nothing more substantial than the possibility that some of the disappearances might be linked to prostitution; that some of the missing women might also be murder victims; and that one or more of their deaths might be linked to the prostitutes whose bodies had been discovered. If I could isolate some thread common to a few of the missing, develop a working hypothesis to structure my investigation around, do some legwork, conduct some interviews ...

I'd begun my previous books with a clear script. Each real-life narrative had climaxed in a criminal conviction before I sat down to reconstruct the characters and events leading up to it.

I may not be so pathological a control freak that I arrange my spice rack alphabetically, but writing always gives me a handle on the unpredictable. Since Pete's death, my compulsion to wrestle experience into coherence through language had taken over. What began as a method for structuring my books expanded into a state of mind, a way of life ...

but now, I have no choice but to let my research dictate what comes next. How far can I let it take me, having packed none of my customary safeguards?

First I need to convince my agent that it's the journey, not the arrival, that matters. Given that her income derives from well-charted literary landings, her enthusiasm might be tempered by pecuniary concerns. Before my euphoria dissipates in the cold light of her pragmatism, I'll write up a convincing proposal for a marketable book. Nothing stands between me and a hefty advance that a wee shot of mendacity can't cure. If I hint that I'm pursuing a strong lead that should force the police to re-open their investigations into the disappearance of several missing women ...

Chapter 13

FRIDAY NIGHT I carefully pencilled in two sable brows like inverted smiles over my eyes, filled in my lips with a hue reminiscent of coagulated blood, then checked out my makeover in front of the full-length mirror.

I'd decided to celebrate Etta's Grand Ole Opening Nite by dressing as Cousin Minnie Pearl, the Queen of Country Comedy. Opryland's Minnie Pearl Museum is one of Mom's shrines, so she ought to appreciate the tribute. Besides, Minnie was the first woman to be named *Billboard's* "Man of the Year" for country music. I had contemplated going as Shania Twain, but hadn't time for the facelift, breast augmentation and navel restructuring.

Most of my outfit came from the Goodwill, which rarely disappoints my inner reluctant shopper. I looked startlingly like Nashville's endearing spinster in my flower-strewn, broad-brimmed straw hat, from which dangled the trademark price tag. My frilly, country-girl dress flounced down to just short of my nylon socks and Doc Martens, more or less sparing me the necessity of shaving my legs. The Goodwill had also yielded my earrings and necklace, tiny masterworks of sea-shell art.

"HEE-HAW," I shouted at my image. I looked like a hundred bucks. No time to puzzle over why I feel more comfortable dressed like an Alabama clown than in your basic black cocktail dress.

I planted a big smooch on Max's nose and headed out to party on Harley. Just past Broadview, we got pulled over by a traffic cop.

"HOW-DEE, officer!" I hoped Blue Boy had a sense of humour.

He grinned. "How-dee, ma'am. You're not in any kind of trouble here. I just wanted to get a closer look. Hope you don't mind."

"I'm flattered. As Minnie once said, 'I wear a hat so folks can tell me and Dolly Parton apart.'" I reached into my saddlebag and produced my straw hat.

"Let me guess. You must be heading for Sweet Dreams. My wife's real upset I couldn't take her there tonight."

"Yeah, my Mom owns the joint."

He was wonder-struck. "Too cool. I can't wait to tell Gloria."

It's not easy, being the daughter of a celebrity.

DayGlo searchlights arced across the face of Etta's edifice. Two exterior speakers blasted an endless loop of "Sweet Dreams of You." A couple were stepping out of a white stretch limo, the guy in a black Stetson, jeans so tight his jewels were singing "please release me, let me go."

A woman in the packed crowd close to the entrance grabbed her girlfriend's arm. "Ohmygawd, Shirley, it's Garth ... GARTH BROOKS."

Maybe Etta hadn't been lying about her all-star lineup. If she owned a race track, I'd be best pals with the Queen Mother.

I drove Harley around to the parking lot behind the bar and used my key on the back door. There stood Etta, giving last-minute instructions to her staff. No less than regal in a white satin gown aswirl in gold sequins, with plunging neckline, slits up to the thigh, and five-inch gold stilettos. Only Etta could carry off a beehive wig the colour of pink lemonade.

Her welcome was subdued. Couldn't be nerves — she doesn't have any.

"Well, you got all the details right, dear, 'cept for the shoes, which should be Mary Janes. But you had to choose Cousin Minnie, eh? Why not Loretta Lynn or Barbara Mandrell — some sex appeal, a little glamour?"

Deep-breathing helped. "Hey, Mom, I didn't come here to get laid." Since I pulled on my first T-shirt and jeans, Etta's been harping on about my clothes.

She softened up as one gold acrylic nail sliced through the wrapping on my housewarming gift. To raise the $190 (plus tax) to make this purchase, I pawned my sound equipment, so Etta's life depended on her being intensely grateful.

"How did you know?" she shrieked.

Like it was the Holy Grail, she clutched the newly-released ten-CD Hank Williams compilation to her ample bosom. The initial run had already sold out (and was nominated for an album-notes Grammy). I love the guy's music, but only a fanatic could appreciate two volumes of annotations, more than 50 previously unreleased cuts, the 1949 radio transcriptions of his "Health and Happiness" shows (including Hank's pitches for the patent medicine Hadacol), demo tapes and studio outtakes.

"How did I know what?" I asked.

"Me and Eddy are flying off to Montgomery, Alabama, in February. They opened up a Hank Williams museum in the old railroad terminal there. It's even got the blue Cadillac he died in."

Different pilgrimages for different folks.

"Eddy?" When it comes to men, Etta's like a kid reckless

with birthday money in a candy shop — so many jelly beans, so little time. She savours each sweet in turn, but her democratic hand never settles on one jar to the exclusion of its mates. Only rarely has she been caught gumming two at once.

"I had to dump Nikos," she confided. "Got a bit of encouragement from his wife. But you know, that very night Eddy walked in here to catch a new band I'd brought in from Halifax. Love at first sight for both of us," she beamed. "He's working late tonight, dee-jaying at the Silver Dollar. Introduce you soon as he arrives."

She planted a wet kiss of thanks on my cheek and tottered off to greet her guests.

Etta's regulars, most migrants from down East, most dressed in plaid flannel shirts, blue jeans and cowboy boots, mingled with local country bands (praying to break into the big time), local celebs, and refugees from Queen Street. A City-TV crew was on hand to document the occasion for urban posterity.

But I wasn't up for the festivities, and headed for the bar. When he saw me approaching, Kenny-the-bartender drew me a pint of Smithwick's. Three other guys steadily worked bar alongside him.

Kenny grinned wide as a mail slot. "Jane, you're looking like a *real* woman tonight. Should try it more often." Etta writes his scripts.

I downed my pint, staring morosely at the replica of Hank's ten-gallon hat in a Plexiglas reliquary. Etta claims it's the original fake, miraculously rescued from the conflagration at considerable risk to her person.

Telling the truth, Mom claims, is not what it's cut out to be. Look where it got Jesus.

By the time things really got humming, I had drunk my

way through my beer quota. Then I stopped counting. Hell, it was a once-in-a-lifetime night.

As I sullenly pondered the virtues of mendacity, some wiseass tugged at the 69-cent price tag on my hat. "Does that buy me the hat — or you?"

Suddenly everything went dead quiet as a classy guy in a tux hopped up on stage. Then she spoke: "A whole lot of us present tonight got our big break right here in this bar. Hell, without the support and encouragement of Etta Yeats, I'd probably be hustling commercials for the beef producers. And you know what a mad cow that would make me."

The whole room broke into wild cheers and applause. She bowed from the waist, and continued. "Back in the early eighties, I strolled into Sweet Dreams in my cut-off boots and square-dance skirt to ask if I could sing a tune or two at one of Etta's famous Friday-night talent shows. Well, I hadn't finished the first verse of 'Hanky Panky' before she gave me the thumbs-up. I've never stopped being grateful. Folks, this woman is pure gold."

She cajoled my reluctant mother up on stage, got down on one knee, took Etta's hand and crooned "Crying." I sobbed my heart out — for Etta, whose joy was palpable, and for me, who, somewhere along the way, had lost track of joy.

And I felt thick as a plank. A couple of years ago, I'd kicked up a storm when Mom refused to hang my k.d.lang poster in her Girl Warblers Gallery because, so she claimed, the singer's Patsy Cline appropriation was mightily offensive. Tonight I saw her refusal for what it really was — a will to keep her helping hand in the shadows, where she knew it belonged.

Etta made her way straight for me, trailing Eddy, her latest Hoochie Coochie man. Turned out he was from the

Mississippi Delta, had migrated north in Muddy Waters' tracks for the Chicago blues scene. Even a bit stooped, he stood about six foot four. Good-looking and a sweet man. Hope he isn't in love with Etta, who doesn't consider any boyfriend a keeper.

Over the protestations of her guests, Etta declined to return to the stage. Seems she didn't want to make herself an easy target for Nikos' wife, who had staggered in armed with a half-empty quart of *ouzo*.

I used to think the romance industry catered to bored housewives. I was wrong. Endlessly questing, yet way too smart to believe she'll find the Holy Grail, Etta cheerily latches on to any vessel without a serious leak. A host of men have found glory with Etta. Not one left without a smile on his face, nor has she shed a tear for any of them.

"I keep trading mine in on a new model 'cause I wasted more years than I wanna remember driving a wreck that only croaked when his liver gave out — long after his piston had stopped pumping. You, why you'd rather walk if you can't get back the first one you ever had."

"It's more complicated than that, Mom."

"Yeah, so's life but that don't keep me from partying."

Chapter 14

MAX BARKED frantically as he pursued the erratic sound track of a rat in turd-dropping flight behind the bedroom wall.

"Murder it, Max, and you get paid in T-bones." Only when my border collie does his atavistic herder shtick can he be considered handsome.

I started the coffee, zapped a frozen bagel in the microwave, and collected the morning paper. After I had digested all three, I tried to assemble a course of action for the day. Motivational trainers would call my impasse an 'organization block.' I knew better.

Six days had passed since I stormed out of Canicatti's, leaving Silver to ponder what a self-righteous jerk I'd morphed into. Being Native, being fat, being a lesbian — hell, being a renegade artist in a culture transfixed on its Magnificent Seven dead landscape painters — had forced her to grow a hide thicker than a buffalo's. But my insensitivity had penetrated even that.

Losing touch with a good friend because she's far away carries an important consolation: I can conjure her in a warm surround of memories. But the sting of absence because I fucked up is unrelieved.

A good jog might give me the clarity to contact her.

My churning brain persisted in scanning my life. Career:

flat-lined, hadn't written even an article in months. Finances: zero, therefore no need to worry about RSPs, mutual funds. Shelter: 25% ownership, renovations flash-frozen in mid-execution, mortgage festering. Romance: love of my life, deceased. Social life: playing insecurity guard at Sweet Dreams, lunching maybe with Silver, drinking beer while pretending to read through the Booker shortlist. Parents: Seamus dead, Etta hyper-vibrant (praise be). Kids: never ... my own prolonged adolescence more than enough.

My classically-depressive sound track ground on, skirting alarmingly close to suicidal riffs. Blinded by my own miseries, I must have walked past Repeat without noticing.

"Star light, star bright. Twinkle, twinkle, little star. Star twinkle bright. There's a moon out tonight." He crooned the words into a lilting lullaby.

He was sitting cross-legged on the wet grass, barricaded within his fortress of plump bags, rhythmically nodding his head as if at prayer.

"Star light, star bright. Twinkle, twinkle, little star. Star twinkle bright. There's a moon out tonight."

I lowered myself to the ground cross-legged. "I'm not seeing the star light this morning, Repeat."

"Star light, star bright. Eyes closed — only dark. We don't like the dark."

I watched him reach for one of his bags in slow-mo, extracting another bag, transparent plastic. He signalled me closer with a frantic flurry of fingertips. Slowly I crab-walked towards him, the underside of my jeans absorbing moisture from the dew-soaked grass. If I transgressed his imagined boundaries by another inch, paranoia would pre-empt our delicate communication.

Repeat's bag was closed at the top with a frayed twist-tie.

His huge hand, fingernails embedded with earth, raised it twirling into sight-line with the sun. Crystal chandelier drops twinkled in a kaleidoscopic dance. Splintering red, orange, purple, green against the thickened arthritic branches of an oak tree, fracturing the spectrum in a fantasy of brilliance.

Suddenly dazzled into remembrance of why I wanted to continue breathing, I instinctively reached to touch his shoulder. Like a terrified animal, he shied away.

"We don't like the dark."

Softly, as I retreated, "You are right. We don't like the dark. Thank you, Repeat. For the sun."

"It's almost dark again."

So we continued. Communication, or none, as our moods dictated. Me bearing coffee and a sandwich, Repeat summoning star shine when he could.

On the way to the phone, I made a warm-up call:

Good St. Dympna, please assist us now in our present necessity, and intercede before God that Silver will forgive me. Amen.

Since Pete's death, I've pretty much lost the will to make and maintain relationships. Something in me fears deep attachment to what can so swiftly be lost. Any setback has me trapped for eternity, staring at a coffin Pete shouldn't have occupied for at least forty years. Silver was as brave as I could get.

I dialled her number. A resolute voice answered, then went silent. I babbled, beginning with "I'm sorry" and ending with "I love you, you know."

"Yeah, I know." Her voice sounded impatient. "And I must love you because your apology *almost* got to me."

"What can I say to convince you?"

"Like you didn't cover all the bases in that long-winded speech? Shit, you white people don't know when to shut up. Ever see a bunch of Indians on a talk show?"

Normally I'd parry with a wisecrack, but I opted for diplomacy. "I get the message. What can I do to make it up to you?"

"You can do what I suggested in the restaurant before you shape-shifted into a born-again virgin. You can pour some enlightenment into that reactionary hole of a brain. There's a woman I want you to meet. She's a sociology prof at Ryerson working on a Department of Justice report on — *ta dum* — prostitution in Toronto. Lenore Tootoosis. Write it down. Here's her home and office numbers — hell, I'll even throw in her pager."

I dutifully inscribed the numbers on a paper towel.

"Lenore's a Cree from the Poundmaker rez. Talk with her and you'll never feel the same way about hooking again. And if you're serious about poking your stupid nose into your neighbour's murder, you couldn't find a better source for the skinny on sex workers. Now, that should speak to your vocational lust for information that normal people leave under flat rocks — should you be disinclined to do penance."

Silver was always way ahead of me. She had it all cooked up, knowing I'd grovel. When I readily consented to sign up, she cautioned, "Just watch your fucking attitude."

"I promise — and many thanks, my friend."

"Yeah. We'll get together after you've seen Lenore."

Within five minutes of Silver's banging down the phone, Lenore Tootoosis had agreed to meet me the following afternoon.

Chapter 15

I SPENT WHAT REMAINED of Sunday poring over the details of the disappeared hookers, and sketching a tentative outline for the book, which contrasted markedly with the proposal I e-mailed to my agent.

Thirty-one hookers known to be missing in the past three years. None took along her personal belongings. None has picked up a welfare cheque or contacted children or family members.

Many people with street experience — Antonia Romanoff, for one — are convinced that these women are no longer alive and that a serial killer is responsible for several of the deaths. Working girls refuse to believe that no bodies equal no murders: disposing of a corpse in a city on a huge lake with many deeply-wooded ravines is easy. They've been encountering a lot more bad dates lately. And the high incidence of girls doing rock drives them to forsake their street smarts just to score.

And the prime suspect(s)? Age: unknown. Sex: unknown. Race: unknown. Height: unknown. Weight: unknown. Eye Colour: unknown. Hair Colour: unknown. Distinguishing Marks/Tattoos: unknown.

Detectives have laboured hard over each file in my possession. But they've been stonewalled — no bodies, no crime scenes, only a long string of missing persons reports. They've found nothing linking these women except that almost all were involved in drugs and frequented the strolls.

The cases have been entered on VICLAS and its counterpart in the United States. They've consulted with the FBI. Investigators have requested dental charts on all the women, and most have been entered on police computers. "America's Most Wanted" recently featured their work, but none of the leads was productive.

Family members and known friends or associates have been interviewed, sometimes more than once. Detective Constable Janet Cole was added to the missing persons section to concentrate on liaising with families and the media, attending community meetings, contacting other police agencies — and on the ongoing investigation of thirty-one files.

Missing-persons detectives conferred with vice and homicide squads, the provincial unsolved-homicide unit and RCMP serious-crime sections. That many of the women disappeared weeks, months or years before anyone reported them missing has made it extremely difficult to determine when or where the women were last seen, let alone find witnesses.

Most were young and unsophisticated, often impaired by drugs or booze, and working heavily-trafficked strolls where their entry into a stranger's vehicle usually went unremarked. Some also had mental-health issues that diminished their judgement and defences.

Easy prey for sexual predators attuned to weakness.

I was tempted to can the whole project. I'm not a real detective, not even a private investigator. My job is to write a book. My best hope was to mount a hit-and-miss investigation, pursuing any promising element I stumbled across. Insight, fortified by bloody-minded determination and slogging, had served me well as an investigative journalist. To that

I could add a personal interest in finding out whodunit to Tina Paglia.

My first chapter would recreate a typical day in the life of a working girl. I'd begin by interviewing someone closely connected to one of the disappeared.

The juices had kicked in. Back again. Feels good.

Memory fades fast as footprints in Toronto snow. So it made sense to start out with contacts for the most recently-missing woman, then work back. Had I noticed a thread shared by a few of the women — a physical type, race, age, anything to suggest a mutual trait, hangout or practice that might have drawn their killer — I would have organized my search around it. But nothing jumped out from the files, except drug and/or alcohol addiction, which seemed more an occupational hazard than a common denominator. Street-smart folks say that a crack whore has two pimps.

I grabbed for the first file.

ROONEY, *Sylvia Lee.*

White female, born 1956, 5 foot 4 inches, 120 pounds, long light brown hair, green eyes, tattoo of butterfly on right shoulder blade.

Rooney is a known drug user and sex trade worker in the Sherbourne and Queen area. Last seen in January 2000 and reported missing in July 2000.

Sylvia Lee Rooney had no known family, was new to the city, had no friends. Reported missing by Family Services, to whom she'd applied for welfare. Bummer.

ANDREWS, *Ellen.*

White female, born 1965, 5 foot 6 inches, 135 pounds, dark brown shoulder length hair, brown eyes, faint acne scars on both cheeks.

Andrews is a known drug user and sex trade worker in the Parkdale area. Last seen in June 2000 and reported missing in July 2000.

Reported missing by her boyfriend, whom cops suspected of being her pimp. Paul Vernon, west-end address. I went online, logged on to *Canada411*, and located a phone number for a 'Vernon, P.' with a Parkdale postal code. The Parkdale stroll is so low-end, it's only worked by really destitute prostitutes.

I downloaded the "Missing Downtown Women" poster from the Toronto Polices Services site, as well as larger photos of the women and additional details on each of them. Before disconnecting, I bookmarked "Searching for Jessye," a linked site set up by a friend of one of the missing.

Something about the wording of the reward poster pointed to authorship-by-lawyers:

The Ministry of the Attorney General and the Toronto Police Services Board have authorized a reward of up to $100,000 for information leading to the arrest and conviction of the person or persons responsible for the unlawful confinement, kidnapping or murder of any or all of the listed women, missing from the streets of Toronto. Upon the arrest and conviction of a person or persons responsible for the unlawful confinement, kidnapping or murder of any one or more of the women listed as missing in this reward poster, a reward will be decided by the Toronto Police Services Board, in its sole discretion, and that decision is final, binding and not reviewable.

Only those people who come forward and volunteer information to the Toronto Police Department will be eligible to receive a reward.

Any persons having information regarding the unlawful confinement, kidnapping or murder of any of the missing women listed in this poster are requested to communicate that information immediately to the Toronto Police Department, Missing Persons Unit.

Sounds so stringent, they'll get away with rewarding the lucky winner a bag of stale donuts.

I taped the poster to the wall and stared at the thirty-one photographs. They fell into two readily-distinguishable groups: grim mug shots, and snapshots harkening back to happier, healthier lives before the mean streets.

None of the women in the snapshots looked cheap, sultry or seductive. All were wearing far less makeup and adornments than Etta dons before her breakfast coffee. Open faces grinned at the viewer — faces straight out of a high-school yearbook.

The mug shots provided a depressing antidote. Almost all the women had been photographed on exceedingly bad hair days, their expressions defiant, resigned or defeated. Eyes dead, downcast or at half-mast. Faces unsmiling and tight-lipped. A few looked vaguely inquisitive, but most seemed disinterested in their plight, well past considering what brought them here.

Fighting back a wave of sadness, I dialled Vernon's number.

"What the fuck do ya want?" challenged a gruff male voice after the ninth ring.

"If you are Paul Vernon, this is your lucky day." *Eat your heart out, Lily Tomlin. Ernestine better give up her day job.*

"Who are you joking, asshole?"

"Mr. Vernon, a lady named — let's see now, here it is — Ellen Andrews filled out a coupon for our lucky draw. The prize is a Total Surround Sound and Motion Entertainment Centre worth $20,000. She wrote down your name and phone number, so I'm assuming you are related. Am I right, sir?"

I could almost hear him hunkering into thought. "Duh ... yeah, she's my sister. But she ain't, uh, home at the moment."

"Perhaps I could call back at a convenient time later today?"

"Like ... uh, maybe I could come and pick it up? She took a ... job in Montreal, eh?"

"Yes, sir, we at PennySmart/LoonieWise would be happy to make such an arrangement. If you'll just bring in two pieces of ID and a piece of mail bearing Ellen's name and address, we'll present you with the Entertainment Centre. And I hope you've got a really big room for it. The TV is so big you could sell tickets for movies and hockey games."

"Far fuckin' out. So where's this office of yours?"

"Goodness, Mr. Vernon. It's far too large for our office. Your prize is being held at our warehouse." I grabbed for this morning's paper and picked out an ad for a funeral home in Peterborough.

"No sweat, lady. That all?"

"Just one more small detail. We do require a phone number where Ms. Andrews can be reached, to get her official consent for you to claim the prize."

Sensing that the vengeful gods had just snatched back his Entertainment Centre, my unimaginative contact morphed into a lunatic.

"I don't have her fuckin' butthole phone number. The bitch run off to Montreal with some nigger pimp. Some folks figure she's dead, but she was too tough to get herself whacked. You wanna photograph the biggest cock-sucking cunt in Canada picking up your fuckin' fancy Entertainment Centre? If she shows up, you can tell the dumb bitch I'll slice off her droopy tits if she ever shows her zitty face in this city again. Got that?"

"Mr. Vernon? Have a nice day."

This genteel exchange led me to conclude that my interlocutor's information was more speculative than empirical.

I moved on.

WILSON, Tracee Anita.

Native Indian female, born 1973, 5 foot 4 inches, 115 pounds, long black hair, brown eyes.

Andrews is a known drug user and sex trade worker in the Sherbourne and Queen area. Last seen in July 1999 and reported missing in March 2000.

Tracee Anita had been alone in the world. Only reported missing eight months after vanishing (the record is held by another woman, who'd been missing for twelve years before being reported). No known family or friends.

One more and I'll give it up for the day.

MURPHY, Daphne.

White female, born 1979, 5 foot 7 inches, 110 pounds, medium blond hair, blue eyes.

Murphy was a known drug user and sex trade worker in the Sherbourne and Queen area. Last seen in December 1999 and reported missing in February 2000.

I lucked out. Daphne's mother had reported her missing. Her number was in the book. She picked up the phone on the second ring. When I explained the reason for my call, she immediately invited me over — even though I forewarned her that I'd be bringing only questions. No new information.

"My dear, I welcome any chance just to talk about my girl."

Chapter 16

HARLEY VEERED ONTO a short street of red-brick bungalows I'd have called 'modest' before I bought 6 Shannon. Sally Murphy opened the door as if she'd been anticipating an $11-million greeting by Ed McMahon.

White female, 5 foot 7 inches, 110 pounds, medium blond hair, blue eyes — an uncanny resemblance to her daughter, albeit twenty years along a gentler road.

"If you were my daughter, I'd be worried to death about you driving around on that big motorcycle."

If I were her daughter, I'd probably be dead.

The aroma of fresh-baked cookies wafted along the hall through air musty with cigarette smoke. Heavy floor-to-ceiling drapes shut out the weak late-fall light. Two pole lamps cast a dim glow over an overstuffed sofa and matching chair against one wall, bridged by a TV table topped with a plastic-lace placemat. In one corner a TV in a huge Mediterranean-style cabinet crushed the plush pink carpet. In the other loomed a gold Naugahyde reclining chair, into which I lowered my butt when Sally nervously placed herself on the edge of the sofa. She faced an unused fireplace, its mantel crammed with framed likenesses of her missing daughter.

The narrow room was stifling, as claustrophobic as the confessional.

A jungle of potted plastic ivy trailed along one wall into

the dining room, most of which was taken up by a table, hugged by eight tall chairs. From its glossy surface rose an enormous cut-glass bowl stuffed with fake fruit and veggies coloured by a brush more psychedelic than God's. A sparkling chandelier hung a fifty-pound warning over the bowl.

Every object hung in dreary suspension.

No sooner had Sally sat down than she leapt up to offer me Nescafé, tea or Diet Pepsi. I asked for a glass of water. She returned with our beverages and a plate stacked with peanut butter cookies.

"These are Daphne's favourites. I bake them fresh every other day, so when she walks through that door I'll be ready with milk and cookies ... just like the old days."

Milk and cookies — of limited appeal to a young woman who sold her body to feed her habit.

Sally noisily sucked up half her Pepsi through a candy-striped straw and lit a Cameo, then squinted at me through a billow of smoke. "You don't look like a writer to me."

"How did you expect me to look?" Why tell her that I look like the child Lillian Hellman and Dash Hammett never had? There wasn't a trace of paper in the room. Not a book, no newspaper or magazine — not even a TV guide.

Her voice took on a huffy edge. "Well, you probably don't think I look like a reader. But I've got a whole bookcase full of Harlequins up in my bedroom. But they never have a photo of the author on the back cover. I've seen some real writers on the TV, though. No offence, but they all look more lady-like than you."

"Perhaps they write fiction," I volunteered.

Sally drained her Pepsi. "Maybe. What do you write?"

Moments like this, I find myself wishing my career came with self-authenticating business cards. *Jane Yeats. Speech-lan-*

guage pathologist. Or Chiropodist. Or Aesthetician specializing in acrylic nails.

"I write about true crimes." I also wish I were a self-publicist who totes copies of her books wherever she goes, hot to thrust them into the interstices of conversation.

Just as I was praying she wouldn't wonder aloud where I get my ideas from, and whether I use a Bic, a typewriter or a computer, she asked, "This book you told me you're researching — what's it about? I mean, you said it was about all the hookers who've gone missing, but how do you write a crime book about women who maybe just disappeared because they felt like it or moved away. Like, where's the crime?"

I quickly swallowed my third cookie. Practice had made them perfect. Etta raised me on TV dinners and Jell-O chocolate pudding. Once she cooked corned beef hash. Thereafter I encouraged her to steer clear of culinary complexity.

"That's a good point, Sally. If only a few hookers had disappeared, I'd chalk it up to personal choice. But thirty-one have gone missing in three years — that's way more than the percentage of other women who disappear. So I got thinking. Put that together with the disproportionate number of murdered hookers whose killers haven't been found — well, maybe some of the missing ones have also ... been killed. But because their bodies haven't been discovered, they're still considered missing. So I decided to research their disappearances in the hope that I'd come across a pattern."

In the pregnant silence that followed, I feared my clever notion was going up like the smoke from Sally's cigarettes.

She blew four perfect smoke rings towards the nicotine-tinted ceiling. "And if there is no pattern?"

I watched the fourth ring collide with the inert ceiling fan. "There will still be a book, because it'll be about pursuing a thread that could go anywhere. When I started writing my other books, I knew exactly where they'd take me — to a conclusion determined in the courtroom. But wherever this one goes, it will document the women's lives ... as a kind of memorial." *So who's being interviewed here?*

"One more question and I'll start answering yours ... maybe. You know, my daughter was a whore. How do you feel about her ... um ... lifestyle? 'Cause your feelings about that are going to affect how you write about the girls. So don't give me any crap you think I want to hear. I've got a real good bullshit detector."

I gave it to her straight. "You asked me how I *feel* about prostitution. A month ago, I could have answered that very simply: selling sex felt wrong to me. No way selling sex is like selling shoes or groceries. If a woman cleans houses, say, or serves tables, she gets paid a pittance for honest work. Trade her self-respect for a couple of blow jobs, she could earn a lot more.

"But then my next-door neighbour got killed. She was a hooker, whom I treated with contempt. When I stared down at her brutalized body I realized that I've never devoted one minute of serious *thinking* to prostitution. That's where I am — thinking, reading, learning a bit more. So I don't have a fixed point of view, Sally. That's why this book: to clarify the issue."

Sally relaxed back on the sofa. "I guess I'm in the same place, caught somewhere between *'my girl's a whore'* and *'that whore is your daughter.'* I love her more than my life."

Without passing it by my inner editor, I blurted, "You talk about Daphne in the present tense. She's been missing for almost nine months."

Sally consulted her watch. "Eight months, twenty-four days and twelve hours. Do I believe that Daphne's alive? My heart says *Yes — she just ran away for reasons I don't understand or she's being held against her will.* That keeps me from killing her with my fear. Then my brain kicks in: *Daphne is dead, probably murdered, maybe OD'd. But definitely dead.* That makes me crazy. So most days I bobble between hope and despair."

My emotions overwhelmed my writerly mandate to dig up whatever I could at whatever cost. "Sally, I don't have kids of my own, so I really can't imagine what you are going through. But I feel I should leave — I'm frightened of saying something that will just add to your grief."

She laughed bitterly. "Since Daphne disappeared, what's crawling around in my head at three in the morning is straight out of an axe-murder movie. Nothing you say could possibly make it worse."

She stared at the ashtray. "Anyway, I stopped fooling myself that she's alive months ago."

"You sound very certain."

"Daphne must be dead. I mean, she was so needy she always got around to contacting me when she was in serious trouble. Usually she wanted money. Knowing what it was going to, I should have refused — but I couldn't. Once she showed up so drugged-out I had to call an ambulance. After that, she'd always come home to detox. For three or four days she'd be throwing up. By the fifth day she'd start to feel better — and head back to the shit that got her into the mess in the first place. She couldn't leave the streets ..." Her voice trailed off.

"When did things start going wrong for her?"

She took a photo from the mantel and handed it to me. "I took this one just before her date arrived to take her to the prom. Dave, nice, clean-cut, from a good home. End of grade ten. She was a straight-A student and a good athlete. But that summer changed everything. In grade eleven her grades dropped and she started skipping school. Some weekends she'd stay out all night, come home looking like she'd been through the wringer. Then she got kicked out of school.

"Just after her seventeenth birthday, an older girl she hung out with got her a job at a strip club. When I found out, I kicked her out. I guess I'll never know what came next — the cocaine or the prostitution. Whatever, I lost my daughter. Maybe if her father hadn't died so young, maybe if I'd been able to figure out what was troubling her so much, maybe if I hadn't thrown her out …"

The rosary of desperate times — as though endless recitation might reverse the irreversible. For months after Pete's death, I spent my nights mentally fingering my own "if onlys."

I tried to get her onto a more productive track. "What made you file a missing persons report?"

"I got scared when Christmas and New Year's passed without me hearing from her. No matter what shape she was in, Daphne always called on Mother's Day, my birthday, the holidays. But instead of going straight to the police, like I should have done, I went looking for her. You see, I was scared that if I got the cops on to her, she'd cut me off. So almost every night in January, I wandered around Sherbourne and Queen showing her photograph to anyone who would look at it. I spent a few nights in Parkdale, too, thinking that maybe she had changed her stroll."

"January was a brutally cold month."

She began to pace the cramped room. "So were many of the people I met. Some of the working girls treated me nice, though. One suggested that I talk to Sandy, the lady who runs Grayce's Space on Gerrard. It's a safe place for girls to drop in any night for a break — just to warm up, have a sandwich or cup of tea, chat, watch TV. Sandy used to be a prostitute herself so she knows … she hands out clothes, condoms, lists of referral services, bad date sheets — she even lends out cell phones so the girls can call 911 when they need help.

"Sandy was really warm and welcoming. Right away she recognized Daphne from her photograph. Said that she had dropped by one really cold night just before Christmas, left about an hour later to meet with a relative of a missing girl. Apparently Daphne was friends with the girl. Sandy remembered her because she was moved by Daphne's willingness to head back into the night to help out.

"Ironic, eh? The last person Daphne is known to have talked to was some poor soul like me. Sandy told me she gets quite a few enquiries about missing girls — but from their friends, not many family members."

My antennae quivered. "The person Daphne went to meet that night — was it a man or a woman?"

"I don't know. I'd make a rotten detective, eh? But the story sounded true because it was the same as I was living."

"Do you know the name of the missing girl Daphne befriended?" I asked, hoping against hope.

"No, Daphne never told Sandy."

"What finally made you go to the police?"

"Sandy said they could conduct a thorough search — *if* they took Daphne's disappearance seriously. She didn't think the authorities had much interest in catching whoever's killing all those women, but I went to them anyway. See, I hadn't come up with a single thing. And the last night a pimp threatened to beat the shit out of me if he saw my face on his turf again."

"Did you tell the police about the person Daphne headed off to meet?"

"No, at the time it didn't seem important. In fact, I forgot all about it until now."

"And what's happened since you reported Daphne missing?"

She smiled sadly. "Oh, the police have been nice enough. One phones me once a month to tell me that they haven't made any progress. He promises they won't close her file until she's found ... now I just wish they would find her body.

"You know, I couldn't get her out of my mind, even at work. I thought about her every minute. I kept showing up exhausted from having been out looking for her and not sleeping. My nerves got so bad my doctor told me to quit — she got me on temporary disability. But I hate being stuck in here by myself. I cry a lot."

She raised her head to scan her photo gallery.

"I'm sure you aren't alone. I'll bet there's a place where you could talk to some of the other moms."

Her face brightened a bit. "I'll ask Sandy."

"If such a group doesn't exist, maybe you could start one."

"That would give me something to do, wouldn't it?"

I stood up and thanked her for her time. She shyly hugged me, then headed off for the kitchen, returning with a big bag of cookies. "Thank you, for caring about what's happened to my girl."

"Sally, if I learn anything that might be helpful, you'll be the first to know."

She squeezed my arm. "Bless you, dear. Each night I ask God to send an angel to watch over Daphne. Tonight I'll ask Him to keep an eye on you, too. Now, be sure to drive carefully."

Through the visor of my helmet, I watched the loneliest lady in the world wave a brave good-bye.

Chapter 17

"**T**IMING HAS A LOT TO DO with the outcome of a rain dance," Silver likes to quip. Timing also had a lot to do with the outcome of what began as a peaceful protest.

Within twenty-four hours of the discovery of Karen Clarke's battered body, Toronto police raided a large home in Parkdale and charged the chatelaine with bawdy house offences. Her crime was renting short-stay rooms to prostitutes turning tricks. Someone inside the force must have tipped off City-TV that the raid was going down. Cameras were on hand to document the woebegone file of women and clients being led out to the waiting paddy wagons. The police claimed that their six-month undercover investigation had led to the arrest of the city's most notorious dominatrix. I guess that makes the streets safer for democracy.

Two days later the police announced the shut-down of fifteen downtown massage parlours, alleging they were bawdy houses. That action resulted in the arrest of fifty-eight people, against whom 245 charges were laid in relation to running a bawdy house, possession of stolen property and drug charges. Charges against eighteen other people were pending. Five of the massage parlours were just a condom's throw from my front door.

A bust on an escort agency revealed that the owner knowingly employed three HIV-infected call girls. The judge imposed a publication ban on their clients, rumoured to be prominent citizens and NHL hockey players. That put a whole new spin on the concept of 'protection.'

Response from at least one sector of the community was swift. Prostitutes' rights advocates rose up in outrage at such a misdirection of police resources. The cops appeared more intent on busting whores than shielding them from violence: prosecuting bawdy houses, massage parlours and escort agencies forces more women onto the streets and into greater danger. On behalf of the city's sex workers, Antonia Romanoff announced a protest march for that very evening. The marchers would wind their way to the steps of No. 51 Division, where activists planned to deliver a defiant manifesto.

With Silver clutching my leather jacket, I sped Harley across the city to the park just off Church Street where the marchers were slated to gather. My buddy was really pleased that I'd asked her to accompany me.

The event attracted street workers, employees of escort services and their owners, bawdy house operators, strippers, exotic dancers. Women, men, gay, straight, from all stations of the sexual continuum — transvestite, transsexual, transgendered and intersexed, cross-dressers, drag kings and queens. Only pedophiles and folks who enjoy intimate relations with Fido seemed unrepresented. I estimated the crowd at about six hundred.

The march to the station was a spunky celebration of sexual diversity, a cold-weather Gay Pride Day without the floats.

Coming to a halt in front of the station, we slowly formed a huge crescent at the foot of the broad stairs. Just as Romanoff began speaking, something happened near the front of the crowd. In a flash, the collective mood turned ugly. Two mounted cops rode into the sides of the crowd. A line of riot police, wielding batons and pepper spray, descended upon us. Demonstrators threw bottles, trash, garbage cans — anything they could get their hands on.

Canadians are not what you would call a warrior class. Something important was happening here.

My worst nightmare was happening all around me and I was trapped dead centre. Since childhood I've managed my claustrophobia by choosing stairs over elevators, reserving aisle seats on planes or in theatres, avoiding shopping malls and rock concerts, driving a motorcycle rather than a car.

Just as I was pitching into a panic attack, someone roughly grabbed the back of my jacket, hauling me away from the oncoming police and rioting demonstrators. My instinct was to swing around and smash my assailant in the face — I didn't give a shit if my fist connected with a cop. But the crowd was so tight I could turn only my neck.

My putative assailant turned out to be Silver. "I'm planning to get us out of this rebellion in one piece," she hissed. "Never forget what they did to Louis Riel."

I succumbed to her tug. Efficient as a snow plow, with her free arm she pushed aside everyone and everything in her path. My Amazon.

She plunked me on a metal bench inside a nearby streetcar shelter. "You going to start breathing again on your own — or do I have to ask the police chief for a paper bag?"

Getting yourself arrested for the first time after you've started collecting your pension cheque takes dedication or stupidity. *Dedicated stupidity*, I emended, grabbing my helmet and jacket and flying out the front door.

Two hours after scurrying back to my sanctuary, I was speeding Harley to the bail court at Old City Hall. Etta had been charged with resisting arrest and assaulting a police officer. She had allegedly struck the young man with a dildo.

My heart flipped in my chest when the lawyer's phone call interrupted my profound slumber. I wasn't even aware that Etta had attended the demonstration.

Metal detectors and three cops welcomed me at the entrance to this grand historic building (saved from a developer's wrecking ball by a group of citizens blessed with civic memory). I headed for Courtroom 101 in the basement, where a justice of the peace would decide if Etta would be released before going on trial. Handcuffed with several other offenders in the glass-walled prisoner's box, she looked seriously the worse for wear.

My wait was mercifully brief. Etta was Case 4 of the morning. When the duty counsel asked for bail, the Crown didn't object. Duty counsel must have had a quick meeting with my mother in the holding cell and cautioned her to behave. Etta listened politely to the justice of the peace, twice muttering an uncharacteristic "yes, sir." After agreeing to put up $500 and promising to avoid protest marches, Etta was set free. Duty counsel suggested that I ensure Etta stayed out of trouble. Duty counsel lives in cloudcuckooland.

Etta was lucky. Striking a cop is never wise, however tempting. Maybe the police considered her age. More likely, they wanted to be spared dealing with her mouth.

She strode towards me, as close to towering rage as a short woman can get. "Don't even *think* about asking any questions. These fools won't take my VISA card for the bail, so you'll have to hit on a bank machine or some friggin' thing."

For once I was a step ahead of the old girl. "It's OK, I

stopped at the bar and took money out of your safe ... but what in God's name were you thinking, Mom?"

Too late, I noticed her damaged acrylic nails. On a bad hair or nail day, Etta is not pleasant. This morning her hair looked like a terminally ill puli's.

She-Who-Bore-Me shouted, "I didn't give it no thought whatsoever. That friggin' cop jabbed me in the ribs with his baton, so I poked him back with mine."

After settling her account, I muttered, "Etta, let's blow this scene before we become the laughingstock of the whole court — and worse, before some reporter shows up and gets your name." I sounded reasonable to me.

"Don't need no reporter. I've decided to call a press conference at Sweet Dreams tomorrow morning. I'd do it today, but I gotta fix myself up." She disbelievingly contemplated her frayed nails.

A lifelong practitioner of free sex, my mother was a passionate advocate of commercial sex. "What I believe in is a woman's right to decide for herself what she's gonna do with her body."

It was the sole principle of Etta's belief system.

Steering us onto less volatile ground, I said, "Mom, I didn't even know you were at the march."

"There's lots about me you don't know," she snapped.

Praise God for small mercies.

"I've been going to them for years. Started when one of our boys in blue ..." she paused to survey the room for a glaring example, "... busted one of my regulars, a very nice table dancer with a voice sweet as Patsy Cline's."

As soon as we hit the pavement, I demanded, "So, when did you go shopping for a dildo?"

She indignantly drew herself up to her full fifty-eight

inches. "Never, you bonehead. I need a dildo like I need two Bibles. Some big, kinda rough-looking girl with a shaved head just thrust it into my hand when the cops started advancing on us."

She paused for a moment's reflection. "Guess she was a lesbian."

Yeah, Mom, maybe.

I knew I'd never dissuade Etta from holding her press conference — easier just to change my name. Wearily, I offered her a ride home to Sweet Dreams.

She looked at Harley like I was the lunatic. "Thank you very much, but do you honestly think my hair can take any more disturbance?" She strode off to hail a cab.

When I got home *The Toronto Post* was lying on my front step. News of the demo blared from the front page, around a colour photo of a cop wielding an industrial-size canister of pepper spray. *Ten arrests. Eighteen demonstrators treated at hospital. Organizers allege police brutality. Mayor calls for calm.* The editorial advised an independent investigation into the police response. Pepper spray is un-Canadian.

Buried in the report were details of what — rather, *who*, triggered the riot. Surrounded by a phalanx of Civilized Majority members, a clean-cut old gent had unfurled a banner reading PROSTITUTES ARE THE ANTI-CHRIST. An overwrought drag queen in a nun's habit promptly threw a cream pie in his face. When the mounted police and riot squad charged the crowd — having first secured the safety of the clean old man and his cohorts — all hell broke loose.

A Civilized Majority spokesperson was quoted as saying, "The very definition of the family is at risk as our downtown streets and neighbourhoods get congested with prostitutes.

Our children must not be allowed to witness their satanic agenda. Mothers must be protected from this revolting spectacle of fallen womanhood. Fathers must not be wrested from the bosom of the family into the arms of these sexual sirens."

When I phoned Silver to elicit some sympathy about Etta's escapade, she just laughed. I slammed down the receiver.

A four-hour sleep did nothing to improve my mood. *Screw Etta. Screw Silver. Screw the human race.* After I'd worked through a few shallow self-affirmations and quaffed two cans of Smithwick's, my inner elder counselled a return to work.

My first four phone calls left my ears bruised by two inane answering machines and two abusive "friends" of missing women. The fifth, however, connected me to Hope Shaver, daughter of JEFFERS, Rita Alison:

White female, born 1959, 5 foot 8 inches, 145 pounds, red hair, brown eyes, tattoos.

Jeffers suffered from mental health problems; was a known alcoholic and sex trade worker in the Sherbourne and Queen area. Last seen in August 1998 and reported missing in December 1998.

Much as she wanted to help me out, the young woman couldn't tell me much. Her mother, a manic-depressive who refused to take her meds, left the family when Hope was seven. In rare moments of lucid sobriety, Rita had been so ashamed of herself she stayed away.

"I haven't seen her for eleven years. Well, I did once, but my father doesn't know about it. Just after I got my age of majority card, I went with some girlfriends to hear a band playing at the Horseshoe. My mother staggered in a few hours later. I recognized her from an old photograph Dad still carries in his wallet. She looked like she could be my grandmother, like totally trashed. When the bartender refused to serve her, she caused such a fuss the bouncer had to throw her back on the street."

"I'm sorry, Hope. That had to be painful."

"More embarrassing than painful. I cried for years after she left us. Then one day there just weren't any tears left."

"So there's nothing that might give me some clue to her disappearance?"

"Nope. Apparently she lived in a rundown rooming house in the east end. The police told me she was last seen in some seedy hotel on Spadina where she took her tricks. I know she must be dead. Maybe it's a mean thing to say, but she's better off."

Even if her mother were alive, what difference would it make to her abandoned daughter?

"You know, I work hard at school — and I work really hard at remembering all the good things before she got so messed up. She wasn't always like that."

I felt close to an ingrate for complaining about Etta — but only close.

Sensing that my mood was getting bleaker, I decided to cut and lay the Formica for my kitchen countertop to B.B. King's "Blues Summit." There's one incredible take — the King of the Blues ripping out "You Shook Me," backed up by John Lee Hooker, Robert Cray and Roy Rogers. But thank the household gods I had the Formica contact-cemented in place before the final cut: "I Gotta Move Out of This Neighborhood/Nobody Loves Me But My Mother."

Chapter 18

JUST BEFORE I LEFT to meet Lenore Tootoosis, Silver called. She was still laughing. The local TV noon news coverage included Etta's press conference, performed from the stage of Sweet Dreams. Flanked by two lawyers, several representatives from the sex trade, and a buxom dominatrix mock-flogging a male hooker in judicial robes, my mother vented her righteous indignation. That she, model citizen and exemplary small businesswoman, should have spent the night stuffed into a holding cell the size of a coffin crammed with a bunch of real criminals and only one toilet was a human-rights transgression unsurpassed in what she once believed to be a free country. She hinted darkly that, next time, thousands of harassed prostitutes and their supporters would rise up in solidarity to resist the state's efforts to regulate desire.

Ye gawds and little fishes. I cut short Silver's recounting of Mom's craftily-orchestrated circus. "We are not amused."

Then I sped over to meet Lenore Tootoosis at one of the student pubs at Ryerson. Here my jeans, biker boots and leathers were not out of place — a minor but irritating concern to me where smartly-dressed people hang out.

A tall, casually groomed woman seated at a table mercifully distant from the bass-grumbling stereo speakers rose to greet me. Her face reminded me of Buffy Saint Marie in her "Indian Soldier" period. But what violent narrative had inscribed the jagged scar from the corner of her mouth to just beneath her left eye?

She grinned as we shook hands. "I recognized you immediately from Silver's description."

"Spare me the details," I groaned. "But I am curious to hear what she told you about why I wanted to meet you."

"She told me to do a convincing impersonation of an elder and to fill your head with whore-lore."

A thin waiter in fatigue pants large enough to shelter a litter of piglets took our orders: beer for me, mineral water for Lenore. It must be true, what I've been reading about in business reports: booze sales are falling. Makes a bibulous girl nervous enough to repatriate herself to the Emerald Isle, where temperance rarely taints social intercourse.

Lenore said she was equipped, academically speaking, to talk about the laws governing prostitution in Canada and their impact on working girls. If I wanted to familiarize myself with the nitty-gritty of actual practice, she could pass along a few names — after checking it out with them first.

I leaned forward, my shoulder muscles tense. "I'm curious about something else, Lenore. I hope you don't take offence, because none is intended. You know Silver's position on government bureaucratic shit: every level of Canadian government has its commissions, committees, task forces, inquiries, position papers, reports — you name it. As a First Nations person, she shuns them all. Now, you're part of this working group on prostitution, so I assume you're comfortable with that choice. Yet Silver would rather go to prison."

"Our mutual friend must also have told you that each of us must choose her own path. Silver respects the work I do because she understands why I do it. My life résumé includes some experiences I've carefully omitted from the academic version. My 'expertise' on prostitution began when my mom died of complications from diabetes when I was in fifth grade. My stepfather started sexually abusing me not long after, when he was drunk — which was most of the time. On my fifteenth birthday, I couldn't bear that shit for another minute. There were two choices: kill the filthy old bastard or leave the rez. So I hitch-hiked all the way from Saskatchewan to Toronto. Soon as my shoes hit the streets, I became a homeless urban Indian who survived by turning tricks — first for food, then for booze and drugs."

I anxiously ignited a Rothmans.

"A lot of girls think they're ending the abuse cycle when they start demanding to be paid for what was taken from them in childhood."

Lenore's face was calm and unashamed. What was she making of my sudden tears? Perhaps she assumed my feelings were as close to the surface as hers. Not a prayer. Mine were tears of shame for having so harshly judged Tina Paglia and Silver. For having judged at all.

"Jane, I was one of the lucky ones. My career as a junkie whore got ended before I got dead."

"How?" I asked. "Did you get busted?"

She roared with laughter at my naiveté. "Did I get busted? Girl, I got busted so often I spent more time in Metro West Detention Centre than on the stroll. But I couldn't imagine doing anything else for a living — until one freezing night I met Silver at Carlton and Sherbourne. She was volunteering with the Anishnawbe Street Patrol, handing out hot soup and sleeping bags from the back of a van. I swear that woman is a trickster. She convinced me to get clean — and then haul my sorry ass back to school."

She leaned back. "So, wrapped up in that cheesy memoir

is my answer to your question about why I now consort with a different set of johns," she concluded with a wry grin.

"What you've survived makes my career, such as it is, look like ..."

Lenore shook her head. "I've sweated my way through enough term papers to recognize writing as real work, even though it pays less than whoring on low track. Besides, Silver lent me one of your books — the one about the judge who killed his wife. It was terrific. I really liked your analysis of how much the criminal justice system gets perverted by the old boys' club. I've been keeping that in mind as I write up my final recommendations to the working group. It's their system that regulates prostitutes' work."

Lenore's praise made me self-conscious enough to light up another cigarette and order a second pint from the boy in the camouflage bag. For more than a year, the only words I'd written were in a brilliantly acerbic letter of complaint I sent to the Health Board regarding Mario Pepino's rat colony. *Was I still capable of practising my sodden craft?*

To avoid answering, I returned the conversational focus to Lenore's field of study. From her brief historical overview, 1851 through yesterday, I learned that the government has attempted to regulate commercial sex with laws ranging from vagrancy through solicitation to communication.

My brain was fried. "I've always thought prostitution was legal in Canada — or at least not illegal."

She laughed. "I don't know anyone who can explain the overall objective of Canadian prostitution law. There's a mind-boggling contradiction at the heart of this part of the Criminal Code, probably because morality drives law — and there's no consensus on this subject ... yet the state still insists on regulating it.

"Prostitution between consenting adults is legal, but the law can criminalize it wherever it occurs. So it's a real brain twister to figure out how a person can prostitute without breaking the law. All the law's accomplished is to drive prostitution further underground, making life even more dangerous for working girls."

I felt obliged to put in a word for your average horny Canadian. "I really don't think many Canadians spend a lot of time fretting about prostitution — just about getting laid."

"You're right — except for the religious freaks who see the Whore of Babylon in every unmarried woman with a sex life. They believe that law should serve God's wrath. Moreover, their numbers are growing by leaps and bounds, and they now have real political clout.

Politicians know they can't be seen to be condoning so-called immorality, especially these days. Bill Clinton got way more media attention for his blow jobs than his legislation, even though most Americans seem comfortable separating private from public morality. So our legislators have stitched together a crazy quilt of laws that tosses thousands of women in jail for a minor urban inconvenience — because they wisely insist on being paid for what Monica Lewinsky did for free."

My inner socialist couldn't resist. "And governments keep denying the links between poverty and prostitution ... which brings me to people who make that link. What do you know about a drop-in centre called 'Grayce's Space?'"

"It's named after Grayce Baxter, a high-priced call girl. God, that woman had style. She had the car and the condo, she earned serious cash, partied hard and had buckets of friends. She'd be screaming down the road in her Mercedes, lining up her next three calls on the cell phone as she headed for a posh hotel to service some wealthy business dude. She specialized in domination. She was murdered by a client."

Lenore sipped her water. "About five years back, PROS — the group that offers outreach services to prostitutes — started up Grayce's Space. It bills itself to the public as a centre run for pros by current and former sex workers, but I'm hearing that's not really the case. Rumour has it that a big power struggle has split them in two — the board of directors, mostly from social service organizations, and the staff and volunteers, many of them hookers. Apparently the executive director, a tight-ass named Rosemary Miller, is making their struggle even worse."

"Yeah, I heard her on the radio last week. Anyway, on Monday I met with the mother of one of the missing girls. She was last seen leaving Grayce's. Can you hook me up with anybody who's involved in running the place — excluding Rosemary Miller?"

"I'm pretty much out of the loop these days, Jane. But I can put you on to a woman who's bound to have the inside track." She reached into her bag for her DayTimer. "Here it is. Chelsea Walker. You might check out her Web site before you call her."

In spite of my plastic being dead, I insisted on paying the bill. That gesture left me with thirty-five bucks from the fifty Etta must have tucked into my jean jacket last week. The pressure of being broke was really gnawing on my nerves. How much worse must it have been for an abused fifteen-year-old Native kid in a strange, unwelcoming city.

Chapter 19

THE SKY WAS SMUDGED with grey clouds. Icy rain splattered against my visor as I cautiously negotiated the few short blocks to Grayce's Space. Better to drop by unannounced than let an appointment alert anyone to my interest. As I turned into a nearby parking spot Harley swerved and skidded on the wet asphalt. I pulled out the key, cursing the unpredictable face of winter in Toronto. Then again, Los Angelenos soak in the sun atop a fault-line.

I opened the door of what might have been an upscale storefront dentist's office between a dry cleaners and an electronics-repair shop. The interior offered a cozy, bright sanctuary from the elements. Peer education posters about health promotion, AIDS and STD prevention, street safety, self-defense courses, police harassment and legal issues covered the walls. Three young women were smoking and drinking coffee as Oprah greeted them from the far end of the deep room. On a sofa, an older woman consoled her dejected seatmate. She spoke a few words into her companion's ear and patted her arm before rising to welcome me.

Sandy Reeder was on the cusp of middle age — in her early forties, I guessed — with a pretty, freckled face and an auburn bob. Her trim body was kitted out in a green cotton sweater, jeans and running shoes.

When she introduced herself with a warm handshake, I

quickly explained how I'd come to be interested in the missing prostitutes. "May I visit for a while and have a chat, if you have time?"

"No problem."

She led me into two adjoining rooms — one equipped with a Mac system and packed to the ceiling with cartons of promotional materials, the second a private sitting room furnished with worn armchairs and a braided rug. She offered me a seat and handed me a mug of coffee.

"I didn't expect to find Grayce's Space so ... well, so inviting."

"Whether they're heading out or leaving the stroll after a night's work, the girls need some place they can feel at home."

"I've heard that PROS has a good reputation among working women."

"Yes, we do," she nodded proudly. "Many of the women who show up here eventually do get off the streets. Those who don't — well, at least they know they're always welcome."

"Those are valuable services," I said, and meant it. "But you do much more, don't you?"

"What you see here is essentially the resource and socializing end of our work. When a girl comes in for help, we get her to detox if she needs it. Then we identify her issues and tailor a recovery program for her. We let her know about related services — needle exchange clinics, medical care, safehouse facilities, support groups. We can help her get enrolled in night school, arrange job interviews, teach her how to write a résumé. Whatever it takes. We do crisis intervention, advocacy and lots of education to raise awareness — especially among high school students."

"Grayce's gets known by word-of-mouth?"

"I'd guess so. Many of the girls are suspicious of do-gooders who wouldn't recognize a blow job if they stumbled on a work-in-progress!" Her laughter was infectious. "We have pros and ex-pros on our board of directors and one full-time worker is an ex-ho — me." She offered a comfortable grin. "So the girls trust us not to moralize or bring them down. But clients are referred here by our outreach workers."

"How does that work?"

"Our van allows us to reach out to street prostitutes who can't or won't come to the centre. Every night a few workers in the van patrol the stroll until three a.m. or so. Some nights we cover the suburban strolls. The outreach workers approach the girls, dispense good cheer, bad date sheets, AIDS prevention information, condoms and the occasional cigarette. If the girls seem interested, they're given one of our cards and encouraged to drop by."

"Sounds expensive. How are you funded?"

"First, we run a very lean operation. Last year an independent assessor declared us a 'model service provider.' PROS is a non-profit charitable organization. Much of our funding comes from the Toronto Department of Public Health, the Ontario Ministry of Health, private donations and occasional bequests — usually from the estates of hookers and feminist activists. Almost from the beginning we've had an operating grant from the federal government, but we know that plug could get pulled any time a self-righteous MP rants on about clean-living taxpayers subsidizing the daughters of Jezebel. Yet sometimes I feel the bureaucratic red tape is more threatening than the moral purity brigade."

Good place to make a subtle insert, I reckoned. "Um, doesn't your charitable status stipulate that you can't mess in partisan politics or proselytize on behalf of any denominational group?"

Sandy raised a knowing eyebrow. "Ah, you must have heard our executive director on the radio last week."

At least she hadn't gone all tight-lipped on me. "And having listened to you, her words seem even more inappropriate. It's not how PROS really operates."

"Although Rosemary does most of our advocacy and PR work, she still gets nervous when the CBC beckons. She figures it's an army of left-wing atheists." Sandy frowned in annoyance. "Sometimes when she's stressed out she just ... loses perspective."

"So your mission does not include converting sex workers into Christians."

Her retort was firm. "If it did, I'd be out of here — along with most of my staff. The board has asked her to tone down her freelance preaching before we lose both our tax exemption and the women we're trying to reach. In July we sent her and another delegate to an international conference in Sweden. Rosemary came off sounding more like a fundamentalist than an activist."

She mused for a moment before adding, "There's a move afoot to force Rosemary's resignation in the hope of making PROS more attractive to prostitutes. It's part of a push to make us more peer-run and diverse."

"Would you support such a move?"

"Sure, but for the moment I'm sitting firmly on the fence — until we find someone with her contacts and her knack for working cash cows like a milkmaid."

I went for the long shot. "Sandy, I recently talked to Sally Murphy. Her daughter, Daphne, was last seen leaving here one night just before Christmas last year. I'm hoping to piece together her movements up to her disappearance." I reached into my back-pack for the photo I'd had blown up from the police poster.

"Good luck. The police and Mrs. Murphy were trying to do the same thing. Poor girl. I remember her stopping by that night because I was struck by how badly she needed her next fix — yet she was willing to help someone find their kid, sick as she felt."

"Might her need for a fix have clouded her judgement about hooking up with a stranger?"

Sandy chuckled. "Hooking up with strangers — that's what we do! But yes, Daphne certainly was in a state where she'd take a risk if there might be a needle at the end of it." She shrugged. "Like I told the cops and her mother, she didn't say anything to indicate who she was meeting that night."

"Tina Paglia was my neighbour. Have you ever had any contact with her? I don't have a photo, but I can give you a good description."

She shook her head. "Don't bother. I saw her photo in the *Post*. Sorry, Jane, but I'm pretty sure I've never set eyes on the lady. I asked around here at the time but no one else seems to know her. A bit of a lone wolf."

"Yeah, because she was and because of the fact that she was killed at home — her death probably isn't related to the others."

"Maybe not. But there's always a chance that the killer is getting sloppy."

We wrapped up our conversation and I thanked her for her time.

"My pleasure. Feel free to come back any time you think I can help. This bastard has to be caught before we lose any more girls."

Outside the sky had grown darker and the rain hadn't relented. At least Harley was getting a good wash.

The Daphne Murphy lead had just gone up in smoke, but my spirits hadn't sunk. Rosemary Miller now headed up my mental checklist — but how to ingratiate myself with her, given our divergent attitudes? Perhaps Chelsea Walker, whose Web site Lenore had recommended, could help.

That promised a fresh start.

Chapter 20

IT WAS A BURNISHED MORNING — the first real sunshine in weeks. And unseasonably cold. Without stopping to buy Repeat's coffee and sandwich, WonderDog and I headed straight for the park. On yesterday's evening walk we had found my unlikely acquaintance quite lucid, his thoughts more organized, his speech fluent. Perhaps the demons had granted him a respite. Maybe today I could lure him from the security of his streetcar shelter to a more sociable human habitation.

"Repeat, I'm cold and my dog is hungry," I spoke into the streetcar shelter. "I'd like to go to that restaurant on the corner, get a coffee, treat Max to a burger. Would you like to come with us? They've got beef stew on today."

For the briefest moment he essayed eye contact, then looked glumly down at his bags. "I can't abandon my stuff."

Parents who take their kids to casinos should be so vigilant. "So let's take all your stuff with us. I'll help." Gathering four bags in one hand, I reached down for the brown one.

Repeat grabbed it out of reach. "My treasure chest," he explained.

We walked to the restaurant single file, tail-wagging Max leading the procession, me behind his shaggy butt, Repeat trailing me like Prince Philip on a walkabout — except for his animated discussion with his voices. His feet moved haltingly, as if each step were engaging the next in uncertain conversation over the icy pavement.

Reckoning that the owner of the restaurant mightn't welcome Repeat's luggage, I suggested we leave them outside and sit at the window table, where we could keep an eye on them — and Max, who would stand sentry. He rapidly nodded his head, depositing all but the brown one. This he stuffed down his jacket. As we entered the restaurant, Repeat now looking heavily pregnant in a lop-sided kind of way, the scrofulous guy behind the counter glared at us as if a giant mutant roach had liberated itself from a tent on the premises.

Repeat nervously shuffled about behind a chair. "They don't like us here. We shouldn't have come. Repeat and Jane won't get served."

"Sit down and make yourself comfortable, Repeat. We'll get served. Trust me."

The owner gave the counter top the only serious wipe it had ever experienced. Approaching with menacing velocity, I reached into my pocket and flashed a card to back up the authority in my voice. My laser printer obligingly chokes out credentials on demand.

"Dr. Katherine Wilkinson, Health Board. I sleep with the guy who decides whether you get to do business tomorrow."

His bacteria-stained rag froze in mid-swirl.

"So, asshole, wipe the grease and crumbs off our table — with a clean rag — and treat my guest like he was Jesus coming out of the desert or I'll have this dump closed faster than the roaches run when you turn on the lights."

Repeat asked me to order for him. Five minutes later, I told the owner to get lost until I signalled. From the moment I had identified myself as somebody who mattered, he'd been hovering like a hummingbird.

Repeat and I dug into our steaming bowls of stew with dumplings, heaped to the rims. Outside Max cheerily slurped away at the bowl I'd taken him. I suggested to Repeat that he watch for Max's big belch.

Repeat giggled. "I know. My dog always did that. And he farted a lot."

"Max loves to fart, too. What was your dog's name, Repeat?"

He glanced up from his bowl, gravy dripping from his lower lip into his beard. "Amazing. Because he made me happy. Never left me — even when everybody else did. Didn't mind when my voices were screaming at me. Like a guardian angel."

Pausing to masticate the huge chunk of bun he'd shoved into his mouth, Repeat quickly turned his head aside. "Father didn't want me. Too embarrassing. Mother loved me, but one morning she died. Somewhere. Not at home. Father took Amazing to the Humane Society before Mother even got buried. After that, I ran away." He patted the brown bag through his jacket. "Never been back."

Swiping his bowl clean with the remaining segment of bun, he fired out another string of words. "I came here eleven years, four months and six days ago. From Calgary. It hasn't worked out very well."

After consulting about dessert, I summoned our reluctant host. "Two apple pie, one with vanilla ice cream. Two coffee and one water in a clean bowl, for my dog." Repeat giggled through the paper napkin he held over his mouth.

One of his plastic bags was stuffed with paperbacks. On the top I'd noticed a worn copy of Kerouac's *On the Road*. "What grade were you in when you left school, Repeat?"

His eyes took on a proud glint. "I was in second year at the University of Alberta. I liked it very much. When I was little, Mother read to me every night at bed-time. Fairy tales, *The Water Babies*, *Peter Pan*, *The Wind in the Willows*, *Alice's Adventures in Wonderland*, *Charlotte's Web*, *The Secret Garden*, *Treasure Island*, *The Jungle Book*, *The Little Prince* ... all kinds of magical stories. My favourite was *Where the Wild Things Are*."

"Hey, Repeat, I named my dog after Max, the little boy in *Where the Wild Things Are*."

He laughed and smiled at WonderDog. "Maybe you should have called him Wild Thing. Anyway, I loved books so much I went to university. I wanted to teach other kids about books."

Suddenly Repeat's head took on a manic life of its own. His right arm involuntarily shot out, rhythmically punching the sugar jar off the table, followed by the salt and pepper shakers, Parmesan cheese and napkin holder. I fired the owner a hasty 'back off' glance.

"... what television does to people. We're just sitting watching the news or cartoons or something ... you'll never know, Max and Jane ... we're just sitting there watching and then they start ... the voices ... we're not doing very well ... "

Forsaking all interest in my pie, I set down my fork. "Repeat ... "

My companion did not reply, so busy was he dabbing an imaginary spot on the table, working the napkin inward with a rapid swirl of decreasing circles.

"The voices, Repeat, do they always come from the TV?"

Just as I was concluding that I should switch topics, his voice re-emerged, softly cautious. "When I don't have a TV, they move to here." He tapped the big growth above his eye. "There's a transmitter inside my head. That's why university didn't work out."

I jumped into the interlude. My motive in inviting Repeat for lunch had been to take advantage of his lucidity and finagle him into getting to a doctor about that worrisome lump.

My inner elder counselled: *Walk ever so carefully. Choose each word with caution, deliver it with solicitude. That narrow opening is closing with every breath.*

Turning the left side of my face in his direction, I asked, "See this tiny scar?" I placed my index finger directly under the raggedy-edged circle on my cheek. "That's where I had a lump cut out six years ago."

His hands abandoned their busy work over the surface of the table. "Did the voices stop?"

"Yes, gone for good. Never heard from them since." Truth was, a very expensive plastic surgeon, who normally plied his knife on aging Rosedale matrons, had excised a sebaceous cyst. "Maybe we could get that transmitter removed from your forehead, Repeat. You'd probably sleep better."

"Hate the voices. Ruin my life. Can't go to the doctor, though." His head flipped to the side. "I'm fine," he insisted. "I don't want anything from anyone. We don't trust doctors. They'll change our drugs again." His hand resumed its obsessive concentrics over the table.

Damn, double damn. I had lost him to the demonic drummer.

As I deposited Repeat's bags back at the streetcar shelter, he grabbed my arm. "I want to show you something." From within his treasure chest, he extracted a small photo frame nestled like a Russian doll within a half-dozen smaller plastic bags.

In a pose that pre-dates Madonna and child, a pretty young woman gazed with pride on the infant she cradled.

"My mother and me." His huge, dirt-encrusted finger tenderly stroked the image.

"Thank you," I said. "She is very beautiful. And you, Repeat, obviously made her very happy."

Startled by a flash of memory, Repeat clutched the photo, its face to his heart. "Go back on your medication ... it's getting dark again."

It was not much past noon and still sunny. As I turned away, assuming him lost to a battery of menacing tongues, Repeat's earthbound voice emerged singular and certain. "Be very careful, Jane. *The truth is out there.* You need to protect yourself. Lock all your doors. Pull down the curtains. Tell Max to guard you well. Your house is surrounded by evil."

Was he afraid of his tentative, growing attachment to me and my dog? Perhaps he feared that we would be snatched from him as surely as his mother and Amazing, by the unseen Force beaming threats from the TV, from receivers in our heads. When we've let down our guard.

Chapter 21

From my second-floor computer cell I looked out on my neighbours' frost-wasted backyards. Crudely-patched roofs; derelict frame garages leaning drunkenly; grapes vines denuded of leaves, suspended like fallen tree branches over elaborate geometries of plumbing pipes; clothes lines strung between rusty T-bars remorseless as crucifixes. Slack Hydro lines superimpose their banal utility on a cloudless slate sky. Occasionally the prospect jerks into motion as a flight of pigeons inscribes a swift arc from their perch on the roof of St. Francis of Assisi and back again. My view is monochromatic rust, a blotch of congealing blood.

Inside the nine-by-five feet room where I shelter my thoughts and my computer from plaster dust, a litter of familiar companions covers my desk top. The omnipresent pack of Rothmans (BY SPECIAL APPOINTMENT), a green Depression-glass ashtray balancing a burning cigarette; a can of Smithwick's; a few books and some fugitive notes scrawled on matchbook covers, napkins and beer coasters.

This space is haunted by the spirit of the old man who died in here just before the house was put up for sale.

To relieve its gloomy interior, I went downstairs to fetch a plant. A Christmas cactus just swelling into blossom, fuchsia, gloriously erotic. The cactus, a gift from Pete, is now a mute *memento mori*. Every year since his death, just before its bloom period, I grow anxious that it won't flower.

I booted up my computer and crawled into the Web. Several minutes passed: in computer years, my pre-Power Mac and modem are geriatrics. I passed the time blowing dust off the tops of my shelved books as my browser snailed to its destination, Chelsea Walker's site.

Just as I was contemplating giving the sink, tub and toilet bowl a scrub, my screen filled. "Searching for Jessye" was lovingly but amateurishly implemented, with a table of contents that ran to seven pages, a confusing welter of facts and emotions that quickly overwhelmed me and the computer. My Mac repeatedly froze as I negotiated between links, forcing me to reboot so many times the bathroom porcelain soon shone.

I downloaded and printed several photographs and whatever information looked useful. Included in the site were items concerning all the missing women: the new poster; a request for information on their whereabouts; dozens of related newspaper articles and editorials; notices of marches, and of prayer and memorial services; links to private investigators, profilers, criminologists; and other missing-persons sites.

What most interested me were those postings special to Jessye Brant, whose disappearance had prompted her friend, Chelsea, to create the site. I immediately recognized the face on the home page from the poster: Jessye's had been one of the rare happy ones. In the photos she appears in a T-shirt, half-zipped satin jacket and shorts. In the first, son on her knee, seated on the carpet of a bright and tidy apartment, she beams confidence and clear-eyed delight. The second photo captured her seated on the carpet, leaning into her wee son, who is planted securely on Chelsea's lap.

The child, who appears to be about eight months old, interrogates the camera, his baby-innocent face uncomprehending, yet preternaturally vigilant.

I read the preliminary article, "How this site began." A rambling and disorganized narrative, what it lacked in structure it made up for in substance. As I worked my way through it, a profile of Chelsea began to take shape. Not unlike me, she felt compelled by strong feeling into conducting an enquiry supplementary to the police investigation. Streetwise, methodical, pro-active and bold, she had the instincts of a born PI. Hers was a profile in strength and self-assurance.

Jessye had been "only" the fourth woman to go missing from the stroll that year. She did not fit the stereotype of a junkie hooker. She had strong ties with her family and friends, and was well-known and regarded in her community. Chelsea began to suspect foul play very shortly after her disappearance and devised a three-pronged search.

She walked up and down the stroll, talking with dozens of Jessye's acquaintances, trying to trace her movements after leaving Chelsea's apartment about eight hours prior to her disappearance. No one had seen her. When the police refused to accept her missing persons report because she was a non-relative, she persuaded Jessye's sister Maggie to file. She met with a detective attached to the Missing Persons Unit to persuade him that Jessye's sudden disappearance was out of character, and gave him a recent photo. Later she initiated a poster campaign, enlisting Jessye's friends to distribute them. Eventually she met Billie Weston, with whom Jessye had been working the street the morning she disappeared. Billie was the last person to see Jessye, just minutes before she vanished. Chelsea took her testimony to the police, Billie being too drug-sick to handle the cops, with whom she was too familiar.

Chelsea finally contacted local and national TV stations and newspapers. My friend, Sam Brewer, was first off the mark with a front-page story, which he followed up on each time another woman went missing. Media coverage increased and eventually she persuaded the producer of "America's Most Wanted" to cover the disappearances. Chelsea felt vindicated: finally people were paying attention.

After submitting Jessye's case to several missing persons' sites and posting information about Jessye into many newsgroups, Chelsea started her own Web site, "Searching for Jessye." Her home page begins: DEDICATED TO THE MEMORY OF ALL THE MISSING AND MURDERED WOMEN. And ends: "We will probably never know what happened that fateful morning at the corner. I'm tormented by that. I miss her ..."

The site was last updated just five days ago. Chelsea Walker was one hell of a friend. I was looking forward to meeting this woman, should she be willing.

I turned to the next article. It was titled "Billie Weston speaks on Jessye, her friend," but was more autobiography than tribute.

Hi, my name is Billie. I am a 30 year old single mother of one. I was the last person to see Jessye alive. We had agreed to meet back at the same spot. When I turned the corner after driving around the block and saw her corner empty, I knew I would not see her again.

The next day I went back downtown to speak with some people she hung out with. No one had seen her. I've spoke with a few officers on the street but no real attempts to question me were made.

If I disappeared today, nothing would happen, but five years ago I would have been front-page news. You see 5 years ago I was one of you — hard working mother in a long term relationship, earning $50 grand a year. I worked hard and I was happy. Then, one day I fell apart. In 2 years I lost it all.

I know now why "they" don't just get a job, go home, go to detox. Do you think when I played with my Barbie that I dressed her up in a spandex mini and thigh high boots and played "junkie hooker?" Of course not.

I don't blame anyone else but myself for my addiction or that to feed it I have to work the street. But I am worthless because of it. I know this because my friends keep disappearing and no one looks for them. Because I was there when Jessye was taken and no one asks me about it.

I would love to go home. But I'm too afraid of losing my monkey — my king kong. I'd go mad.

Someone please, make it safe for us to stand in that dark lonely place.

Jessye, I miss you — you called me your friend and in 18 months you're still the only one.

— Billie

Billie's forlorn voice went straight to my heart, but it contained no clues to further my investigation. Her next item, "Billie's statement of events leading to Jessye's disappearance on April 14, 1998," sounded more promising.

Jessye and I left the Munroe Hotel on Jarvis after getting ready for work and got to Allan Gardens around 1:30 in the morning of April 14.

We fixed ourselves. Working dope sick or worrying for the coming "terror" is not my idea of fun. Then we walked from Allan Gardens down Sherbourne Street towards Dundas.

Jessye stayed on the NW corner by the variety store. I walked across to the SE corner by the hardware store. We stood around for about 15-20 minutes. Several cars drove by — a light-blue four-door with a white vinyl roof drove by slowly and went around the block, I presume, and pulled up to me. I got in.

I looked back to see if Jessye had got picked up. She hadn't. My date and I proceeded around the block and talked business. We agreed to disagree and he turned back on to Dundas from Parliament and dropped me off. I looked for Jessye. She was gone.

The whole street was empty. No cars, no people, no nothing. I felt really scared and alone. I knew she was gone.

— Billie

I'd give Billie the interview the police weren't interested in.

Then I read the note Chelsea had appended to Billie's two contributions:

"Billie speaks on Jessye, her friend" was specially written for the memorial for Jessye and the other missing women.

Unfortunately Billie was not able to attend the memorial. She died of a heroin overdose the day before. Police said that the heroin in her body was very pure.

Instead of firing off an e-mail, I picked up the phone.

Lenore Tootoosis greeted me warmly. "Of course I've got Chelsea's phone number — she's big in activist circles ... one great lady. But her number's unlisted. After setting up her Web site, she got so many crank calls her friends and clients had trouble getting through."

"Do you think she'd be willing to talk with me?"

"She's very keen to communicate with anyone who might help her. I'll ask her to call you right back if she's interested."

Ten minutes later, I grabbed the phone on the first ring.

Chapter 22

I WAITED IMPATIENTLY for five Hamlets blocking the door to decide if they wanted to enter or not to enter The Metropolis. A young woman with maraschino hair and an entire jewelry boutique piercing her face and ears read from the menu posted in the window.

"What's a quesa-fucking-dilla?" growled one of her cohorts, shoving past me to peer at the menu. He jabbed his finger under the Cold Tapas section. *"Hummus, tzatziki, harissa, pitas* — what is this shit? No fucking fries and no burgers. Let's go to the Can. They got Canadian food."

Even the lesser deity Trendy has his youthful dissidents.

The café was surprisingly empty. In the evenings it's packed with Gen X refugees from the suburbs, well-dressed, well-heeled and hot-to-trot.

A server in T-shirt and jeans was lounging on a bar stool near the cash register, while a cook in T-shirt and jeans listlessly hacked at some veggies at the end of the bar. Both were youthful, skinny and pretty enough to be Gap models. Both were enjoying a good hair day.

From wall-mounted speakers Etta James lamented "Love's Been Rough on Me." Too early in the day. Two low-rent types were laughing and shooting pool at one of the tables in the back.

I walked past the bar to the only occupied table, where

a casually-dressed, very attractive woman I instantly recognized from the "Searching for Jessye" photos was seated, her head bent over *The Globe and Mail* Challenge Crossword.

She looked up and grinned. *"Getting up in the morning is revolting* — six letters?"

"Hey, I can't even get the Quick Clues, let alone the Cryptic. But I totally agree with the sentiment."

She laughed. "I thought you said you were a writer."

"Did I make any claim to being smart?"

"No. Lenore told me that part."

The waiter glided over to our table, asked if we wanted it wiped (I said 'yes,' just for the pleasure of watching him grimace), tossed down two menus, took our drinks order — pint of Guinness for me, Kilkenny for Chelsea — and disdainfully cantered off.

I scanned the booze side of the menu, counting 27 offerings of single malt. "Wish I'd thought to order us the Dom Perignon — a bargain at $150. Something tells me this place attracts people who earn serious money."

"Actually, Jane, I fall into that category."

"Ah," I replied, at a loss for any intelligent reply.

My 'ah' came out sounding more like 'aaargh.' Hardly the time to launch into the stock harangue about starving writers, although my inner socialist advises that I should be earning say, as much per hour as a competent dentist.

She raised her glass, interrupting my reverie. "Lenore also told me that you are a talker. So let me guess what's pitched you into this uncharacteristic silence. Is it 'that' or 'how' I earn my serious money? I've got to tell you, girl, if you have issues with 'how' — including being too polite — then this conversation has N-O-W-H-E-R-E to go. So lighten up."

My blood pressure began a slow descent to normal.

"Thanks. I was scared shitless of saying something that might offend you."

"Hope you don't take that attitude towards your friendships."

"No," I admitted, "my friends tell me I'm subtle as cheap perfume."

She grinned wickedly. "Well, with that crap out of the way, we can get down to business."

'Business' — is she expecting me to pay her for her time? Why, I ask, do conversations already fraught with tension then get loaded with ambiguity?

Etta James passed the mike to Billie Holliday. "Body and Soul" filled the room.

Chelsea's eyes brightened. "I've managed to stay more Nina Simone than Billie Holliday — you know: *You don't have to live next to me / Just give me my equality.*"

Notwithstanding my tone-deafness and inability to carry a tune, I ventured a couple of lines.

"I love the self-assertion, Jane, even though you've fried my ears."

I rose to my feet, curtsied, excused myself and headed for the can. As I voided a pint-plus-a-drop into the appropriate bowl, all the while keeping my naughty bits well raised above the seat (Etta's only enduring lesson), I studied the walls. The Metropolis' selection of graffiti runs from soft and saccharine (mostly baby dykes coming out), to this charmer:

YOU ARE A STUPID PIG DOG / SHIT FACED CRACK WHORE /
WHO FUCKS FOR A BEER / RACIST LITTLE BITCH /
DROP DEAD CUNT

If this is sisterhood, hand me a chain-saw.

I returned to our table to find our pints replenished. We ordered some food, none of it recognizably 'Canadian.'

Chelsea told me about the last time she saw Jessye, significant only in retrospect — two close friends meeting to gossip. On Monday, April 13, Jessye came over to her apartment for a short visit just after six. They talked, watched *Jeopardy* and ordered in Chinese food. Jessye, who stayed at the Munroe Hotel and stored some of her stuff at Chelsea's, filled a pillowcase with clean clothes, and Chelsea drove her back to the hotel at about 8:30.

"The last words she said were, 'Be cool my friend. I'll call you.' I'm still waiting." Her voice trembled. "Jessye was a very sensitive, complex person. She had this great sense of humour — and a wild laugh. I miss her like hell."

"Chelsea, do you think you will ever see her again?"

She vigorously shook her head. "Hell, no! Right from the start I knew my search was futile. Jessye was terrified to leave Toronto. It was the only place she felt like she belonged. She was really close to her mother and her sister — who, by the way, are raising her two kids. She had always made it a point to stay in touch with her family. She would never, ever let them worry. Something terrible happened to her.

"People say that women like me and Jessye choose to be prostitutes, often drug addicts too. Jessye never *decided* to become a drug addict or a whore. She became addicted and started pulling tricks to pay for her habit. She desperately wanted out of the life, but heroin owned her. Ever seen a mouse trapped on one of those glue pads? The harder they struggle, the worse they get stuck."

The more such stories I heard, the more drugs began to look like the real pimps. I wanted to ask Chelsea what had driven her to the life and what kept her there, but I had no right.

Chelsea's pager started vibrating on the table. She

excused herself and headed for the pay phone. "Sorry for the interruption, but that's a client. Since life on the stroll got so dangerous, I've been doing 'in' calls — you know, businessmen or whatever in town for a few days. I go to their hotel rooms."

When she returned, I got straight to the point.

"Chelsea, as well as studying your Web site really carefully, I've read tons of newspaper and magazines articles — and some of the police files. Can you think of anything that hasn't been reported? Has your search uncovered anything you didn't include in your site?"

"Yes, two things — both related to this pager. Last June I got a call saying that Jessye had been spotted at the Vie en Rose Hotel in Montreal. I couldn't tell if it was a man or a woman speaking. Maybe the caller was trying to disguise his or her voice, or had a cold. But it sounded legit. So the next morning I loaded a box of posters into a rented car and drove off. I contacted outreach organizations in Montreal, supplied them with posters and information and contacts. I went with the police to the Vie en Rose to check with the manager and tenants. No one recalled ever having seen Jessye. She had never been a resident there. I drove around all the working strolls and handed out posters to sex workers to distribute. One woman translated the poster into French for me and had a few hundred printed up. But — not a soul recognized her. After a week, I headed back to Toronto. The call must have been a hoax.

"Then in September I got three pages on a Sunday morning, back-to-back. I think it was the same voice as the first call:

'Jessye's dead. There will be more girls like her dead. There will be more prostitutes killed. One every Friday night. At the busiest time.'

Then,

'You'll never find Jessye again. So just stop looking, all right? She doesn't want to be seen and heard from again. So, bye. She's dead.'

The last one said,

'This is in regard to Jessye. You'll never find her again because a friend of mine killed her, and I was there.'"

She spoke slowly. "I knew in my guts that I was listening to her killer, the sadistic son-of-a-bitch."

"So you think that reference to a 'friend of mine' was bogus?"

"Sure, just like all those people who write in to Dear Abby. 'A friend' is into bonking poodles or sniffing knickers — stupid wankers who can't even admit their perversions to themselves."

The second item on my agenda she dispensed with as quickly as Sandy Reeder had. "Nope, never heard of a Tina Paglia. I know so many of the working girls, she must have kept a low profile." Her face went serious. "Obviously not low enough."

She extracted a manilla envelope from her backpack. "Here's something I photocopied for you. It's a few pages from Jessye's journal — the last entry she made, and a poem she wrote after one of the other girls' bodies was found."

We polished off our food and, pints in hand, headed for the pool tables. I racked up the balls. Chelsea picked up a house cue from the wall rack, checked the tip, then held up the cue like a rifle and sighted down its length while slowly rotating it. Shaking her head, she exchanged it for another, subjected it to the same test. Second one passed.

A few months ago, as the keystone in my new fitness regime, I bought a copy of *The Complete Idiot's Guide to Pool and Billiards*. I must have skipped the cue chapter.

She chalked up, made a few warm-up strokes, and executed a spectacular break shot, straight and smooth and solid, hitting the front ball full in the face.

"How did you do that?" I marvelled.

"That's the great thing about pool. Because you don't need to be big, strong and fast to win, women aren't at a disadvantage. You just need to work on your control."

"Is that all?" I muttered. Finally, I got a shot. Self-conscious as hell, I tried to emulate her stance and bridge. My jerky, unsure stroke drove the cue ball right off the table. Red-faced, I retrieved it and handed it over to my opponent. With a string of pocketed balls, she cleared the table.

"I've been playing since I was ten," she consoled me. "Would you like me to help you with your bridge, and show you a couple of good drills?"

We chatted as I practised my closed-loop bridge and ran through some basic drills. Taking advantage of our more relaxed mood, I ventured into item three on my agenda: asking her help in getting me into some camouflage gear so I could spend a few hours on the stroll. "Um, what are you doing tomorrow night?"

She burst out laughing. "I've got tickets for the opera. Richard Gere is my date."

I really wanted to reply that I'd been trying to treat her as though she had a life beyond her job. Instead I grabbed for my beer.

She flashed a wicked grin. "Why are you asking — you want a date?"

I recovered quickly enough to explain my idea. She agreed to help only on the condition that I first speak with a woman named Dee-Dee. "She's a twenty-year veteran of the life, who will do her damnedest to dissuade you. If you can talk your way past her, then I'm on board — but only if you promise not to get in a vehicle and if you let me watch over you from the opposite corner."

As Chelsea bent over to demonstrate a combination shot, a mocking laugh rang out. Sitting at the back of the café, a pitcher of beer between them, were the two guys who'd been shooting pool when I arrived.

"Shee-it, man, I am not believing my eyes!"

"Like, what?" asked his monosyllabic but attentive buddy.

"See that bitch at the table — the black one — I fucked that chick, man."

For the first time, Chelsea blew a shot, catapulting the cue ball into a pocket.

"Should be a law against broads playing pool." The boys guffawed.

Gently I nudged Chelsea's bridge hand with my cue. Slowly her eyes rose to meet mine.

"Hey, girl," I said, "hope you left him broke. I'd make that piece of trash pay big to get into my Hanes."

Sudden tears flooded her eyes. "Thank you ... and I'm sorry I ... embarrassed you in your neighbourhood."

"Don't flatter yourself, Chelsea. Nothin' you could do would depreciate my reputation more than I've already done."

I collected balls from the pockets and loaded them onto the tray, anxious to leave before I lost it.

A loonie bounced on the felt.

"That should cover a BJ, Peaches."

"Head straight for the cash and pay our bill — I'll finish up here." My suddenly commanding tone startled Chelsea into action as another loonie came to rest beside my hand.

In full combat mode, I planted myself in front of the prime offender.

"Hey, cowboy, stand up for a minute."

Buddy Two chuckled, "I think he wanted the blow from the other broad."

As Buddy One lumbered to his paws, I proclaimed, "Blows are my specialty." Full in the nuts with the toe of my Doc.

"Devil made me do it," I muttered to Chelsea as I hit the front door at a run.

"Girlfriend," she chortled, "you under-rate your network: *God* made you do it."

Chapter 23

INSIDE THE MANILLA ENVELOPE were ten photocopied pages, eight of them a long excerpt from Jessye's journal, evidently her final entry. There was also an untitled poem, neatly written, not marked up with changes. The author had spent some time revising and recopying the text.

    Woman's body found beaten beyond recognition
    you sip your coffee
    taking a drag of your smoke
    turning the page
    taking a bite of your toast
    for you it's just another day
    just another death
    you've already forgot.
    It's not just another day
    not just another death
    she was a broken down angel
    who touched my life
    she was no whore
    but somebody special
    who lost her way
    fighting for life
    trying to survive
    a lonely lost child who died
    in the night all alone
    scared, gasping for air

Jessye had written her own epitaph.

Sudden sorrow overwhelming me, I headed for my beer stash, prepared to induce a state of temporary amnesia. A wiser self turned me from the fridge door and brewed coffee instead.

The eight journal pages were written in a more hurried hand. Jessye's frantic pen seemed driven — dredged-up memory fuelling her compulsion to witness. The entry was undated and prefaced by what appeared to be a false start: "Down here it's different ... a fine line divides your world from mine and yet there is so much that you people wouldn't understand: our rules must be followed."

That declaration echoed the Us/Them fissure that cleaved her poem deft as razor wire.

I tried to explain this to that stupid religious bitch at the demo who kept nagging on at me about how we all choose our realities. She was carrying this placard that read JESUS COMMANDS YOU TO STOP SELLING YOUR BODY. Like, maybe she thought I could choose to be a brain surgeon? Choice means you've got options.

Then the journal explodes into raw pain, her words brutally evocative as a snuff movie. Jessye documents the savage beating and rape she received at the hands of a bad date — a nightmare exacerbated by subsequent police indifference. It concludes:

Some nights I dream and I could swear that I'm there. I actually feel the blows and kicks to the head. I wake in a panic and in tears. It was so dumb of me to fight back. But in my heart I know he was definitely trying to kill me. Good thing a car came along and scared him off.

I paged Chelsea, who got right back to me. No, she didn't know when the entry had been written. Jessye had told her about the assault, though, which occurred about four weeks prior to her disappearance, but she couldn't name or describe her assailant — only that he wore triple-soled Dayton boots. A blue van, maybe a Chevy or a Dodge. No plate number. Yes, the police had the journal, which Jessye had left at her place, along with some other valuables. When she went missing, Chelsea turned it over to them. Jessye was too wrecked to report her bad date to PROS, but Chelsea gave them what little information she had.

Might Jessye, unable to shoulder any more pain, have killed herself? Possible, but not likely, Chelsea replied. If she had, where was her body? Far more probable was that her attacker tracked her down, abducted her and finished what he'd started when she fought back.

Finally, I asked her if she'd give me the bad date sheets from the past three years.

"Sorry, Jane. We keep really tight control over their circulation. Prostitutes won't trust any BDS that gets outside the business. Anyway, the reports are anonymous, so you couldn't track down any girl who provided information. They're only meant to help other prostitutes avoid dangerous situations."

"Who collects these reports? She must keep records of the girls' names and numbers."

"Sandy Reeder publishes the best BDS in the city. You could give her a try, but I doubt she'll reveal any of her informants. She's refused to let the cops access the entire list."

Instead, I urged her to phone DeeDee, my would-be trainer. She had already done so.

I kept my head on by reminding myself that I was a writer — with a strong urge to produce a book that wouldn't change the world, but that might be witness to such violence as Jessye endured. I turned back to her journal.

Having regained consciousness and dragged herself out of a ditch — only to discover that her assailant was still cruising in search of her — Jessye flagged down a Good Samaritan:

He drove me to the police station — against my will but I had no fight left. I had only one thing on my mind, a fix. The pain and the sickness were killing me. My eyes were almost swollen shut. Their response was what I expected. I felt like a total cheap junkie whore standing there stark naked, beaten to a pulp and they told me I got what I deserved. No clothes no bus fare no help, no sympathy. Part of what they said was true. And I still remember that tone of voice and that look as clear as if it were right now. I walked out trying to keep my head up high ...

A chapter on police response to violence against prostitutes began to take shape.

Chapter 24

"ARE YOU SURE YOU WANT TO DO THIS?" DeeDee Whitney sat at my dining-room table sipping Red Zinger tea. "I only take in calls," she'd explained. "So I prefer to get out as much as I can when I'm not working."

DeeDee's classy appearance toppled yet another of my stereotypes. She was in her mid-thirties, tall, elegant, her black hair Sassoon-sleek, dark brown eyes and oval face subtly made-up. White silk tank tucked into a deep grey linen skirt, matching jacket. She could easily be a lawyer heading into court. What had I been expecting — street-hooker drag in the middle of the day on a woman with a client list of corporate CEOs?

After a slice of small talk, I went for the main chance. My clever idea, that I go "undercover" on the stroll to get firsthand experience of the backdrop to the murders and disappearances, struck DeeDee as very dangerous.

Who could blame her for not wanting to feel responsible for any harm that might befall my dumb ass? I tried to persuade her that my proposal, however foolhardy, was not frivolous.

"DeeDee, the setting of my book is everything. The stroll isn't just where the action happens to take place. We're looking at fifteen unsolved murders, twice as many disappearances. Every one of those women worked the streets. Most got picked up on the track and lured to their deaths. These women got into trouble in a relatively small area. The way I see it, the stroll is part of the plot — the magnet that keeps pulling the killer back."

DeeDee nodded. "I hear you. But tell me, why can't you just *imagine* where the action takes place? I bet lots of writers never go to the places they write about. They probably just read travel guides."

"You're right, but a serious reader can tell the difference. I have no idea what it's like to be walking the stroll alone at two a.m., how you screen customers, what kind of johns and bad dates you encounter, who you hang with, what you talk about. I need to make my reader see, hear, taste, smell and feel the street action. That's something I can't do sitting safely at home behind my computer."

DeeDee's brown eyes deepened. "Still, I don't want to have any hand in sending you out there — at least not without one last effort to dissuade you. I haven't survived this long without learning how to trust my gut. A street whore has a minute or two, tops, to assess the risk of getting into a john's vehicle. That's why it's so bloody important that she hit the stroll clean and sober. Her life depends on keeping a clear head and sharp reflexes."

"A veteran cop once told me how a rapist sizes up a potential victim," I replied. "He reads her body language for all those tell-tale little signs that reveal if she's good victim material. What you're describing sounds to me like the flip-side."

"Exactly. Your typical rapist is tracking a woman who seems ill-prepared to take care of herself. A street-smart whore is always on the alert for a john who can't get his rocks off without hurting a woman — and, believe me, there are hundreds out there. Developing that awareness takes a whack of nasty experience you don't have."

She sucked deeply on her cigarette while her eyes read my face. "But I don't think that writing a good book is your only motive. Aren't you also hoping to root around for clues to the murders — maybe even luck out on tripping over the killer?"

No way DeeDee was going to be suckered by my usual bag of verbal tricks. "You're close. I want to see if anyone knew Tina Paglia. Maybe I'll get a lead on some disappearances ... which may be linked to some of the murders."

"Just by posing as a whore, you're inviting deep shit, Jane. At best you could get busted for communicating. First offence, you'll get off with a fine and a warning. At worst you end up in the morgue — especially if some bad date figures your real motive."

I couldn't let my brain hold on to that thought. "Please, DeeDee, just give me your best advice about how to keep out of trouble. I'll follow it to the letter. I won't take any dumb risks, and I have no intention of getting into a stranger's car."

She raised a skeptical eyebrow. "And how are you going to avoid doing that?"

Seemed clear to me. "Well, can't I just turn a guy down because I don't like the look of him?"

"Sure, we do it all the time — otherwise even more of us would be dead. But you're going to get hit on fifteen, maybe twenty times, in a few hours. If you turn down all the johns, you could be setting yourself up for trouble."

"I'll take a lot of coffee breaks. And maybe I could arrange to have a male friend pose as a john and pick me up."

"I hope none of your male friends would even think about helping you out — once he knew what you were up to."

She had a point.

"I really appreciate your concern, DeeDee, but I am determined to do this. Look at it my way: forewarned is forearmed."

"Please, don't encourage me to look at anything your way. I value my butt." She walked over to the window, then grinned. "Okay, I give up. But the makeover could turn out to be pretty dangerous in itself." She glanced at my Doc Martens. "Do you ever wear high heels — I'm talking *very* high heels?"

Encouraged by her change of direction, I confessed, "Not since my grade twelve prom, but I couldn't get through the evening without taking the bloody things off every time I wanted to dance. I had to go home in my stocking feet. My date never asked me out again."

"Then you're just going to have to practise 'til you get the hang of it. Big heels are part of the uniform. And you can't just limp along the street: you have to shake your ass in–vi–ting–ly." Her demonstration cracked me up. "Maybe we can get you into platform boots instead. Anyway, I'm going to phone a friend and book you for seven tonight. That will give him time to package you for the stroll. And I'll see that Chelsea watches your back."

As she was putting on her coat, I asked why she'd changed her mind about abetting my scheme.

"Because dead women can't write."

Several hours later I made my way up a dark flight of stairs to the second floor of an old brick low-rise apartment building on Jarvis Street: Miss Lucy's Finishing School for Boys Who Want To Be Girls.

"Hi, you must be DeeDee's student," a thin man in an

Armani greeted me at the door. "I'm Miss Lucy, principal of Toronto's premier male-to-female cross-dressing academy."

He ushered me into a large, dimly lit room, decorated entirely in Ralph Lauren chocolate brown: ceiling, walls, carpet, furniture. Only the art relieved my oppressive sense that I'd fallen into a Hershey bar, or worse. A six-foot-high reproduction of Michelangelo's David stood beside a life-size cardboard Bette Midler as a mermaid. Beanie Babies nearly filled the velvet brocade sofa. I cleared a space before I sat down so I wouldn't smother the herd.

Male-to-female? "But I'm a woman," I blustered. "Jane Yeats."

My confession did not faze Miss Lucy. "DeeDee always knows what she's doing, dear. She was quite right to place you in my capable hands. I do adore a challenge." After giving me a hasty once-over, he delicately essayed, "It seems you're not totally at home with the ... ahem ... *femme* aspect of your nature."

"What has that got to do with being womanly?" I snapped.

He wagged a finger at me. "Do not mistake the Academy for a shrine to feminism, dear. Our goal is Total Slut. Most guys find trashy a turn-on. Now, makeup and clothes are important, but there are some essentials you'll need to master, like walking and posing seductively. I'll coach you after I've worked my cosmetic magic."

My only preparation had been to scrape my legs and underarms. Miss Lucy took care of the rest. Forty-five minutes later, he had me prancing about in a strapless black leather mini dress and short, red fake-fur jacket. He tried to talk me into purple fetish spikes with six-inch heels, but a trial stroll around his dining-room table had me hobbling bent-kneed.

Lucy confessed they were comic relief — designed for sitting or posing with your legs in the air. Ye gawds. I assured him that my feet would never leave the ground tonight, but I wanted to be shod so as not to impede a fast get-away.

When I dubiously eyed his collection of tacky wigs, Miss Lucy assured me that my hair was sensational enough. Some serious backcombing and a can of hair spray later, the wigs looked classy by comparison. He contoured and darkened my eyebrows, tinted my lids to match the jacket, lengthened my lashes until they could dust knick-knacks, and painted on a glossy scarlet mouth. As a finishing touch, he wound a long double string of fake pearls around my neck and tucked the rest into my cleavage.

I quickly snatched them off. "Like if some nutbar wants to strangle me, I'm going to provide the weapon?"

Miss Lucy marched me over to his gilded full-length mirror: Total Slut.

"Now that I've got you all frocked up, we can work on your *allure*."

Another forty-five minutes later, Miss Lucy acknowledged that he had taken me as far along the road to glamour as the recalcitrant materials allowed. "You definitely will do. Really, you've got major curb appeal."

DeeDee showed up as planned, congratulated Miss Lucy on his magic and led me by the arm down to the street. My nostrils convulsively sneezed out Beanie Baby fur.

"We're going to set you up on the corner close to the donut shop two blocks south of here. Don't try any other location. Territory on the stroll gets distributed through seniority and power — and you've got neither. Make your way to the donut shop at midnight. A lot of the girls drop by for their coffee breaks. I'll introduce you to a few of my friends. Meanwhile, Chelsea will serve as your 'watch' from the opposite corner. When she used to do this with Jessye, she'd record the customer's licence number whenever her partner went off to service a trick. But this is not a working night for her. She left the stroll after her friend disappeared. Tonight she's here at my request. Don't count on her to rescue you if you do anything stupid."

The underwires cantilevering my breasts towards the Milky Way were driving me crazy. As I did a passable imitation of walking, while tugging the top of the minuscule dress up and the bottom down, DeeDee gave me some safety tips, a menu and my prices.

"Advertise your services without being pushy or you'll get busted. When you first approach a john, don't mention sex or money — just offer to show him a good time. Now, you look classy enough to demand fifty bucks for a hand job, seventy for a blow and a hundred for intercourse. Do not offer bargains. If you undercut the competition, they'll retaliate. Always demand the money up front. Tell them that you don't suck or ride bareback, you don't swallow or permit anal. A lot of them will drive off as soon as they hear the bad news. You'll have to figure out how to deal with the rest. But keep one arm across your chest to ward off any sudden blow if a situation goes sour. You're a writer — get creative."

To keep from cancelling the whole gig on the spot, I swiftly blocked all graphic images of actually performing those acts with a stranger. *How desperate would a woman have to get?* I'd sooner take my chances foraging for Kraft Dinner at a food bank and sleeping beside Repeat in the park.

Then again, the draft tap hadn't yet run dry.

We passed an emaciated girl leaning against a street sign

as she struggled to maintain her balance. Raising her skirt above her thighs, flailing her shaking hands slowly, rapidly, then slowly again, she tried desperately to attract a john.

"How are you doing, Rainbow?" DeeDee asked.

"Fuck off, bitch!"

My instructor turned to me with a shrug. "Heroin. She'll be dead in a few months. Even the outreach workers won't go near her. She carries a needle she claims an AIDS carrier shot up with. Poor kid can't be more than thirteen."

DeeDee stationed me on the south-west corner. "This is a good spot to pull a date. Traffic has to stop before turning onto Wellesley."

A dull blue van cruised past us for the second time. "Don't waste your time trying to attract the circlers — guys like this who do laps around the block leering at the girls while they jerk off."

She patted me on the back. "You're on your own, babe. Be smart."

Chelsea waved from her post across the street. Shivering more from fear than the bite of the night air on my exposed legs, I lit up a cigarette. While my eyes trolled the scene, I pasted a world-weary expression on my face. *Been there, done that, got the T-shirt. Nothing new under the sun.*

Because my favourite camera shop is nearby, I know this area by day. By ten p.m. the atmosphere alters beyond recognition. Lean menacingly morphs into mean. There are far fewer pedestrians, most of them male — none looking for a camera or a pawn shop. Some vehicles are being driven slowly, as if a frightened parent was in search of a wayward daughter, so carefully do the drivers scrutinize every face.

A police cruiser creeps past. The cop glances in my direction. *Hah, bet he can't recognize a writer when he sees one.* That stupid reflection reminds me how much I cling to my hidden identity as a woman whose work is marginally more respectable than sucking dick.

Act the part, Jane.

To appear nonchalant, I begin to recite Emily Dickinson to myself. Hoping they might impart a rhythmic impetus to my strut, I select two lines with a jaunty ring.

Bees are black, with Gilt Surcingles — Buccaneers of Buzz. At twenty-four steps, I swing round. What the hell are 'surcingles?'

"Whore!" shouts a teenager in a grey Lexus. "Slut!" shouts another from the car's rear bleacher. I ignore them, hoping they don't manage to hunt down a gay boy to bash.

Bees are black, with Gilt Surcingles — Buccaneers of Buzz. Bees are black ...

Chapter 25

"**H**EY, YOU WANNA STAY there talkin' to yourself or are you in the mood for some fun?" A slightly slurred invitation from a Jeep Cherokee perched on jacked-up tires.

DeeDee forgot to warn me about elevated vehicles. Wondering how I'd lean down sexily into a utility vehicle, I approached the driver. In spite of the satin baseball jacket, the guy looked seriously out of shape, his gut competing for space with the steering wheel. Mid-thirties, thinning curly black hair begging for shampoo and scissors, chubby face, couple of chipped teeth. A moist pocket of stale sweat and beer-reek popped close to my nose.

I painstakingly recited my menu, exorbitantly elevating my rates while assuring that my offerings didn't sound too palatable.

"Ya give me a blow without a rubber and we got a deal."

Be still my churning stomach. "Sorry. No love without a glove."

"Fuck you," he spat, speeding off without so much as a wave.

With an eloquent shrug, I resumed my strut. *Bees are black...*

After six more rude rejections, I headed back towards Coffee Time. Two of my six suitors had refused gloves, the remaining four aspirants found a sour variety of ways to let me know what they thought of my fees. One quipped that he wouldn't pay that much to fuck the Queen. *Well, who would?*

I couldn't see Chelsea.

I had to get my feet out of these boots before I wound up knuckle-walking through life. For sure, the underside of my breasts would carry to the grave a half-moon imprint. Just before I reached Gerrard, a red Pontiac Grand Am bearded with rust pulled up to the curb.

"Hop in quick — there's a cop watching the car," its occupant commanded as I terminated Emily Dickinson.

I frantically scanned the street for Chelsea. No luck.

Before I realized what I'd done, I found myself sitting beside my would-be client as he swiftly turned the corner on to Dundas. The lock on my door clicked.

Even his mother could not describe my date as an attractive man. He had beady eyes, a thick, crooked nose, thin lips and a body by junk food.

"Glad you changed your mind, babe." He squeezed my left thigh with a fat hairy paw.

Where's Hugh Grant when you need him?

"I'm sorry, but I did not change my mind. I just didn't want to get busted."

His look was not encouraging. "Too late now, babe." This wannabe stud was driving quickly, but still within the speed limit. I missed the name on the street sign as he lurched around a corner, raced down a pocked laneway alongside a deserted factory, and ground to a halt in an empty lot.

I couldn't see the street — the parking lot was very deep and unlit. Staring through the slush-splashed windshield at a chain-link fence, I reckoned that sprinting my way to safety hobbled by these damn boots was a no-go. Bluffing my way out appeared my only option.

"When you were turning that corner, I pressed CALL

RETURN on my cell phone."

Right, like my skimpy outfit could conceal anything bigger than a mole. As I tugged down my skirt, my goose-pimpled breasts suffered even greater exposure. In a panic, I summoned less palatable strategies. I could bite it off. *Yuk.* Cut it off — if I could extricate the retractable knife tucked into my right boot. *No ... risky as it was revolting.* The guy could be carrying a weapon.

Unzipping his fly, Prince Charming tossed a few rolled-up twenties into my lap. "What I'm havin' to pay, ya better give fantastic head."

Definitely time to execute Operation Bluff. Pitch a seizure.

Clutching my bosom, I lurched towards the dashboard, emitting a long, drawn-out wheeze.

"What the fuck — this part of your routine?"

"Asthma," I gasped, "having an asthma attack." Another lung-rattling wheeze, compliments of Rothmans of Pall Mall. "You got a dog?" That was a reasonable bet, given the suspect hairs embroidering his sweater.

"Yeah, a pit bull, but I didn't bring him with me. What do you take me for, a pervert?"

Doubling up, I held my breath until my face flushed fuchsia. "It's those dog hairs. You gotta get me to a hospital. Tongue's swelled up, throat's closing, can't — EEEEEEEEEEEEE — breathe. Don't have my EpiPen. Dead in five minutes." I slumped heavily against the car door.

The jerk panicked. "SHUT UP. WILL YA? Okay, I'll get you to the fuckin' hospital. That cop mighta took my licence number. They find your body here, could look like I whacked ya."

Clearly the peckerhead had my best interests in mind.

Rapidly zipping his disappointed member back into his polyester pants, he accelerated out of the parking lot, speeding north towards Wellesley Hospital. Two hot minutes later, he pulled up to the Emergency entrance and leaned towards my recumbent form to shove me onto the pavement. What the hell, the last time a man opened a car door for me Elvis was still breathing.

Not a totally wicked man, once a girl got past the genital urgency, I consoled myself. I'd place serious money on him now heading straight home to the wife and kids.

Just inside the doors, a woman hooked up to an IV, her complexion the colour of dirty snow, lit up a cigarette.

"What the fuck are you staring at?" I shouted, picking myself up and scurrying back to the street, bruised and scraped, but with that critical pinch of dignity intact.

Well, maybe not. I gazed down. One of my boobs had liberated itself. Yet another occupational hazard.

I flagged down the first cab to come along and instructed the driver to drop me off at Queen and Sherbourne, hub of the crack trade. No way was anyone ever going to hear about this escapade.

En route to the coffee shop, I stilled my drumming heart by deep breathing.

A power-walker quickly passed me and approached a huddle of women.

"Scarlett! Y'all seen my ho Scarlett?" he shouted.

Instinctively, the women shielded their faces with their hands and turned away. Maybe they already had a pimp or made do without one.

"I'm not hasslin' y'all. I just want my bitch."

Chapter 26

THE CROWDED COFFEE SHOP felt safe as my own home — before the roof collapsed. DeeDee waved me over to a booth mid-way along the aisle. She and the three women drinking coffee and smoking with her seemed totally composed — hair in place, makeup intact, faces collected. *Can sex with strangers become routine as brushing your teeth?* Although I donated my virginity to a good cause when Michael Jackson was a black man, I still find locking naughty bits with an intimate, let alone a stranger — an ... agitating experience.

Blowing a huge smoke ring towards the ceiling, DeeDee observed, "Shit, honey, don't you look like something the dog drug in."

"I slipped on some ice."

She introduced me around the table. "Jane, meet Ruby, Marilyn, Janet. Girls, Jane is friends with Lenore and Chelsea." They smiled me a lukewarm welcome.

"Love your dress," said Janet, a slightly-built woman with short dark hair and raccoon eyes.

"Thanks," I blushed, "but I'm not sure it's me, if you know what I mean."

"Finish telling us about the jerk in the van," DeeDee encouraged Marilyn.

Marilyn, a blowzy woman whose best feature was her shoulder-length blonde hair, extracted a big wad of bubble gum from her mouth and married it to the underside of the table. "So, the prick agrees to fifty bucks for a blow. Soon as I get in the van, he goes, 'Ya got big tits?' 'You're only paying for my mouth,' I says. He goes, 'Tell you why I'm askin'. I like to make movies. Thought you might be interested.' I tell the goof, 'If I wanted to be in movies, I'd have moved to L.A.'"

"He was a director?" I blurted out.

Eight world-weary eyes stared at me like I'd fallen from a tree still gumming a banana.

"Porn, Jane, porn. Dirty movies," DeeDee explained. "The guy wasn't looking for Julia Roberts."

Eyeing me suspiciously, Janet asked how long I'd been in the biz. No way I could fool this panel of experts. "Actually, I'm a writer," I stammered, shoving down my wayward boob.

"Yeah, and I do brain surgery afternoons," Janet retorted. "How long have you been a whore?"

"I guess that depends on who you ask." I laughed nervously. "Seriously, I don't do it for money ... I mean, really I am a writer ... true crime books. Tonight I'm sort of ... uh, doing research."

"Girl, we all had to start some time," Ruby offered.

DeeDee came to my rescue. "Jane looks genuine because Miss Lucy did her up. She really is a writer. Chelsea asked me to help her out because the book she's working on is about the shit going down on the stroll. One of the murders hit real close to home. Tina Paglia's body got dumped in Jane's front yard. You can trust this woman, eh? Lenore says she's got a good take on the life."

Ruby, a big black woman who looked like she could chew glass without blinking, shrugged. "I've got no problem talking to you, girl. Hell, anything, if you think your book might help catch that son-of-a-bitch." She briefly studied her fingernails. "So, what do you say, girlfriends? Between the four of us we could teach Prostitution 101. Let's give the broad a break."

In the brief silence that ensued my ears picked up some surrounding conversation. A boy pleaded with a dealer for a hit of crack. The man refused, but not because of the kid's tender age: the kid couldn't pony up. Two girls no older than the desperate boy each produced the requisite fifty dollars. "Only two-and-a-half BJs," one joked.

Then Marilyn and Janet nodded in unison, although Janet didn't look much like she was prepared to be co-operative. I asked if any of them had known Paglia.

Janet shook her head. "Never heard of the poor bitch 'til last week."

Marilyn busied herself searching her bag for more bubble gum. "Nope. Don't think she ever worked our stroll."

I ventured a few more questions. Either none of them had anything to offer, or they weren't talking. Then I dredged up the sole nugget I'd gleaned from Sally Murphy. "Have any of you been approached by a relative of one of the missing girls — mother, father, sister ... whatever?"

Janet snorted as she ground her cigarette butt into a tin ashtray. "Like our families give a shit?"

Ruby tried harder. "Girl, unless you got a good description of this person, you're outta luck. I run into these poor broads every week. Mostly mothers, trolling the strolls, bars, restaurants, trick hotels, shelters, soup kitchens ... you name it, they're looking, hoping, *If I can just talk to her, I can turn her life around.*" She rolled her eyes. "Yeah, right, and if I could carry a tune I'd be Aretha Franklin."

I gave them each my card, with a request that they call me if they picked up any information.

As we were paying our bill, a scuffle broke out across the street. It first looked like a man helping a young Native woman to her feet, but then he shoved her back down to the pavement and kicked her in the stomach. Everyone in the restaurant watched the brief scene as though it were on TV.

DeeDee grabbed my arm as I charged for the door. "Stay right the fuck where you are. Guy's an undercover cop." As her assailant drove off, the girl picked herself up and tottered off clutching her stomach.

Ruby spoke to me, her voice harsh. "Girl, you know what we always tell the new kids? *If we could weed out the undercover cops and the nut cases, this wouldn't be a dangerous job.* That woman won't report the beating. Like, who do you call after a cop beats the shit out of you?"

"And if they ain't beating or fucking you, they're busting your ass for communicating," Marilyn wearily added.

As I reached into my jacket pocket for my house key, my fingers touched the wad of rolled-up twenties. My night on the stroll yielded more than I'd earned in months. I'd donate it to PROS.

The bloody phone was ringing. It was Chelsea, eager to confirm that I'd made it home safely. She apologized for having slipped off to relieve herself of two coffees. "I remembered your promise not to go off with a john," she explained. No problem, the evening had been remarkably uneventful, I lied, and quickly ended our conversation.

I put Max on his leash and wearily headed back out the door, Baggie in hand, for what I hoped would be a quick dump. How I wish my dog were toilet-trained.

While Max romped about, I fretted. Who in hell had I contrived to be — a Halloween hooker, a one-night no-trick wonder with no need to put her mouth around a stranger's cock for the price of a good meal?

Then it struck me, harder than the shove from my putative john: I had been so busy protecting from contamination the "shrine" that is my body (into which I suck death-defying quantities of nicotine and alcohol), that I had risked my life. Didn't take a shrink to tell me that this wanton disregard for my own safety took root following Pete's death.

Who draws this gossamer-thin moral line between "good girls'" sex and commercial sex?

I thought back to the friend whose mother confided to her that for thirty years my friend's father had insisted on "consummating" their marriage nightly, whatever her mother's inclination. "Since menopause," her mother had sobbed desperately, "it hurts me even more ..."

Now, Jane, force yourself — think back. Eight years old, lying bewildered on my narrow bed. The night you overheard your own mother's small voice, so tentative compared to today's commanding bark. "Please, Seamus, not tonight. I'm not in the mood." Later, his inebriate snoring muffled Etta's whimpers.

Whores at least get to choose their tricks.

And then that other memory: crisp sunlight, flooding through my studio windows on two sex-glistening, kneeling bodies. Pete's eyes locking mine, our fingers interlinked. Wondrous, a flash of glory on the sheets.

Getting paid for getting laid. Making love. In the middle, the sexual favours exacted by husband from non-consenting wife or snatched by power from innocence, priest from choir boy, sports coach from young player, father from daughter, uncle from nephew...

I fell into bed, lonely, vulnerable, exhausted — clinging to an enchanted memory.

Chapter 27

SUNDAY AFTERNOON, I parked Harley behind All Souls Anglican Church at the south-east corner of Dundas and Sherbourne. Daylight cast a deceptively benign veneer over the streets, but did little to assuage my fear.

Poverty rubs unwelcome shoulders with prosperity in this urban combat zone. Young professionals' gracious Martha Stewart restorations hold up shabby rooming houses, where folks fortunate enough to escape the streets huddle in the temporary refuge of dingy, overpriced rooms.

Mornings, middle-class mothers en route to daycare scurry their offspring past dealers smoking up with working girls. Nights, I know about.

Self-mandated to gentrify the streetscape, alarmed home owners organized themselves into a powerful residents' association to do battle with the riff-raff. Most of their indignation centres on the local prostitutes, whom they perceive as magnets for all the other garbage. They posted on their Web site licence plate numbers and descriptions of cars driven by johns. In response to their barrage of complaints, the police department assigned a special unit to patrol the intersection. All Souls installed six surveillance cameras. The recent murders of five working girls in the vicinity fuelled their determination to drive the whores into someone else's neighbourhood. "We are not a vigilante group," said their spokesman, a real estate agent.

Hearing her flock described as the "scum of the earth" at a heated residents' meeting, the priest at All Souls retaliated by opening up her huge old edifice to several non-profit groups — volunteer angels hell-bent on aligning themselves with the "vermin," as a posh bed-and-breakfast proprietor dubbed them.

It was the shit-disturbing Reverend Sharon Thompson I'd come to see. Getting Repeat to a doctor for treatment of the growth on his forehead was something I couldn't achieve on my own. He once mentioned that he sometimes comes here for hot meals — and shelter on those rare occasions when he's feeling secure enough to accept it.

The architecture of this lovely structure is Victorian Gothic Revival. Its red brick walls rise in a steep triangular wedge to a high bell tower above the west gable. Entering the main door through a small porch on the west side, I found myself inside the nave. The vivid illumination of stained glass fell upon age-darkened timbers and oak pews incongruously lined with sleeping bodies. A woman in jeans and a bulky blue sweater knelt on the crimson carpet of the central aisle, leaning towards a young man's recumbent form. Smiling warmly, she rose to her feet.

"I'm Sharon Thompson." She extended her hand. "How may I help you?"

She was expecting me to ask for some form of charitable assistance, I could tell. Last night I had scrambled to assure the hookers who'd mistaken me for one of their sorority that I was really a writer. Today my inner Queen Victoria rushed to correct the priest's misconception.

"I'm Jane Yeats, Reverend Thompson," I replied, alert now to my name as a signifier of my worth. Repeat has never told me his real name — first or last. Only what the streets christened him for his linguistic tics.

Was I gradually being tutored in the humility of dispossession, of utter unremarkability?

"Please, just call me Sharon. The 'Reverend' bit gets in the way." She opened her arms to her church and its unlikely congregation. "I paid attention to my ratings. Coffee, a good hot meal and someplace warm to sleep are a much bigger draw than my sermons," she laughed. "John Donne I ain't."

"Must your flock sing for their supper?" Piety brings out my churlish side. Blame it on the nuns.

"Hell, no! You must have been looking for God in all the wrong places, Jane. The modern ministry — at least the way some of us practise it — simply attends to people's needs, no strings attached. I'm just carrying on the tradition of All Souls as a people's church." She relaxed. "Why don't we grab a coffee and talk about whatever brought you here?"

Seated side-by-side in a rear pew, I summarized my chance introduction to Repeat and our subsequent meetings. When I mentioned my now habitual provision of coffee and sandwiches, Sharon interrupted to ask why I bothered to seek out his company, let alone feed him.

I told her about Repeat's crystal chandelier drops, how he had flashed them to ward off the black cloud of depression that trailed me into the park one bleak morning.

She nodded in recognition of his gentle deed. "So you must be Repeat's 'angel.' He showed up here a few weeks ago, very frightened and disoriented. Repeat so hates any kind of shelter, any space that even vaguely hints of an institution. I knew something serious had happened to drive him here. After a meal and a night's sleep, he calmed down enough to assure me that soon he'd be fine back in his streetcar shelter — now that he had his guardian angel watching over him. Wouldn't tell me what had scared him, though."

Given that Max and my writing are the only responsibilities I've assumed in adult life, Sharon's revelation increased my anxiety. "That's what drove me here — Repeat's trust in me. I'm not sure I'm up to it, though. I'm just beginning to learn how to communicate with him without setting him off. That growth on his forehead might be malignant. The poor man needs medical attention."

"Sure he does, but his reluctance to seek it out is well-grounded. Last month, some incensed citizen complained about him sleeping in the streetcar shelter. Apparently he was in a bad state ... paranoid, gesticulating, shouting obscenities at passersby. The police responded by taking him to the hospital, where he was forcibly administered his meds, then released back onto the streets, terrified as ever. No wonder Repeat believes doctors are messing with his brain."

"So what can I do?"

Her hand gently grasped my arm. "Just keep on being his friend. But make sure he understands your boundaries. Something he said before he left here made me think that he knows where his angel lives. Neither of you would be well served by his camping out close to your house, Jane."

This news startled me, but then I recalled Repeat's parting message to me after our lunch. *Be very careful, Jane ... your house is surrounded by evil.*

"Maybe he followed you home from the park one day. Think of his paranoia as a sudden tornado that sucks everything essential about him into its vortex when it touches down. He's left diminished in its horrible wake, but with his intelligence and wariness remarkably intact. Maybe he witnessed something untoward close to your house. Or it could be that his voices sounded a horrible alarm when he was nearby. I have no doubt that *something* occurred, real or imagined, but scary enough to make him alert you."

I gripped the back of a pew with clammy hands. "Two weeks ago a woman named Tina Paglia was murdered in the house adjoining mine. Her body was dumped in my front yard. Do you think Repeat might know something? That would be enough to terrify him. It sure as hell scared the wits out of me."

Sharon's eyes widened. "What day was she killed?"

"Two weeks ago today — probably early Sunday morning. Her body must have been dumped some time after three, when I arrived home, and six, when my neighbour spotted it."

Her voice grew urgent. "That's the very Sunday he showed up here for the first time in months. He was in such a terrible state I considered phoning for an ambulance. But as I said earlier, he did manage to calm himself down enough to eat supper and get some sleep. Came back to sleep for three or four more nights."

"That accounts for his absence from the park."

Sharon paused for a moment's reflection. "But I could be over-reacting. About five hundred people use church outreach services every day. One provides health care to juvenile prostitutes. I like to think that a few of them find comfort just being in a church. News of Tina's death would have spread rapidly along their grapevine. So Repeat could easily have picked up on it right here."

"Perhaps," I replied, unconvinced.

I needed time to think this through. Maybe I had dismissed Repeat's warning too readily, as just another weird artifact of his fevered brain. But it was beginning to take on the unwelcome contours of a chillingly significant fact.

As I opened the oak door onto the street, I felt an old familiar feeling — entering church a reluctant seeker, only to depart more confounded.

Repeat's transmitter was still safe in its pod. Mine crackled an ominous warning.

Your house is surrounded by evil.

"Tell me what you smoke." Repeat withdrew a bag stuffed with cigarette butts from his jacket pocket. "They have to be longer than an inch-and-a-half counting the filter or I don't pick them up. Not worth the trouble."

A few hours after returning home from All Souls, I'd come to the park to have one last go at persuading Repeat to get his tumour looked at.

"Rothmans — but how do you know I smoke?" I never indulge outdoors. Etta once warned me that respectable folks would take me for a vagrant.

Chuckling, he replied, "Easy. Every time I light one up your right hand gets nervous." He carefully selected a handful of Rothmans butts from his stash, rubbed each one between his thumb and index finger until the tobacco fell onto a clean cigarette paper, which he deftly rolled.

Passing me his handiwork, he repeated the operation. "I'm not fussy about the brand. Mix them all up for myself."

After mulling over my suggestion that we visit a clinic together, he shook his head. "Nope. The first time I got sick the police called an ambulance. I thought that the aliens who were communicating with me sent them to transport me into the future. When I got to the hospital, it was worse. The nurses and doctors were plotting to kill me. They choose certain special people and remove their brains. Then the researchers slice them up, put them under a microscope and figure out how to make everyone's brain into a transmitter so the aliens can take over the world by yelling at people and making them do wicked things."

"I see. What happened when they let you out of the hospital?" I kept my tone of voice flat and was careful not to make eye contact.

He plucked frantically at his beard. "I tried to stay on my medication. It sometimes worked for a while, but the demons always came back. I went back to university but I couldn't concentrate, I couldn't read, I couldn't understand the lectures. I thought the professors were all talking about me, so I stopped going to classes. I daydreamed and slept all day. One day I realized the drugs were poisoning me. So I quit taking them. Then the craziness came back. That was the end of my education."

Repeat had talked himself into a black hole. Thinking some exercise might haul him out, I asked him if he'd walk around the park with me and Max. I set off slowly while he pushed his bags into the huge cardboard box he made his shelter. Today he was in a mood to leave them there. The brown bag he carried with him, though.

Only after a long interlude of companionable walking did I speak again. "Now I understand why you don't want your transmitter removed. I won't bother you about it again. I promise. But if you ever change your mind …"

"I'm fine," he shouted. His head swung away. "I don't want anything from anyone."

We finished our stroll in a silence muddied by his mistrust. He scanned the ground for cigarette butts as we circled the valley, frequently picking up the longer ones and occasionally adding a pine cone or acorn to his collection.

Noticing his fingers were shaking in the cold air, I removed my grey wool mittens. "Please keep these. I've got more at home."

He examined one closely, repeatedly pulling away the

Velcro flap at the end to reveal four glove fingers. "Wow," he marvelled with childlike delight, tugging them on. "My fingers thank you."

I had almost given up asking him why he had warned me about the danger surrounding my house. But I had to know if he had really seen or heard anything first-hand around the time of Tina's death.

I waited until he was walking just behind me. "Repeat, sometimes I see you writing in a notebook. I am a writer, too."

"What kind of stories do you write?"

"Mostly I write true stories about people who commit crimes. And I wrote two books about the police." Banking on the fact that my words hadn't visibly agitated him, I added, "Right now I'm working on a book about some prostitutes who were killed or went missing here in Toronto."

"I keep a journal. I write down my thoughts. Sometimes I make up word games."

I inched a step closer. "Do you ever write about what happens to you? You know, people you meet, or things you see?"

"Nothing happens," he replied, shuffling back down the valley to his home.

I called after him, "Repeat, maybe you should find somewhere warm to sleep tonight. The radio says it's going to get very cold."

Silence.

Shortly after I returned home, my answering machine recorded an unforeseen call. "Hello. This is Rosemary Miller calling at 6 o'clock. I read in yesterday's *Globe and Mail* that you're writing a book about all the missing prostitutes. I have something of a reputation as an expert on the sex trade. I'd be very happy to meet with you and share my knowledge. Your research really can't be complete until we've talked. My phone number is 416-558-8998. God bless you."

Writing occasionally stretches one's patience more than the mind. My agent must have been cementing my commitment to the new book by issuing a press release. Now every nutbar in the city could just call my number and while away a few lunatic minutes badgering me.

Look on the bright side, woman. Maybe someone with some useful information might think to call. Miller, though, hadn't claimed to know anything about the missing prostitutes. She seemed to be volunteering to mentor me, presumably in the hope of influencing my take on the subject.

Soon I'd follow up on Miller's invitation. If nothing else, she promised some much-needed comic relief.

Chapter 23

A HUGE TREE LIMB crashed onto the roof of a parked car across the street. From my bedroom window I watched a vicious north wind scoop up an empty garbage pail and deposit it with a clatter several metres away. The faded tricolour Italian flag hung at the front of Dominic's Pizzeria during the last World Soccer Cup was whipping itself to shreds against a downspout. A few sheets of newsprint rattled against my wrought iron railing, and the road and sidewalk were spackled with hoarfrost.

Winter's first major wake-up call is always shocking. One year a sudden avalanche of snow prompted the mayor to call in the army to clear the streets, much to the amusement of the rest of the country. This being a pacific kingdom, we were afforded the rare diversion of seeing soldiers in the flesh; ordinarily we glimpse them only on the late-night news, peace-keeping, boozing or raping in far-flung lands.

Usually we get zapped by winter when we are at our most vulnerable, just days after family gatherings, New Year's Eve celebrations and the flu have knocked out our immune systems. This year it has struck early.

My toilet belches when I prompt it to flush. Downstairs, I crank up the thermostat to recapture some of the heat the house leaked overnight, then turn on the kitchen tap to fill the kettle. Nothing happens. The pipes are frozen.

As I open my front door to collect the morning paper, freezing air lacerates my T-shirt. One sharp intake of breath draws a road map of my respiratory tract. I tug at the paper. The headline remains stuck to the sidewalk. Across the street the amputated tree creaks ominously. If it topples it will crash the entire length of my house and come to rest with its crown well into the back yard. No more renovation expenses.

As I scurry inside, CBC Radio announces that overnight a fierce Arctic front plunged the temperature to −42°C with the wind-chill factored in. Frostbite will occur in two-and-a-half minutes.

I picture Max, his penis flash-frozen by a graceful arc of piss to a fire hydrant, pedestrians glacialized in mid-stride, bringing traffic to a reluctant halt.

The City of Toronto has issued another extreme-cold-weather alert. Not much use to those living in cardboard dens under bridges or huddling within donated sleeping bags over heating vents.

I hope Repeat sought some accommodation more protected than his appliance box or the streetcar shelter. But his body thermometer is seriously out of whack. On hot days, he's often cocooned in enough layers of clothing to see him through a polar expedition. Cold weather can find him wearing only a ragged T-shirt or unbuttoned flannel shirt.

It's impossible to read the paper without a mug of coffee. I bundle up, grab my thermos and head for the Second Cup. The city's paved floor has contracted, leaving widened cracks in a surface glazed with a pewter wash. I slip crossing the street, recover my balance with a curse.

Cold undermines civility and community — the world shrinks into the narcissistic clasp of survival. Neighbours, their heads tucked into collars, pass one another without recognition or acknowledgement. Even on the College Street strip, looking cool gives way to staying warm. Markers of age, race and gender disappear under hoods, bulky jackets, mittens and boots. Eyes stream in the narrow gap between wool toque and scarf. Workers headed for the office or factory troop glazed as ants towards the streetcar stop. The shouts of school kids layered thicker than the Pillsbury Dough Boy are muffled under moist wool. Through their steamed windows, drivers smug in their metal cocoons appear out-of-focus.

I can't stop wondering about Repeat.

Returning home, I made a fast decision. "Boyfriend, gird your loins. We're taking an early walk."

Max squirmed and growled as I forced on the Black Watch tartan coat I bought him for days like this. He knows it's mightily undignified and unmanly.

I let him run free down near-deserted streets towards the park, pausing to catch my breath at the streetcar shelter. I found no sign of Repeat. If he hadn't gone to a shelter, he must have spent the night inside his appliance box. Gasping shards of frosty air into my lungs, I regretted not wearing a scarf.

We moved on to grass brittle with frost. My excited manner alerted WonderDog to danger. Instead of racing forward, he trotted smartly beside me, making inquisitive little canine whines high up in his throat. I bent over to pat his flank. Pointing down to the valley, I commanded, "FIND REPEAT, MAX! FIND REPEAT!"

Speeding south, he was soon lost to a wilderness landscape not yet touched by the rising sun. Running towards his excited barking, I caught sight of him circling Repeat's cardboard box, sniffing at one end, then backing off.

Bitter swathes of icy air raced lunatic as a stoned snowboarder up and down the sides of the valley. Not a sound issued from within the box. Max's frenzied yelping was loud enough to wake up the dead ...

"REPEAT," I screamed into the silence. The sides of the valley picked up my voice, echoing "REPEAT REPEAT REPEAT" like a cruel joke. "It's me, Jane. Max and I brought you coffee."

Banging and kicking the side of his carton, I kept screaming his name. My arms felt strangely frozen, paralyzed by fear of what I might discover when I opened the flaps.

Chill out, woman. He's probably snoring away on a pew at All Souls.

As a child, I learned that fear of what you anticipate is almost always worse than fear of what finally happens. *Almost always.* With Max at my side, I pushed aside one flap, then the other.

The thin beam of my flashlight revealed only a mound of stuffed plastic bags. Relief dissolved into panic as I spotted the brown bag. Repeat would never abandon his treasure bag. Flashlight in my left hand, I reached in with my right.

Lifting the bag, I stared in horror at the blue hand stretching towards me in a frozen claw. Crouching down, I cleared away enough bags to expose Repeat's head and shoulders. My strength surely augmented by terror, I tugged his big body from the carton.

He slid out stiff and unresisting on to hard ground. Turning him over, I brushed the hair away from his face. The gloves I had given him were clutched to his chest. I removed my own glove to close his eyes. Zipped up his jacket. I said good-bye. It was so cold.

Max was whining, reluctant to leave our friend. As I snapped the lead to Max's collar, I picked up the brown treasure bag, fully aware that I might be removing evidence the police could use to identify his body. Repeat would hate that it be treated as garbage. This was no murder case, *ergo* no crime scene. Unless death-by-hypothermia has finally been deemed governmental manslaughter.

From the phone box at the corner I dialled 911 and reported a body in the park. Gave its precise location. Refused to give the dispatcher my name. Slammed down the phone and hurried north before a police car could arrive on the scene.

Stumbling homewards, tears freezing to my cheeks, I stopped at the life-size, chipped alabaster statue of the Blessed Virgin outside St. Francis Church. She sits atop a high stone platform flanked by potted shrubs and a vase of plastic flowers and a few votive candles in glass jars. With her right arm she shelters her child; her left is raised in greeting.

Usually when I pass I salute the BVM with a cheeky wave. This morning I paused to contemplate her gentle face.

Mother of God, pray for Repeat.

Then, to Dympna, for charity:

You are celebrated St. Dympna, for your goodness to those who are mentally disturbed or emotionally troubled. Kindly secure for Repeat some measure of your own serene love … Amen.

Chapter 29

SIPPING A MUG OF HOT MILK fortified with a double shot of brandy, I watched Max dozing in front of the radiator. I worked myself through some deep breathing, a few shoulder and neck rolls. The initial shock of my discovery diminished, leaving me to cope with the tumult of emotions surrounding my relationship with Repeat, my grief that he had died so young, so alone.

Tina Paglia's funeral Mass had sounded a grace note for the passing of a troubled life. Repeat should not suffer the final indignity of a pauper's burial. With a guilty start, I remembered that my possession of his treasure bag would stall decent funeral arrangements. Perhaps he had family. Certainly he had an identity beyond his street name.

I collected the brown bag from the front hall and sat down on the living room carpet. First I removed his cherished photograph, then gently emptied the rest of the contents. Among his treasures were those precious chandelier drops, a bag of multi-coloured sequins, another stuffed with pine cones and acorns, a worn rabbit's foot on a chain, a woman's watch with a cracked crystal, two pencil stubs and a Bic pen, a near-empty box of Smarties ... and his dog-eared notebook. But no name — no driver's licence, social insurance or health cards. The absence of bank and credit cards was a given.

Quickly scanning his notebook, every page but the last

two dense with doodles, word games and inscriptions, my eyes picked out nothing that might reinstate his birth name. Then I got thinking — had Repeat been a stranger, I never would have refused to identify myself to the 911 dispatcher. I'd have stayed near him to describe the circumstances that led up to my discovery of the body. By contacting the police, I had fulfilled only a part of my obligation. At the time, I hadn't been thinking clearly — I just had to flee the scene. But now I had to work things through. Repeat's flight from the neighbourhood two weeks ago might have been triggered by something he'd seen near my house — maybe something related to Tina's murder, so keeping my relationship with him a secret from the police had seemed a good idea. I couldn't handle the hassle of trying to explain why he might have chosen me for an intimate.

But this didn't help establish who he was. How do I — eureka, Sharon Thompson. I'd phone the church with the sad news. Maybe Sharon knew of some agency Repeat had turned to for help, or where he had been hospitalized. Some record containing his name and something of his background must be filed somewhere.

When I told Sharon, she wept softly. "For some silly reason, I'm glad it was you who found Repeat, Jane," she finally said.

No consolation there. "I sure fucked up as guardian angel, didn't I?"

"It wasn't in your power to save him. I look around my church and wonder why all the angels have fled," she said, disconsolate.

I don't speak angel talk. "What will happen now? I was kind of wondering ... well, if you will help me claim the body, we can arrange a nice funeral service." Since Pete's death, I've secured access to my heart like it's a crime scene, but Repeat's tragedy was releasing long-interred emotions. Forcing me to feel human again.

She readily assented. "I'll be very happy to help. I wouldn't be surprised, though, if he hasn't already been identified. The police in your area picked him up several times and had him hospitalized under the Mental Health Act. So some of the officers are bound to recognize him — and they'd have a record of which hospital they took him to. Normally when a homeless person is found dead, the police send the body to the coroner if the person has no known next-of-kin. If the coroner determines that the death was from natural causes, the police contact the government undertaker to arrange a pauper's burial, paid for out of public revenue."

She added quietly, "I'm pretty sure that Repeat has no surviving family."

"You sound horribly familiar with the process."

"Most of the people who use our services are poorly nourished and need medical attention — mental and physical. So they die — often young and in preventable circumstances — like Repeat. But the government doesn't give a serious damn and people don't care enough. Drugs, assaults, murders, car accidents, hemorrhage, hypothermia — we've lost friends to all of them."

I really needed to get my brain on a more proactive track. "But he will have the best damn funeral we can give him — right?" My belated gesture felt superfluous, and I knew I sounded like a child. My education didn't include understanding mental illness or how to communicate with people's skewed brain chemistry.

Sharon ignored my needy tone. "I'll phone 14th Division, tell the police we're concerned about one of our clients, and describe Repeat. Then I'll accept responsibility for the body. I'll phone you back as soon as we've made arrangements."

"We?"

"Repeat was a likable guy when he wasn't possessed by his demons. He made a lot of friends around here. I'll get everyone involved. Meanwhile, you think about readings and music for the service."

That evening found me pounding on the door of Silver's studio. Repeat's sudden death had me a heartbeat away from plummeting back down to the abyss that was Pete. The night Pete died Silver cradled me in her arms until dawn, singing to me in a language I never knew she knew. But that was an exception to her general practice of not allowing people to swallow up too much air time wallowing in their own miseries, when she has her own preoccupations; besides, she disapproves of wallowing on principle. Other folks find this trait unnurturing, especially in a woman. I needed her capacity to distract me from my woes.

In Silver's studio, form marries function tight as a Shaker chair. Objects are arrayed in the large warehouse space according to the dictates of work. She paints in front of the huge east-facing windows. The surrounding walls prop up her canvases. Other needs are relegated to the margins — except for sex, with its curious habit of leapfrogging boundaries. Good fences do not make good lovers, she avows.

Inside the door I received her full-on-the-mouth signature kiss and bear hug. She scorns white folk's air kisses and glancing body-greetings.

Scrutinizing my face like she would the night sky, she asked in a voice well short of her usual bark, "So who died?"

When I told her about finding Repeat's body, she went

straight to the fridge and pulled out a Blue for me, a Coke for herself.

"Ain't a thing you can do about your friend being dead, love. All you got now is what those academic types call 'the plight of the urban homeless.'"

Silver never wastes a hot minute getting to her point.

Lenore Tootoosis had told me she'd first met Silver handing out blankets and hot soup from the back of the Anishnawbe Street Patrol van. "I guess I could sign up as a volunteer for some program like Out of the Cold."

"Good idea. It would keep you out of the pub one night a week."

That part of our conversation was clearly over. As I swigged on my Blue, something riveted my eye: a large artwork on an easel. At first I hesitated to ask about it. Silver normally shields her works-in-progress fierce as a lonely child conceals her imaginary friend.

The focal point of the piece is a painting of a young Native woman, black-and-white, starkly executed in the style of a missing-person poster. Her left breast has been slashed away to reveal a DayGlo sacred heart. The portrait is messily pasted over a rough plywood surface littered with seemingly 'found' objects — a broken feather, a stem of sweetgrass, a scrap of Hudson's Bay blanket, a faded document that looks like a school report card, a crack vial, a couple of condoms, a torn, out-of-focus photograph, a crushed beer can: rage mediated by craft.

"It's part of my new show. The whole lot of them I'm calling 'Raven Series.'"

"That's incredible ... I don't know, but it fucking blows me away."

"Seems you haven't turned art critic," she mumbled. "Before your friend died, you were snooping into your neighbour's murder. Found out anything?"

"Not a damn thing. But all I've really done is ask a bunch of people connected with the sex trade if they know anything about her. They don't."

"Talking heads. Not too creative an approach."

"I got sidetracked by other stuff — like investigating the prostitutes who've disappeared."

"Whatever," she summarized. "So why don't you get off your ass and do something?"

I stared at her startling collage again, fumbling for a nice way to phrase the obvious question. My friend loathes 'nice.'

"Silver, on the rez, at residential school — were you abused?"

She rose to her feet. "I have to get back to work."

At the door, I pulled her close. "Thanks for being here for me. It matters."

Her face relaxed into a huge grin. "Yeah ... well ... us Indians gotta repay you white folks any way we can."

I punched her. "That bit of sass lets me ask a favour — or gives you another opportunity to express your gratitude to the master race. Will you go to Repeat's funeral with me?"

"Pick me up on your way."

Chapter 30

REPEAT'S FUNERAL WAS SCHEDULED for Thursday morning. By Tuesday afternoon, my mind was screaming for diversion. I first prescribed some renovation work, but my brain kept buzzing along as I exhausted the rest of me in a flurry of paint stripping. While I cleaned up, Rosemary Miller's phone message beckoned a welcome distraction — that's how bad a day it was.

And that's how it came to pass, six hours later, that I found myself walking into Juice for Jesus, a "soul" restaurant just east of Honest Ed's Bargain Warehouse. Had I not been preoccupied with Repeat's death, I'd have thought to come in drag. If I was spotted in a place like this, my bad-girl reputation would be toast.

The ceiling sported a beguiling detail from the Sistine Chapel, Adam's finger reaching to God's, ET-style, his naughty bits concealed by a powder blue Huggie. The walls were cloud-patterned, with the vertiginous effect of creation aslant. Paintings by lesser talents than Michelangelo depicted revisionist Biblical scenes on a health-food theme — Jesus merrily dispensing whole-wheat loaves and fishes, saints breaking gluten-free bread with colleagues, a marriage feast sans wine — no miracle there — and a Last Supper straight out of *Diet for a Small Planet*.

Cursing the hairshirts who'd created this demi-Eden, I

mentally slapped myself upside the head for failing to quaff a Beer for Beelzebub prior to leaving home.

A woman rose from a table beside the Last Supper. I grumbled my way towards her outstretched hand. "You must be Jane Yeats." Beguiling as a shark, she flashed me a tall-toothed Colgate smile.

"And you must be Ms. Miller," I replied, seductive as a dog turd.

Her dry hand wilted in mine. *"Mrs.* Miller," she corrected me.

My would-be mentor appeared to be in her mid-thirties, although her hair and clothes shrieked accidentally retro. Locks from Madame Tussaud's waxy tribute to Dame Margaret Thatcher, a suit that made matronly look good, and shoes that could give 'sensible' a bad name.

A waiter disguised as a guru materialized with the drinks list. Rosemary ordered a Divine Mango Smoothee. "I'm feeling naughty today," she giggled. Look out. I opted for the Quaker Shake, a mixed fruity concoction that, with four fingers of rum, might pass for a real drink.

"A wise choice," Rosemary assured me, the perfect sommelier.

She spoke with a Betty Boop voice the Creator normally reserves for our fine-feathered friends, hyper-pitched at a level that could shake leaves loose before their sap expired. Can you get to heaven and be kept out of the choir?

She slid effortlessly into her born-to-be-chairing-the-meeting shtick. "When I read the notice announcing your book, my heart thrilled. I pride myself on keeping up with all the latest research on prostitutes."

What could I say? Some people collect empty beer bottles.

"God gives each of us a mission in life. Our shared interest in 'ladies of the night' makes us soul mates, Jane — sisters in scholarship."

My failure to affirm our sororal bond did not discourage her. "Allow me, dear, to explain my interest in these women." She smoothee-ed her throat with evident relish. I stared at my glass, which looked like it held the consequence of puréed prunes.

"I trust you are familiar with the Bible. No one could presume to write about prostitutes without studying the Scriptures."

She began to quote in uppercase, her voice vibrant with conviction, her eyes taking on that visionary gleam normally due to booze or drugs. "HOW IS THE FAITHFUL CITY BECOME AN HARLOT! IT WAS FULL OF JUDGMENT; RIGHTEOUSNESS LODGED IN IT; BUT NOW MURDERERS." *Sotto voce*, she appended, "Isaiah, chapter 1, verse 21."

I glanced around at the other diners to see if anyone else was finding her harangue an embarrassment. I found myself alone. Briefly I considered striking a bargain with God. *Beam me up ... or lower me a beer and just one cigarette. In return, I promise never to ...*

"You will agree that Toronto has fallen to whoredom."

Presuming my consent, she sped on. "I refuse to just sit back and watch the city of my birth slip into iniquity. The moment I heard about Mr. Chretien's plan to eradicate child poverty, I received a vision of what Toronto could become if prostitution — the root of so many evils, including child poverty — were eradicated."

Not without trepidation, I interrupted. "Forgive my ignorance, Rosemary, but *what* is the connection between prostitution and child poverty?"

"Many men who turn to prostitutes are husbands and fathers. The money they pay for sex should be going to better their children. And many prostitutes have children of their own, most of whom wind up with Children's Aid, supported by taxpayers' dollars."

Briefly I mulled over suggesting that maybe she had her chickens and eggs in the wrong sequence, that poverty forced many women into the sex trade. Before I could weigh the relative drawback of provoking her wrath against the benefit of amusing myself with the spectacle of her reasoning running holes faster than a pair of cheap tights, she resumed.

"The very act of having sex with someone to whom you are not married, and with no intention of creating a child, is *fornication*. The only lawful sexual connection is the marriage bed." She pronounced 'for–ni–ca–tion' like it was a nasty gum disease, rather than something you might do for the sheer fun of it.

She patted the side of her helmet. "Of course I'm inviting ridicule from feminists and other subversives who consider themselves 'progressive' — unfortunately, a few of them sit on our board of directors. But that problem will soon be solved. My directions come from a Higher Power." Her accompanying smile snatched the enigma prize from Mona Lisa.

"Were you always ... uh, religious, Rosemary?"

"Catholic by birth and by confirmation," she affirmed. "But when Rome gets too liberal, I turn to the fundamentalists."

Presumably Rome would have been more appealing during the Inquisition.

The waiter flourished menus. "Are you ladies hungry tonight?"

Funny he should notice. I'm starving for a rare sirloin, garlic mashed potatoes smothered in gravy and a keg of bitter.

A swift glance down the menu confirmed my fear — there was no escape from green and grainy.

"No, thank you. I've already eaten," I muttered. Breakfast.

My companion ordered the Garden of Eden salad plate. May a serpent be coiled beneath the lettuce.

Soon she was tugging a mango string from some teeth near the back of her busy mouth. As she paused to spear some greens, I took advantage of her evident belief that a lady shalt not talk when her mouth is full.

My inner investigative journalist surfaced. Noting the absence of a wedding ring, I volleyed, "Are you married? Do you have children?"

The spinach garlanding her teeth imparted a whimsical air to her humourless demeanour. "One husband. No children." No surprise there.

"What does your husband do?" *Apart from plot how to slip antifreeze into your smoothees.* People who trash sex make me crabby. Hey, I am Etta's daughter.

"Andrew is a high school English teacher — but he still makes time to help with my work. He's absolutely committed to getting young prostitutes off the street. He's so supportive I can't imagine what I'd do without him."

Wash your own socks, maybe.

Rosemary, speaker in paragraphs rather than tongues, munched contemplatively on a carrot, as she stared uncertainly at my Harley T-shirt.

"Are you a Christian?"

"What a peculiar question! I've just been elected president of the Toronto chapter of Bikers in Christ. I thought you might have known."

She looked only mildly impressed. "Lovely, dear. Now

tell me why you've chosen to write a book about the prostitutes who've disappeared. Why not put your talents to better use — like writing about missing children?"

The stench of sanctity made me do it. "I'll be absolutely open with you, Rosemary. My income derives solely from royalties. The more books I sell, the more money I earn. There's a much bigger market for a book about prostitutes than one about missing kids, most of whom get kidnapped by non-custodial parents. Besides, it's looking more and more like some of the missing women are victims of a serial killer — now that's a sensational subject. The book will fly off the shelves." I smiled apologetically. "Call me greedy, but I've just mortgaged my soul to the bank."

She notched up her precisely pruned eyebrows. "That many people really *care* about a few dead whores?"

I shook my head. "Of course not, but most people do love a good mystery. Take Jack the Ripper, poster boy for the modern serial sex murderer. Shelves of books speculate on his identity — not that many people can name one of his victims."

Rosemary shrugged. "Why would anyone want to?"

Time to shake her tree and watch what peaches fall to ground. "Isn't that perhaps a rather callous attitude for a social worker? Don't your views get in the way of your work with PROS?"

"I've always been a highly effective social worker, if I do say so myself. And my 'attitude,' as you call it, only facilitates my work as executive director."

Why did I think anything but an over-ripe ego would shake loose? "Oh, I don't doubt that for a minute. I meant no offence, Rosemary. But has your work brought you into contact with any of the missing or murdered prostitutes?"

"No. I'm no longer a front-line worker. I raise funds and public awareness."

She signalled our guru for the bill. "Let this evening be my treat. In exchange, may I have your business card? I'd like to send you some literature."

In a move I regretted before I'd completed it, I pulled my wallet out of the back pocket of my jeans. From my collection of business cards, I extracted the only legitimate one, a soiled, frayed-at-the-edges thing I carry because I still can't always remember my new phone number.

She received it with her left hand, and fluttered her right in a Queen-like farewell. "I'll be in touch, Jane — and do feel free to contact me if I can help you any further."

All my many egregious sins against man and nature, in this life and all those past ones, do not warrant tonight's grievous penance.

I mustered something close to a smile. "Rosemary, there's a fig leaf between your front teeth."

Chapter 31

THE POWERFUL DEAD GET TRANSPORTED to glory in a flurry of pomp and circumstance. Royalty, Popes, heads of state, corporate barons, movie celebs, hockey players — each receives ceremony commensurate with his status. Ralph Eric Bradshaw was borne into All Souls Church on a cold sunny Thursday morning by six of his street buddies, in ill-fitting shirts, ties, suits and leather shoes. During the service for the Burial of the Dead, his simple pine coffin rested at the foot of the altar. Atop it stood his treasured photograph: Repeat and his mother, smiling out from a new pewter frame.

The Reverend Sharon Thompson spoke a warm and lively sermon to the mourners, many of whom lined the side aisles. The pews were packed with homeless people, hookers, social services and shelter workers, members of the congregation. So Max wouldn't distract anyone, Silver and I remained close to the rear doors. Freshly shampooed and brushed, WonderDog behaved with absolute decorum throughout (apart from when he sang along with the choir). Chelsea sat beside me.

The priest's words of recollection made Repeat a somebody again. A young woman, who accompanied her own soft voice on a guitar, sang "The Streets of London" in place of a final hymn.

Did Repeat rage against the dying of the light? I doubt it. He died as he had lived for years, impoverished, alone, visited by demons so often his life must have felt like one long relapse. At my request, the stonemason chiselled five words below his name, birth and death dates: *A certain slant of light.*

Emily Dickinson's phrase. Word-sorcerer to word-inebriate. My gratitude for crystal chandelier drops.

After thanking Sharon for the beautiful service, Silver and I left the church. Chelsea stood waiting outside. Silver diplomatically excused herself — not without a nudge-wink. Chelsea and I headed off to a nearby café. I told her I had uncovered no useful leads, either in Tina's murder or the disappearances. I asked if she would post a request for assistance on "Searching for Jessye." Perhaps I could snag some new information — or tempt the murderer into making a traceable boast, threat or declaration. She agreed and suggested that I also post my message to the discussion group.

Together we drafted the request:

I am writing a true-crime book about the missing women. If you have any information on the circumstances surrounding any of their disappearances or on their present whereabouts, please call my voice message pager (416) 558-7394 with your facts. If you want to talk directly with me, leave a number where you can be reached. Confidentiality is assured.

We spent the next hour shopping for a cell phone and pager, two bits of gear Chelsea said belonged in any snoop's tool kit. A woman foolhardy enough to embark on such an investigation should at least have a lifeline, as a dangerous situation was bound to happen, probably sooner rather than later. The new phone boasted a bevy of features: clearglo blue backlit display, vibration alert and multiple ringer styles, 300 phone book entries. The pager was simpler, but more ominous — it could track me down anywhere, anytime.

Farewell to my reclusive ways.

Never, never, never would I give Etta my new numbers.

Back home, I plunged into Repeat's journal.

Word-inebriate, indeed:

> The street's full of garbage, people-garbage dumping night people, I was alone in the desert of garbage for a long time. The gospel is garbage dumped on the desert. The world couldn't receive it because it was already blocked with garbage. New sights were planted in my mind by evil powers. I'm here and not here — they think I can't see them because they don't see me. They're here and I'm not here — in the same garbage dump. Bars were everywhere. They dump garbage into the van. They dump garbage on to the lilies. Then they all leave in the van all at the same time for all who litter must leave in all the vans into the time that is no time, they escape time, escaping time is dumping hours like littering. I know the cure for littering, that is my great discovery, it's not making garbage, no time for all time which is now that time which is now forever ... The next time they dump garbage-people I'll throw them into a pail.

Bless you, Repeat, but ... hey ... this passage seemed the only one even remotely relevant to Tina's murder. It first appeared that a few recurrent word associations sent his mind careening off into a torrent of non-sense. But there was a curious subterranean logic at work beneath the random flow. Although his delusions would render him a totally unreliable witness in court, it did seem likely that he had seen Tina's body dumped in my garden the night of her murder.

They dump garbage into the van. Had "they" been loading something prior to dumping her body?

From the start, I'd found it baffling that Tina's killer would dump her body in a site that would ensure its discovery shortly after sunrise. Leaving it at the crime scene would have delayed its discovery only until her boyfriend dropped by.

Dumping it in my front garden just briefly diverted attention from the crime scene — and it seemed unlikely that her killer would do something so risky as a warning to other hookers or users.

Probably the killer's original intention was to dump her body far away to deflect police attention from her apartment. Had the body remained concealed, the search for Tina would be dropped. Hookers often move out or go missing, sometimes permanently. Advanced decomposition would destroy or contaminate much of the trace evidence, should her corpse ever be found. Dumping her in the lake would appear to link her to the three hookers found floating close to shore.

On Repeat's — no, Ralph Bradshaw's — 'evidence,' it seemed likely that an attempt had been made to move her body to a waiting van — after something else had been removed from her apartment or somewhere else in the building. Something unexpected must have occurred between the front door of her building and the back of the van, they panicked, and flung Tina over my short railing. A neighbour peering from a bedroom window? Most of my neighbours would never admit to witnessing anything untoward. See no evil, hear no evil, speak no evil. *Omertà*.

The person they probably spotted was Repeat, watching them. Crouched in the laneway alongside Nina's house, he would have seen everything through five rows of fencing: Bars were everywhere. What were their options — give chase to Repeat with a naked body in tow, or toss her into the back of the van and give him both a head start and time to raise the alarm, or ... had they identified him as a homeless person, and evidently mentally ill, they might have figured that he probably couldn't intelligibly communicate what he had witnessed — even if he wanted to.

Whatever had been moved out of the building that night (in addition to Tina) must have been incriminating. Unless the perps were very stupid, which I wasn't inclined to discount, they'd have realized that removing evidence — a blood-soaked carpet or sofa cushions — would be fruitless, given the trace evidence that would persist.

So, whatever they took out must have directly pointed to her killer or to another crime, possibly related to her murder. Mario Pepino owned that building, as well as the one housing his sandwich shop. Mario, my arch-enemy, Ratmeister with a temper that makes Mike Tyson an amateur. Twice he has threatened to kill me, most recently as payback for my letter to the Health Board shortly after I discovered he tossed stripped beef and veal carcasses into a shed behind Tina's house, which leaned against my backyard fence. There they decayed until garbage day, hosting a symphony of blue-bottles and a cacophony of rats, and creating a stench that made sitting in my yard a dead-ringer for no-man's land at Ypres. On the other hand, it doubtless accounted for much of Max's delight in being alive.

My letter did eventuate in a visit from the health inspector, who suggested only that I bury some broken glass and sprinkle some warfarin, like he took me for a demented voodoo queen. Later I heard him laughing with the don over a bottle of wine. After the inspector's departure, I opened the door on Mario's furious pounding. "You make trouble for me, I make meatballs outta you." I slammed the door in his foolish face. Small man, big roar. Very early the following morning, Silver retaliated on my behalf by painting a tantalizing image on his shop window, a large Italian bun sandwiching tomato sauce, sliced mushrooms, melted mozzarella and a rat.

Mario's first death threat had been more spectacular.

The fence running along the property line at the back sagged into my side of the yard, its timbers so rotten I pulled them away with one hand. I replaced the fence, cementing new posts into the holes left by the old ones. Storming out into the yard, rake in hand, Mario expressed his gratitude for my free labour and materials: "Put one fucking toe on my property again and I nail you like Jesus to the cross." Finding little to choose between crucifixion and the meat grinder, I did nothing to escalate the situation.

The man definitely was afflicted with a powerful need to dominate his own territory. *Did Mario have something other than rats to hide?* Repeat's journal seemed to confirm my suspicion that he had witnessed Tina's body being removed from the house. Now it remained to discover what else might have been removed — and why.

There was only one sure-fire way to find out. Weeknights Mario closed up the shop at midnight and drove off in his battered station wagon north-west of the city. I knew where he lived because once I ventured to suggest that he might take more interest in maintaining his buildings if he lived in the neighbourhood. "Now I know for sure you are a crazy bitch. Me — I live in a big castle in Woodbridge. This neighbourhood is for nobodies like you, missus."

Most women dress up for special occasions. I'm generally an exception to that rule, but it's not every night I do a break-and-enter. I opted for your basic black — elegant Harley-Davidson T-shirt under turtleneck sweater, jeans, socks, boots, even the underwear. And I was perfectly accessorized — black gloves, and hair tucked into a black baseball cap.

"I used to be Snow White," said Mae West, " ... before I drifted."

Chapter 32

GETTING INTO THE EMPTY HOUSE next door shouldn't be a problem. An addition on the back left a six-foot high wall facing the narrow walkway from my kitchen door. Putting my aluminum ladder in place, I climbed onto the roof of the extension. This placed me level with the kitchen window of the first-floor apartment. Security bars shielded the first-floor windows, front and back. These I could have crow-barred aside, but I couldn't afford to waste any time. Although only a few neighbouring windows overlook the site and it was one in the morning, I didn't want to attract attention. One of the priests from St. Francis might be glancing out the rectory's bathroom window while enjoying a leak. And I was hoping to get in and out without leaving any eye-catching traces of a break-in.

Hauling the ladder up to the roof, I raised it to the kitchen window of the second floor apartment. The rusted aluminum windows yielded quickly to my screwdriver and I eased my body sideways into the kitchen sink.

I detected no movement or sound, but I hadn't expected to. Walking from room to room beaming my flashlight briefly around the walls and floors, I discovered not a single sign of Tina's occupancy. Gone were the sorry bits of furniture I'd seen her moving in just two months ago. The forensics team must have collected every pathetic trace of her life except the dark stain of her death soaked into the worn living-room floor.

The ground-floor apartment yielded nothing more interesting than liberal sprinklings of rat poo and roach tents. I descended the uncarpeted basement stairs, their treads worn to concavity by a century of traffic. I had noted that the door leading to the basement, now open, had been fitted with locks. Maybe only the landlord was permitted access.

I scanned the wall at the foot of the basement for a light switch. The two windows, which opened on to deep window wells, were covered with rectangles of cardboard secured by duct tape. I hit the light switch. Flickering fluorescent tubes dimly illuminated an ancient oil tank and huge octopus furnace. Halfway along the concrete block wall between the house and the sandwich shop, a door frame had been cut. Thick with flaking grey enamel paint, the door readily yielded to my crowbar.

The basement of Mario's sandwich shop was frigid as the morgue. Same vintage heating equipment, same blocked windows with security bars, same rust-stained cast iron sinks. I flicked on the light. Columns of stacked cartons nudged the ceiling beams. A huge freezer occupied one corner, dozens of olive oil buckets filled another, tins of Greek olives rising in staggered tiers behind them. Salamis and pepperonis hung in greasy purple fingers from hooks on the beams, next to thick tubes of mozzarella cheese and braided buds of garlic. Enough cans of tomato sauce to float the Empress of Ireland. Giant jars of marinated mushrooms, artichokes, sun-dried tomatoes, red peppers, anchovies. Huge string bags bulging with onions. Bags and bags and bags of white flour ...

So far I'd cleverly detected the makings of a La Scala-size pizza.

I made my way around the room, diligently searching for anything that might not be what it appeared. All the cartons were empty (except for roaches), as was the unplugged freezer. When I tugged a flour bag towards me, two rats scurried out of the jagged passageway they'd nibbled into its side. This inspired me to similarly damage each bag so I could sample the contents. Pure, unadulterated flour. I shook each tin of olive oil in turn. Nothing dubious.

All that remained were a few dozen thirteen-kilo mustard-yellow tins. NATURAL GREEK OLIVES. VERY NUTRITIVE AND HEALTHY FOOD FOR EVERY AGE. THE IDEAL COMPLEMENT FOR YOUR TABLE. DIGESTIBLE, APPETIZING, AROMATIC. The tops were sealed with circular metal lids, like paint cans. I pried one off with my screw driver.

Staring back were what appeared to be kilo-bricks of the ideal complement for your nose. I carefully poked a small hole near the top of one plastic-wrapped bag and placed a moistened finger inside. Barely had I noted its bitter taste when the tip of my tongue went numb.

My little grey cells clicked in. A few years ago, I'd written an article on the role of biker gangs in drug distribution. Pure cocaine gets shipped in bricks from Colombia and other producer-countries to wholesale cocaine traffickers. The stuff is then repackaged in retail quantities or converted to crack and sent out to crack houses, bars and street corners.

I stood up and steadied myself against the wall — Mario was pushing more than sweet veal. This could account for the store's hitherto inexplicable busyness. His sandwiches couldn't be that big a draw. It could also account for Tina's murder, if had she twigged onto his operation. This could be what Repeat had seen being moved into the van the night of her murder — after all, leaving drugs next door to a murder scene would have been dumb. Perhaps the perps had relocated them until the heat was off.

I had no idea how much was hidden down here, let alone its street value. But keeping it a secret had already cost one life.

I decided to steal a brick to have the contents and relative purity confirmed. Quickly replacing the lid, I rearranged the stack of olive tins, with the violated one at the bottom. When Mario discovered the missing brick, he'd assume his supplier had shorted him or that one of his dealers was trying to go big time. The man had no reason to suspect me of anything beyond aspiring to a rat-free abode.

Swiftly retracing my steps to the open window, I carefully made sure everything looked as undisturbed as possible. I returned the ladder to my basement.

I headed upstairs and fell into a profound sleep.

Chapter 33

JUDGING BY THE BRICK I was staring at, that one olive tin must have contained at least 12 kilos. I had stepped into something extremely dangerous. Nobody gets his hands on this much blow freelance. Mario must have connections. If my brick proved to be cocaine, then the Mob had a stash house sixteen feet north of my front door.

I would turn over what I knew (and my chunk of proof) to the cops — well, to Ernie Sivcoski. Before joining homicide, he spearheaded a three-month operation targeting street dealers selling crack from North York striptease clubs. I couldn't risk bestowing my hoard on a cop who might be dishonest.

But before contacting Ernie, I intended to put my purloined brick to work. Maybe I could use it to extract information about Tina's death from Quasimodo, if I could locate the little weasel. He was reputed to be a street dealer — lower in the pecking order than Mario, his likely supplier. I'd concoct a story to persuade him to exchange what he knows for enough of Mario's blow to retire in a style to which he was decidedly not entitled.

First, I had to get a sample analyzed and determine the bricks value. *Where to go?* Independent drug-testing labs must have to contact the police if someone shows up with a prohibited substance. I've heard of a quick field test for assessing the purity of coke and heroin, but I'm not intimate with anyone who buys or sells drugs in bulk.

I racked my brains. Drugs. Addiction. Treatment centres. Eureka — The Addiction Research Foundation. My dad the drunk. Etta grew so tired of his antics she had him admitted for a month not long before his fried liver finally solved all her marital problems. Like a fool, I visited him every day, hoping my support would keep him sober. One afternoon I bumped into a guy named Martin Sweet, who had married a friend from university days. Over coffee he jokingly asked why I'd chosen to hang out at ARF, when I could be drinking beer in the Waverly Hotel across the street. He worked in an on-site lab, testing blood and urine samples from addicts entering rehab programs. I hadn't kept in touch with my friend, but maybe her husband would do me a favour for old time's sake.

A phone call to ARF quickly confirmed Martin's ongoing employment, currently as director of his unit. To my surprise, he answered the phone himself.

"Hi, Jane, it's been a long time. I hope your father's not in trouble again."

"Well, he did relapse after his release, but he's been sober for five years. Hasn't touched a drop since he croaked."

He laughed nervously. "I take it you're no longer in mourning ... um, what can I do for you?"

My answer called for a liberal dash of fiction. "My sister, Caitlin, is nearly hysterical with worry, Martin. Yesterday she found a small bag of white powder tucked inside her daughter's pillow. Before she hauls Cindy off for treatment, she wants to find out what it is — but she's not willing to involve the police. My niece is in medical school and my sister knows that any hint of addiction will end her career. Cindy has been losing weight and sleeping poorly recently. My sister figures she must be on something."

"So you want me to test this powder and give you the

results? Jane, that's a very ... unorthodox request."

"I'll understand perfectly if you say 'no.'"

"I can easily get a GCMS run for you — we run tens of thousands of tests through my lab a year — as long as you don't have any other motive that would ... raise ethical issues."

What a prick. "Heavens no, Martin. If Cindy is in trouble with drugs, I just want to get professional help."

"Okay, then why not drop it off later this morning? My office is on the third floor of the north wing. I'll do the analysis myself. Perhaps we could have lunch."

Very least I could do. "Great idea. You can bring me up to speed on what's been going on in your lives."

"Life," he corrected. "Julie and I got divorced three years ago."

"Oh ... I'm sorry to hear that. I've been out of touch with a lot of old friends in the last few years."

That evening, Martin phoned with the test results. The gas chromatography, a separation technique, had positively identified my substance as cocaine. Pure cocaine. Street dealers, he told me, increase their profits by cutting their cocaine with similar-looking substances — cornstarch, talcum powder, sugar. Illicit cocaine has become purer over the years, but it is rare for the purity to average more than 75%. In all likelihood, he said gravely, my niece was dealing the drug.

"Thank you so much for doing this, Martin." I paused. "Um ... do you have any idea what the stuff is worth?"

"In Toronto, the wholesale price of a kilo is $40,000. Cut for street use at the gram level, you're looking at $160,000. Well, I'm sorry the news was bad. Good luck, Jane. I hope your family gets your niece turned around fast. She'd be safer in the hands of the police than with the kind of people who supply her."

"I promise to do everything in my power to get to the bottom of this." That was no lie.

When I plunked the brick from which I'd scraped Martin's sample onto my kitchen scale, the needle came to rest at a hair under a kilo. I quickly stuffed it back inside my plaster Elvis bust. The King's street value had soared — not a bad return on the five dollars I'd laid down for him at a garage sale.

The phone interrupted my unethical musings on how best to exploit my stash. It was Sam Brewer, my old drinking buddy. His news assured me that his planned 'retirement' from crime reporting hadn't severed his contacts within the police force.

The cops had just made a big arrest, scheduled for media release at a press conference tomorrow morning. Murder charges had been laid against Richard Harris, 22, currently resident with his mother in Scarborough, in the deaths of the three prostitutes found dead over the Victoria Day weekend. Apparently young DickHead went on a spree after his girlfriend dumped him.

He had another go last weekend. Mistaking a young woman on her way to a rave for a whore, he snatched her off a dark street into his van and took her to a condemned building. There he grabbed her from behind, held a knife to her neck, choked her until she pretended to pass out, and hit her repeatedly with a two-by-four. He fled at the sound of a distant police siren. Immediately following her release from hospital, she was taken to the cop shop, where she honed in on his mug shot faster than a fruit fly to an over-ripe banana.

We nattered a bit and agreed to meet for lunch the next week.

Fifteen hooker murders minus three solved equals twelve — including Tina's. Be ever grateful for small mercies: one more freak off the mean streets.

Thirty-one disappearances minus zero solved equals thirty-one — including Jessye's.

Good guys: 3. Bad guys: 43.

Chapter 34

THE FOLLOWING MORNING I was not thrilled to discover an electronic missive from Rosemary Miller. "Glad tidings" pealed the subject line. Nor did the body of the message much stir me:

Your warm encouragement during our lovely dinner together encourages me to solicit your help. I have just written a pamphlet proving that recovery from prostitution addiction can not be maintained without faith. Before sending it off to the printer, I'd like you to edit the pamphlet (I find reading Scripture more rewarding than proofreading). I will, of course, credit your efforts, which may bring you some freelance work from the Christian community.

Yours in Jesus,
Rosemary

Shit. She really had gone off the deep end. I fired off a rapid reply explaining that my book deadline necessitated my turning down any extra work, however worthy the cause.

So, back to work. Chelsea had suggested that Sandy Reeder might hear my plea for bad date sheets. I grabbed for the phone.

Two hours later I stood with Sandy in the PROS admin office. When I explained that my investigation had dead-ended and that Jessye's journal entry now stood as my only lead, she made a swift decision.

"My hooking days have given me an infallible bullshit detector. So here it is — Operation Central for the best goddamn bad date sheet on the track. It's the most effective outreach tool we've developed." She pulled up an impressive database on her monitor.

"I started this thing up shortly after I got the job here. Our outreach people talked up the idea on the street and pros immediately got it. Before long the reports were coming in, mostly over the phone. Street pros desperately need this kind of information. They'd always warned each other by word-of-mouth, but a BDS could broadcast the bad word to a helluva lot more women."

"Can you give me a ball-park figure on how many reports you've received?"

"More than 450 entries since we launched the list five years ago. That's only the tip of the iceberg, of course."

"How much attention do the cops pay to these sheets?"

"I never call the police without the consent of the pro — no matter how brutal the assault. And I never try to convince a pro that she has to give the sexual assault squad a report. If she chooses to, I go to the station with her for support and as a witness, to ensure that she gets treated seriously. Some of the sheets inevitably fall into the cops' hands. They claim to read every BDS that crosses their desks and to make serious efforts to arrest abusive johns. The truth is, most cops don't give a shit. So a lot of pros don't bother to report assaults. That's what makes our up-to-date bad date sheets vital. I don't give the cops access to our entire list even when they're looking for a suspect. They won't warn pros about a deadly john because they need the suspect to reoffend in order to lay charges."

Before I could pose my next question, a gentle knock

sounded on the office door. "Sorry to interrupt, Sandy, but I got your message."

"Hi, Andrew," she greeted the tall man leaning against the door frame. Prematurely grey hair, deep-set grey eyes, grey sweater — but a Technicolor aura. My hormones screeched. We were introduced. So this was Rosemary's husband.

"You're not the Jane Yeats who wrote 'Blue Boys?'"

I nodded, amazed that he had the title of my crabby book on the Toronto Police Services on the tip of his tongue. *Banish immediately all thoughts of the tip of his tongue.*

"A terrific book. I've read it twice."

"Thank you." I came damn close to curtsying. "It didn't win me a lot of friends on the force." My royalty statements tell me the odds of my bumping into a fan anywhere other than a signing are less than being struck by lightning while I empty a pint — way less, if God turns out to be vindictive as Rosemary believes.

He turned his polite attention back to Sandy. "I'm just passing by to pick up a disk for Rosemary — some new pamphlet she's working on. And to let you know that I'm fine for driving the van tonight."

"Our regular driver is down with the flu," Sandy explained to me. "I can always count on Andrew to fill in at the last minute."

"No problem," said Shy Guy. "I'll be back by 8:30 to stock up the van. Who's volunteering tonight?"

"I've scheduled Ron, Meagan and Rhonda. Meagan promised to pick up extra lube and Trojan golds."

He blushed. "Saturdays nights, they fly off the shelves."

My hormones took another leap when he reached to shake my hand. "It was a real pleasure meeting you, Jane. I hope we see one another again."

He turned at the door. "I just had an idea. Rosemary tells me you're researching a book on the missing prostitutes. Maybe one night you'd like to ride the outreach van, if that's OK with Sandy."

Be still, my naughty bits. You don't do married men.

Sandy nodded her assent.

"Thanks, Andrew. I'd like that."

I waited until his comely back exited the front door and my knees got back to supporting me. "That can't be Rosemary Miller's husband."

"The same," Sandy giggled.

"Shit. What was he on when he hooked up with her?"

"Hey, we'll find the key to eternal life before we crack the mystery of sexual chemistry. But Andrew Miller is no fool. He's a fabulous teacher — great rapport with his students. And with young hookers, which makes him pure gold for us. Funny, he always rationalizes Rosemary's excesses by reminding us that she 'means well.' But he is absolutely devoted to the cause of rescuing troubled kids."

In vain did I rack my brain for any mission that would justify a life shared with that humour-challenged harpy, then I snapped my focus back to my own mission. "What do you ask for when a woman reports a bad date to you?"

"Any details that will help other pros identify the assailant before he gets a chance to hit on them — time, place, appearance, vehicle, licence plate number. And, of course, what went down — and if she's OK. When I put together a new monthly sheet, I conclude it with a reminder that our hotline service is available 24/7. It helps relieve the helplessness."

"How sophisticated is this database?"

She chuckled. "Not very. You'd be better off taking all the sheets home with you. Searching this dinosaur will drive you bonkers. The fields need some serious tweaking to make searches faster and easier. I've applied for a grant to design a quick reference booklet. I want it to be organized first by vehicle (car, van, truck, taxi), then by colour of vehicle — with tabs so you can open it right up to a vehicle description."

"You must keep records of who gives you the info for the sheets."

"Of course — if she offers her name and number. That information is kept secure, though. If I publicized it, a pro's address could be verified by anyone with access to a reverse directory. That would totally fuck up our whole purpose."

"Have the police searched it?"

"They never asked to."

Sandy handed me two crammed legal-size envelopes. "The reports are in chronological order, starting with the most recent. And I use a rotating colour scheme to make each new sheet recognizable." She patted my back. "Fortify yourself with a stiff drink before you go through that stuff — it's not light reading."

I couldn't leave without telling her about my dinner with Rosemary and the e-mail request I'd unwittingly provoked.

Sandy looked more melancholy than perturbed. "Remember I told you I was sitting on the fence on forcing her resignation? You've just confirmed the board's suspicions. The poor woman is becoming a total nutcase. I'll throw my weight behind getting her removed. Maybe we can persuade her to get some help. But I doubt it."

Chapter 35

IT WAS WELL AFTER DARK Saturday when Max yelped at an unexpected knock on the door. My hound more than earns the small fortune in Science Diet and liver treats he wolfs down. But for his threatening presence, I wouldn't have opened the door. Something about having a stash of cocaine makes a woman jittery.

Hammer Hopkins stood shivering outside, wearing his latest crime. His barber had given him a mullet. Shoulders hunched, hands in the pockets of his ski jacket, shuffling his meager weight from foot to foot, he was edgy as hell.

"Hi, Hammer. Would you like to come in?"

Glancing at Max snarling behind me, he muttered, "I just come to tell you something, but I'd sooner meet you somewheres else. I don't like dogs and this place is too close to where Tina got killed, eh?"

"Of course. Why don't we meet at the Can in ten minutes?"

He nodded. "See you there."

After giving my alpha male a liver-treat fix for his surly guardianship, I pulled a brush through my hair and threw on my jacket.

Entering the restaurant, I got bashed with "Do Wah Diddy Diddy" from the Hyperbeam Laser Disc. Good, no chance our conversation would be overhead. A few neighbours were bound to spot me meeting with Hammer and telegraph the grapevine that I hadn't the decency to wait until the poor girl was cold in her grave before hitting on her boyfriend. Worse things have been said.

Hammer, hunkering under a cloud of smoke at the table nearest the jukebox, stubbed out an Export 'A' and poured the last of a Blue straight down his unshaved throat. As I sat down, he signalled a waitress exiting the kitchen with two plates of pasta in one hand, a gargantuan pizza in the other.

"Gimme another," he said, pointing at his empty bottle.

"Glass of Nut Brown, please," I appended.

Hammer was staring at the ashtray, disinclined to talk. Maybe he was having second thoughts, so I cut to the chase. "Last time we spoke you had a court appearance coming up, Hammer. How did it go?"

He shrugged, eyeing me warily. "OK, I guess. Me and Salvatore — that's my buddy, right? — we got our case postponed on account of the asshole lawyer screwing up the paperwork. So I'm on bail for a while yet." He blew some smoke down the neck of his empty bottle, doubtless in deference to the environment.

As the waitress set our drinks on the table, Dean Martin came to overly-amplified voice on the jukebox. "When the moon hits your eye lika bigga pizza pie, that's *amore*." A young woman with a hot pink buzz cut wandered over to inquire politely if she could "borrow" one of our chairs.

"No," snarled Hammer accommodatingly. "You escaped from the fuckin' zoo or what?" She scurried off.

"How do you expect things to go when you finally get to court?" I asked Mr. Manners.

He lit another cigarette. "Not good. The kinda record I got, I'm looking at a long stretch. But getting busted got the cops off my back. I mean, it wasn't like I could have been in jail and killing Tina at the same time, right? But, next job I ain't takin' Salvatore with me. Fuckin' moron."

"Hammer, you had something to tell me?" I prompted.

"Yeah. That night you and me had some beers after the memorial for Tina ... ever since I been thinking. You said that you'd do everything to help find the bastard that killed her. Well? You done anything? The cops sure ain't."

"I've been busy. But I've hit the same wall as the cops. They have conducted some interviews and checked out a lot of people on the stroll. But Tina's world was pretty small, so they don't have much to go on. You know that she lost touch with her family years ago and didn't hang out with the other girls. She was a bit of a loner, eh, Hammer?"

"Just in the last few years, since she became a junkie. Before that she was real normal."

"I'm not a huge fan of the police, but they have been showing more concern about all the deaths and disappearances in the sex trade. Maybe it's public pressure, maybe it's political, who knows. But in the past few weeks, they've got the guy who killed the three prostitutes. They've posted a $100,000 reward in another case, and they've got a task force reexamining all the evidence to see if it points to one or more serial killers."

"Yeah, yeah ... next thing you know, they'll be calling in the Cold Squad." Hammer isn't the only one who gets pissed off because reality fails to live up to TV. Guess that tells you something about who gets to script reality.

"But whatever resources they pour in, I don't think their investigation is going to turn up Tina's killer. From what I hear, there's not a shred of evidence linking her death to those of the other prostitutes. In fact, I believe that she was killed for reasons that had nothing to do with her sex work."

He looked up suspiciously. "Reasons like what?"

"Reasons like we talked about last time. I've got a strong suspicion that maybe Tina's murder had something to do with drugs ... um, I guess you don't know who Quasimodo's supplier is?" I tried to make my question sound off-hand.

Hammer pulled a few napkins out of the chrome holder and began shredding them. "Nope. She didn't give a shit about where her blow came from so long as it kept snowing. And that's not a question a broad's gonna ask if she cares about her butt, eh?"

Now wasn't the time to inform Hammer that I valued mine, notwithstanding the evidence to the contrary.

He shot a lascivious glance at the imposing breasts of a passing waitress. "But he's still in the neighbourhood. Some guy told me that a buddy of his bought some dope offa the peckerhead last weekend."

My eyebrows shot up. "The cops haven't picked him up for questioning?"

He glowered at me like I was stupider than Salvatore. "How the hell would I know? It's not like they tell me what's going on, is it? Maybe they haven't been able to find him. Maybe they ain't looking. Even if they are, none of his junkies are gonna squeal on him, right? Anyways, Quasimodo's got a rep for taking care of anybody who pisses him off. He was born twisted. Got expelled from St. Lucy's in grade one for breaking a kid's nose. Used to torture and kill cats. When he got bored, he started on kids — burning them with cigarettes, stuff like that. Raped a girl when he was twelve."

He gathered the shredded napkins into a small mound, balled them up and tossed the wad into a white plastic urn holding a terminally neglected spider plant. Hoop dreams.

The waitress replenished our beer, splashing mine as she plunked it down, and ignored the overflowing ashtray, true to the Can's emergency-only service protocol.

"Hammer, I'm kind of surprised that you haven't tried to find Quasimodo. I thought you were hell-bent on killing him."

He slammed down his beer bottle. "I still wanna see the peckerhead dead, but I changed my mind about taking him out myself. That was the beer talkin'. Like I'm already headed back for a stretch in the joint, unless some judge takes pity on me 'cause I got an asshole for a lawyer, right? So I been listening to my mother. She figures if I ain't smart enough to rob a house without getting caught, then for sure I ain't got the brains to kill Quasimodo and get away with it."

He seemed comfortable with his mother's assessment of his aptitude for a career in crime.

"Makes sense to me, Hammer," I agreed. "So you decided to tell me where Quasimodo's been hanging out lately. You're hoping that I'll follow up?"

"I got no problems telling you where he is — if you're gonna do something about it, eh?"

"Hammer, when I told you that I thought there was a connection between Tina's murder and drugs, I wasn't just farting in the wind. I'm on to something. Your girlfriend was a junkie. Quasimodo was her dealer. Before she died, she told you she had something big on Quasimodo ... I think I've discovered what that something was. You tell me where I can find Quasimodo and I'm on to it."

"I'll tell ya and I'll tell ya why I'm tellin' ya. I seen your mother on the news the other night — she's the old broad who got busted for smacking a cop, right? If you got her attitude, I figure you can take care of Quasimodo."

"My mother. Etta Yeats. She owns Sweet Dreams, the

country joint in the east end."

Other women get to claim, "My mom's on the symphony board." But then, their mothers get to claim, "My Charlotte's a corporate lawyer with Blarney, Blather, Bluffer and Bullshit."

Hammer stuck a fresh Export 'A' between his thin lips. Blew the smoke at the faux-marble tabletop, raising a duststorm of cigarette ash. "This buddy of mine that knows one of Quasimodo's customers? He told me where the prick is stayin' — above the shoe repair store on Manning ... you know, just north of College."

I hoisted my glass to give me time to rehearse the only scenario that came to mind: I drop by Quasimodo's, hopefully catching him off-guard and alone ... no, he wouldn't open the door ... I set up a meeting with him, pretend I know more than I do, bribe him for more information with my purloined cocaine ... any way it goes, for sure I need more backup than Max. Scratch that: I would never knowingly endanger my dog.

"Hammer, I know what Tina had on Quasimodo — and I've got my hands on something that will pry it out of the bastard. But I'm not stupid enough to try on my own. I need a man to back me up." I stoked his sense of chivalry. "So, are you up to coming along with me? We'll both feel a whole lot better knowing that we helped get him caught. Tina deserves it."

Actually, I knew only that a big stash of virgin cocaine was resident in Mario's basement and that Tina, who found out about it, had connected the blow to Quasimodo. Precisely how those two facts added up to her murder, I did not know. But leaning on Quasimodo would help me connect the dots.

For the first time, his defeated eyes lit up. "Yeah, sure — so long as it don't get me in no more trouble."

"To be honest? No guarantee."

But when I told him what I had in mind, he signed up on the spot. Vengeance is a potent motivator. Still, I hoped it wasn't just the beer talkin'. Given Quasimodo's temperamental quirks, maybe when Hammer sobered up he would regret his commitment.

I drained my beer, settled the bill and headed out the door, leaving my cohort shredding paper napkins and muttering darkly to the ashtray.

When I arrived home, I had too much on my mind to pay undue attention to the e-mail (plus attachment) that littered my in-box:

Jane, dear:

Please check out my new Web site. I know you'll appreciate the roses. As you must know, the word 'Rosary' means 'Crown of Roses.' Our Lady has revealed to several people that each time they say a Hail Mary they are giving her a beautiful rose and that each complete Rosary makes her a crown of roses. As the rose is the queen of flowers, so the Rosary is the rose of all devotions and is therefore the most important one. The Holy Rosary is considered a perfect prayer because within it lies the awesome story of our salvation.

I've taken the liberty of attaching the unedited text of my new pamphlet. Won't you please reconsider? Just enter your changes and e-mail it back to me.

Yours in Jesus,

Rosemary

This had to stop. I had no desire to impale myself on her thorns. I fled through cyberspace to Rosemary's virtual incarnation. Her site opened against a background of long-stemmed red roses forefronted by a detailed guide of How to

Pray the Rosary. I skimmed through her informational beads — not one of which mentioned the murdered and missing prostitutes.

With growing impatience, I opened her attachment, snappily entitled "The REAL Mary Magdalene: Just Who Was This Mysterious Woman?" Intending to read only the first and last paragraphs (as I do instructions for how to program your VCR and letters from Revenue Canada), I quickly found myself drawn into her article.

Some strong compulsion to broadcast the glad tidings that Jesus' favourite female companion was never a prostitute must have propelled Rosemary's exacting research. The poor lady (Mary), cited by all four Gospels as being present at both the Crucifixion of Jesus and the Empty Tomb on the morning of the Resurrection, was — at worst — only demon-possessed.

Now, I had always believed that Mary Magdalene was history's most famous sex worker, but I wasn't about to research the topic.

The moral of this revisionist take had to be Miller's own: no way ever would Jesus have consorted with a prostitute; indeed, he'd made it his mission to redeem harlots from sin.

I had to get this woman off my back and out of my computer forever. I posted the following back, muttering a fervent prayer that observing human antics over the course of two millennia had made even God a bit irreverent:

Your article did not change my mind about Mary Magdalene having been a prostitute.

Life is full of mysteries, not the least of which seems to be the true identity and profession of Mary Magdalene — surely as intriguing a puzzle as any Agatha Christie conceived.

A feminist or otherwise progressive scholar might be

tempted to suggest that The Two Marys, Jesus' mother and Magdalene, originally may have been one, in accord with the pagan bipolar disorder which causes men to regard women as virgin/whore. Now, no man likes to think of his mother as a tart. Decency demanded their separation.

The Creator is the author of the universe. I, too, am a writer. Having given Jesus two nice parents, it remained only for God to add a powerful love interest. And what could lend greater authenticity to his narrative than making her a whore? Jesus' attraction to such a woman would prove that he was a real man, whereas falling for a nice Jewish girl would seem too formulaic and ... unmuscular.

As to the thornier issue of the precise nature of the relationship between Jesus and Mary Magdalene ... well, let's not go there ...

I'm sure you will agree that I am not the right editor for this text.

— Jane Yeats

Chapter 36

RENTS AND PROPERTY VALUES are on the rise in Little Italy. Yet the blue-collar streets off the College Street strip, with its seventy restaurants and bars, haven't yet suffered the blight of gentrification.

Manning Shoe Repair operates from an eight-foot-wide storefront at the south end of a neglected turn-of-the-century building. Slabs of concrete with weed tufts sprouting between their fissures pave over the front yard. A disabled air conditioner tilts precariously above the door. But the proprietor has an exalted notion of the value of his enterprise. Mildewed plywood conceals the glass on the entrance door, secured by two deadbolts and a padlock. Four steel bars run in both directions over the store window, the grime effectively blocking off the interior. Three pieces of cardboard taped to the base of the window bear sloppily inscribed, sun-faded messages: *Come in we're open. Open at two most days. Out for lunch.*

Rumour has it that rich Italians, long since migrated to posh suburbs, return with their wounded shoes and handbags to this highly-skilled artisan, who freelances as the neighbourhood bookie.

The flat above the store was accessible only by a fire escape at the rear. Hammer had set up a meeting with Quasimodo through the buddy who knew one of his customers. Only Quasimodo was expecting his customer — not me and Hammer. As we walked through the narrow, unlit laneway to the back, a bitter wind in our faces, I psyched myself up. Be brave, remember to breathe, close your eyes and think power. You are woman, you are invincible. Tonight my mantra worked no better than it does when I'm confronted by the dentist's drill.

Only an old pickup truck leaning into a deflated front tire occupied the asphalt parking lot. All the windows were dark. The rusted fire escape loomed like a stairway to death. I glanced nervously at Hammer, who looked too scared to take care even of himself. I asked him if he was carrying. He had good news and bad news.

"I don't believe in weapons. Anyways, I'm short-sighted."

What had I been thinking of? Given the right back-lighting, he looked more threatening than anyone else I knew, except for Etta — but truth was, I don't know another human stupid enough to do escort duty on this mission.

I glanced at my Swatch: it was now or never. Quasimodo's instructions to his customer had been clear: *Show up exactly at nine. Knock four times.* I pulled up my hood, took a deep breath, and pounded on the windowless door. When no one answered, I put my ear to the wood. Not a sound, but something signalled his presence. Then I heard what might have been a dog whining.

Finally Quasimodo opened the door just a crack. "What the fuck?" he shouted when he saw us.

I shoved my boot in the door to dissuade him from slamming it. "No cops, Quasimodo. It's just me, Jane Yeats. Tina Paglia lived next door to me. And you know her boyfriend, Hammer, right?"

He glared over my shoulder at Hammer. "Yeah, I know the asshole. What are you two doing here? I was expecting somebody else."

I spoke quickly, trying to ignore his trademark facial scar. "I know, but I've got a much, much bigger deal to offer. Trust me, you do want to hear me out."

"Benito. Come." A massive rottweiler that probably snacked on newborns while pumping iron flew to his side, flashing enough teeth to shake a shark's self-assurance. Poor Hammer, if Max made him nervous, Benito must have him leaking into his jockeys.

Having satisfied himself that we were weapon-free, Quasimodo opened the door just wide enough to let us in. "Move slowly and don't make any sudden moves. You don't want to upset Benito." He was right about that. A master of the understatement.

Quasimodo hardly looked like he'd been holed up for weeks. Hair sleeked back into a ponytail at the nape of his neck. White shirt open at the neck, Armani jacket, Versace jeans, black leather loafers. Cartier watch, heavy chain, bracelet, two rings.

He turned on an overhead light, illuminating sparse furnishings from the Goodwill, the '50s kitsch that's dear to people too young to have suffered it first time around.

"I'm just staying here temporarily," he remarked. "You two sit on that sofa, where I can keep an eye on you."

As Hammer and I lowered ourselves onto an orange Naugahyde horror manufactured before Hank Ballard introduced The Twist, Quasimodo seated himself across from us on a soiled mustard armchair. Benito circled the sofa like a sentry at a labour camp — except for the uniform. Benito was sporting a Gucci dog collar and sterling silver dog tag. Max wouldn't give such a poof the time of day.

Hammer placed a trembling hand on either knee to suppress the jittery dance of his lower appendages. Before my bodyguard pitched an anxiety attack, I had to persuade Quasimodo to get the damn cur out of sight.

I feigned a chain of convincing sneezes. "Could you please send Benito to another room? I'm very allergic."

To my surprise, he immediately obliged, closing a bedroom door behind Fluffy.

"So why are you here?"

My stomach gave a nervous flutter as I launched into my sales pitch. "I want to make a trade — something you know for a kilo-brick. I badly need that information and you can buy your way into the good life."

He leaned forward, eyes aglitter with interest. "Go on. I'm interested. Ever since that broad got iced, I've been trapped in this dump." Hammer stirred ominously at the rough reference to his lady. I'd warned him to keep his mouth shut while I did my shtick. He was to turn menacing only if Quasimodo got physical.

"A friend brings me food and stuff, but I can't maintain my business without being on the street. Even my girlfriend doesn't know where I am."

"You could get the cops off your back by giving them an alibi for the night Tina was killed. If you had nothing to do with the murder, there can't be any evidence linking you to it. No evidence, no arrest and you could resume business."

He barked out a rude laugh, then abruptly narrowed his eyes. "So tell me two things — and don't fuck me around with any bullshit. First, show me the blow. Unless you've got some very big-time connections — which I doubt — there's no way you could get your hands on that much cocaine. Second, what the hell do I know that's so valuable?"

"Show you the blow?" I snorted derisively. "Am I a total jerk or what? You frisked me thoroughly enough to satisfy yourself that I've got nothing on me except clothes. If I brought the cocaine with me, what's to stop you from stealing it? I'm not about to part with it without the information I came for. So tell me what I need to hear and I send Hammer to fetch your reward. I'll stay here with you and Benito until he returns. Then I'll give you twenty-four hours to get out of town before I act on what you've told me. On the other hand, you do me or Hammer any harm once I've handed over the blow, faster than you can spell 'life sentence' this place will turn blue with cops. If I'm not safely home by 10:30, my best friend is on the phone to Homicide and the narcs."

"Why should I believe you even have the stuff?"

"I'll tell you how I got my hands on it, then you'll believe me. I broke into Mario Pepino's basement and removed it from a tin that should have been packed with Greek olives."

He leapt straight out of the chair. "You *stole* it from Pepino? You fucking *stole* a kilo? Then you got a whole lot more to worry about than me, lady." He paced, muttering *sotto voce*, "Mother of God. Shit. I don't believe it. I do not believe this."

"Sure you do. So, moving right along ... what do you know that's worth a brick? *You know who murdered Tina Paglia and why.* I'm not saying you killed her, but you were there and you were seen helping to remove her body from the house. For some reason, maybe because you spotted the person who was watching you, you and your companion dumped her body over the fence, instead of taking it away in the van."

He sank back down into his chair. "So why hasn't this witness reported what he saw to the cops?"

"For good reasons that are none of your business."

"If I do tell you what happened, what are you going to do with it? And why do you care? You got some kind of detective complex?"

"I want to see Tina's killer locked up. If you didn't kill her, you have nothing to lose by incriminating whoever did. You'll be collecting a Florida suntan by the time he gets arrested. Even if you do get caught, you can plea bargain in exchange for your testimony. In fact, I wonder why you haven't thought of that already — hire a good lawyer, turn yourself in and bargain your way through to a reduced charge? Makes much more sense than living here cramped up like a hamster."

"You really think the cops are my problem?"

I reshuffled my deck. "Look, it's getting late," I said, glancing conspicuously at my Swatch. "You want to deal or not?"

"If I had any cash, I would have blown this town before Tina's body got discovered. I probably make more in a week than you earn in a year, so you think that I have thousands lying around. In my dreams. I can't put big earnings in the bank without attracting attention. I have to invest in businesses, pay cash for everything."

We should all have such financial woes.

"The week before the murder I laid down seventy-five grand on a Porsche — 911 Carrera 2 Coupe. Fuckin' thing's sitting in my grandmother's garage. Old lady doesn't even have her driver's licence. I can't leave this apartment, so I haven't been able to deal, except small, to the few guys I totally trust — not that I got much anyway. I never keep more on hand than I can sell in a few days. Too fuckin' risky."

"Quasimodo, we really do have to pick up the pace. How did Tina die?"

Hammer chose this critical moment to rally his courage and ask if he could smoke — a social first for him. Maybe because Benito seemed to be rearranging the bedroom furniture.

"Smoke, if it will keep you talking," our host obliged. Figuring I need both hands free in the event of an emergency, I didn't light up along with my insecurity guard. Also a social first.

Chapter 37

QUASIMODO SAT DOWN, removed a long black hair from the arm of his shirt, and looked at me through frigid eyes. "So listen up, Miz Yeats. I did *not* whack the broad. Sometimes I get a bit violent — real violent. Beat up a few people who maybe wished they were dead by the time I was done. That's all part of taking care of business. But I have never killed anybody.

"When Tina got herself between me and Pepino, the shit hit the fan. She phoned me that Friday night all twisted out of shape. She'd been on a run for a couple of days, she smoked her last pebble and crashed. But she had no cash. And I don't do freebies. She cussed me loud enough to loosen her teeth. I slammed down the phone.

"About a hour later I go over to a buddy's, toss back a few beers. I'm leaving — my bike's gone. *My seven-thousand-dollar bike I'd a sold my grandmother for.* I mean, that bike don't even need a lock, right? So, I ask myself, who's the only asshole in the whole 'hood stupid and desperate enough to even think about touching my bike? I head over to Tina's place, look through the front door and there's my bike. God did not give this woman a big brain."

My bodyguard shot to his feet. If he was about to defend Tina's IQ, I'd sic Benito on the dumb bugger myself.

"'Scuse me, but may I go to the bathroom?" At least he didn't put up his hand.

"Yeah, but the dog gets to baby-sit."

"Then I'll just hold it — I mean, I'll wait." The action of sitting down again made him change his mind. "I mean, I'll go. I have to go."

I scanned the ceiling for my guardian angel.

"Low-life dipshit." Quasimodo jerked his thumb towards the bathroom door. He did not summon Benito to guard Hammer's underwhelming presence.

"Next thing, the cops show up. I get my bike back. Tina gets a lecture. Scene two. Saturday night — very early Sunday morning, I'm in bed with my girlfriend when Tina phones again. Seems she figured out Pepino was distributing from the sandwich shop. Maybe she seen or heard something going down, maybe she snuck downstairs when he was getting a delivery. Who knows? So she tells me, if I don't *give* her free blow forever, she's going to call the cops, they'll bust Pepino and dry up my supply."

"But if her crack came from you, how did she figure …?"

"The bitch was in no shape to figure out what fucking year it was."

Hammer plunked his bony ass back down beside me. I couldn't believe he'd chosen a piss over Quasimodo's story. But I'm blessed with a durable bladder.

"So I stall her, say I'll be right over. Then I got on the phone to Pepino up in Woodbridge. Tell him it's an emergency. Tina's so drug-sick she could phone the cops any minute. An hour later we meet at the store. I tell him all about it. He totally loses it — like, *totally* loses it. Storms into the kitchen, pulls on one of those white lab coats he wears when he's working, pair of rubber gloves, grabs a cleaver for big joints of meat, and tells me to follow him.

"All the way up the stairs to Tina's, I'm telling him we

could do this thing better — feed her some pure stuff, she ODs. Cops wouldn't waste an hour on her. But he's crazy as a bull with a hard-on. Charges into the living room — she's sitting buck naked staring at some TV infomercial. Pepino grabs her by the hair, slices into her throat like she was a hunk of veal. Fuckin' blood hit the ceiling."

Both hands over his mouth, a gagging Hammer fled for the bathroom, without permission.

"Then Mario tells me to help wrap her up in the carpet. He says, no point in cleaning up, cops will find traces of him everywhere anyway. He's the landlord, right? I want to ask, *Fine — what about traces of me?* but this is not a good time to rattle his cage. He's still holding the cleaver. So we lug the carpet down the stairs. He pulls his van around to the front. There's nobody in sight. He says, first we've got to move some stuff into the van. After we load up the olive tins, we pick up the carpet.

"Halfway to the van, we spot that Looney Tunes in the laneway staring at us through the fence — like we're doing a scene from *Law and Order*. Pepino says, 'Help me get her outta the carpet and toss her over the fence. Give that bitch Yeats something good to complain about.' While we're dumping her, Looney must have scurried off down the laneway leading to the back of the church. Pepino tosses the carpet into the van, goes back into the house, comes back — doesn't even lock the door — gets into his van, his cleaver all wrapped up in butcher paper. Tells me to bugger off, he'll phone me in the morning before he goes to Mass."

When he reached the end of his charming narrative, Quasimodo was as composed as a deportment class. *Had he given me the straight goods?* My bullshit-detector wasn't fibrillating.

There I sat, in the company of a man who valued his

mountain bike and his dog more than a woman's life — two, if you count his grandmother.

Hammer sat rigid, staring at the opposite wall.

"So how did you end up on the run from Pepino?"

"When he phoned me the next morning, he tells me to lose myself for a few weeks. Guess he was afraid I'd turn him over — like you said, plea bargain for a reduced charge. Promises to give me a bigger role in the organization when the heat is off."

"What organization?"

A hush fell over the cathedral.

"Lady, there isn't enough blow on the planet to make me go there. Anyway, I agree and disappear."

"Have you heard from him since?"

"Yeah, he called me ten days ago. Wanted me to meet him up in Woodbridge at one of his other businesses. I put him off by telling him I had the flu. Bastard didn't know I'm onto him. Get this: the day after he slit Tina's throat, he hires one of his associates to kill me. What he doesn't know is, the hitman tells a buddy of his. Buddy happens to be married to my sister. Hey, Pepino's *paesano*. How could he forget Little Italy is one big family?"

With this touching affirmation of community, Quasimodo relaxed back into his chair. "There's your story."

I should have stopped right then, but no. "OK. Before I send Hammer out to fetch your brick, I've got one more question — just curiosity. The way I see it, you must have known Pepino would kill Tina when you told him she was threatening to expose his operation. The man erupts sure as Vesuvius at the slightest provocation. And you stood by and watched as he nearly separated her head from her body. Then you helped him dump her body like a bag of garbage." I took a deep breath. "Tell me. What vital piece of human equipment were you born without?" I could not have stopped myself. Rats make my flesh crawl too, but that's their job.

He jumped to his feet. "Fuck you. That bitch *was* a bag of garbage. A wasted old crack ho. You think the world is going to miss the douche bag?"

Hammer exploded into a human cannonball across the room, scoring a direct hit. He landed on top of Quasimodo, knocking them both — and the chair — backward. Benito set about snarling and snapping as he flung himself at the bedroom door.

Boys will be boys. Hammer was pile-driving Quasimodo's head into the hardwood. Quasimodo had both hands locked around Hammer's throat. Benito hadn't given up on the door.

I cast my eyes around the room for a weapon — to stun whoever surfaces first. If Hammer kills Quasimodo, there goes the only eyewitness to Tina's murder. If Quasimodo manages to strangle Hammer, God knows what he'll do to me, once he realizes he's in even deeper shit than before.

Just as I yanked out the plug of a tall lamp with a lime green ceramic base molded in the shape of a buxom mermaid, Benito projected himself through the bottom panel of the bedroom door in a flurry of slobber and splintered wood.

Grunting and cursing, locked tight as hurried lovers, the two men rolled over and over across the floor. At the precise instant Quasimodo and Hammer came to rest in the missionary position, Quasimodo on top, his legs splayed to pin down his thrashing assailant, Benito flung himself into the air graceful as Nureyev, and clamped his jaws on his owner's naughty bits.

As Quasimodo howled in agony, the enterprising

Hammer sucked in a few lungsful of air and shimmied out from under. Before he could orient himself, I swung the lamp in a wide arc and mightily whacked the dog upside his confused head.

In slow motion, Benito rolled off his master and onto the floor, limp as a sack of flour.

Quasimodo's anguished howling diminished as he drifted into shock. I inched closer to examine his distressed crotch, my view facilitated by Benito's having ripped away a sizable chunk of denim and white cotton. The blood did not conceal that something vital was missing.

Oh shit.

Benito was resting tranquil, a contented grimace twisting his ugly face, the tip of a fat sausage-seeming appendage drooping from the side of his mouth.

"Guess I really fucked up," squeaked Hammer.

I dialed 911.

Then I phoned the emergency vet line. To all appearances, Benito was a flat-liner.

Hammer stopped blubbering long enough to light up an Export 'A.'

Chapter 38

THE SAVE-A-PRECIOUS-PET Lifeline ambulance arrived five minutes after the two paramedics, who had attended to Quasimodo's grievous wound and placed him on a stretcher ready for export to Toronto Western. Although Benito was still out cold, both paramedics refused to rescue the victim's penis from between his clamped jaws. They ignored my pragmatic solution, that they put the dog on the stretcher beside his erstwhile master, haul the duo off to the hospital and make it the surgeon's problem.

The vet was naturally more concerned about Benito, but obliged the paramedics by injecting a fast-acting muscle relaxant into his thigh. Soon his jaws went slack enough for the vet to dislodge the peripatetic member. He wrapped it in wet gauze and sealed it in a plastic bag, which he submerged in a second bag full of ice cubes.

"Why didn't you tell me on the phone about this ... this situation?" he complained.

As I replied pleasantly, "Would you have come?" two cops made their way into the apartment. Not that I had requested their presence. My tense call to 911 had specified the nature of Quasimodo's injury. Perhaps the dispatcher assumed I was the vengeful girlfriend.

"Well, I'll be damned," remarked the female officer as the paramedic flashed the bag's insubstantial contents.

Vulnerability is only one of many reasons Freud had it wrong about penis envy.

The officer signalled the paramedics to get Quasimodo to the hospital. I recognized her partner as young Constable Macintosh, the beat cop who'd been at my house the morning Tina's body came to rest on my prize hosta.

Macintosh greeted me less than enthusiastically. "You seem to be a magnet for violent men." Like Cleopatra on her burnished throne, Benito was transported on a litter borne by the indignant vet and his assistant.

"Think he'll make it?" I asked the vet, hoping that Benito would pass immediately into the company of the angels who, it is rumoured, possess no genitals.

"Where do I send the bill?" he snarled.

"John Wayne Bobbitt Relief Fund."

"What the hell happened here?" asked Constable Choy as she slammed the door behind the Precious Pet missionaries.

"Quasimodo and Hammer Hopkins —" I gestured towards my companion. He was still fighting rigor mortis on the sofa. " — got into a fight when Quasimodo dissed Hammer's dead girlfriend. The rottweiler broke through the bedroom door and stole his owner's jewels."

"Go figure," muttered Choy.

"So this whole mess is connected to the Paglia case," Macintosh concluded in a lightning leap of logic. "You two better come down to the station. Homicide will want to talk to you."

I helped Hammer to his feet. His bladder had betrayed him.

The unexpurgated version of my story I confided to Ernie Sivcoski, while another homicide detective fussed over the volume control on the tape machine.

    Ernie did not look disgruntled at being summoned out of bed in the middle of the night. In fact, he appeared positively gleeful that I had my ass in hot water again. When I reached the delicate bit about how a kilo-brick had come into my possession, he rhymed off a partial catalogue of what he could charge me with: break and enter, theft over a thousand, possession of stolen goods, possession of a controlled substance, trafficking in narcotics ...

    He mistook me for a woman who caves in to bullies. "Ernie, my heart was pure, my intentions worthy. As God is my judge." My dear-departed, drunken father, Seamus, so invoked the Supreme Court whenever he lied. "All I intended to do was snoop around a bit and see if I could come up with a motive for Tina's murder."

    "Guys like me get paid to investigate homicides."

    "I had nothing you would have taken seriously. And I figured you had too many other higher profile murders to put more effort into Tina's. If your team had been keeping an eye on the crime scene, it wouldn't have fallen to me to discover Pepino's stash. Shit, Ernie, your officers took almost twenty minutes to respond to my 911. Even the vet was quicker."

    Ominous silence.

    "Look on the bright side," I chirped. "Quasimodo confessed his role in Tina's murder, named the killer and, were he not otherwise engaged, would be confessing in exchange for leniency at this very moment. And you get to bust Pepino for trafficking. Who knows where he might lead the narcs? The guy seems to have Mob connections. So call me immodest, but it looks to me like my nosiness paid off."

    "Next you'll be recommending yourself for a commendation from the Chief."

"Actually I'm recommending that I go home. If Max doesn't get out for a run soon, his bladder will burst."

"After tonight's shenanigans, you could be looking for a permanent home for that pathetic mutt."

"I am not the bad guy, Ernie, so cut the crap. I have co-operated with you completely — didn't even call my lawyer." I omitted to mention that a lawyer would bankrupt me faster than home renovations. "I've gone over my entire story twice. Every single word is true and I left out nothing. Hammer's account will confirm mine. I've offered to testify in court. I'm turning over the cocaine. The department will take all the credit for solving Tina's murder and making a big drug bust. What's your problem?"

Ernie stood up to answer a knock on the door of the Inquisition room. I heard him arguing with someone in the hall.

Several minutes later he came back into the room even more exasperated. "I've been instructed to send you home in a cruiser with two officers. You will turn the cocaine over to them — every particle of it."

"Ernie, as you know, my drug of choice is beer."

"I already know far too much about your lifestyle. Leave, fine, but on one condition: we want you back here Tuesday morning at ten. Without a lawyer."

Whenever he's trying to appear bulky and imposing, Ernie hunches up his shoulders like King Kong, a trick he must have picked up from World Wrestling Federation apes. It seriously stresses the seams of his costly jackets.

"Why would I drag my sorry ass back here *without* a lawyer if you plan to charge me with everything except plotting to assassinate the premier?"

"Given your politics, you've probably got that in the

works, too. The reason you'll drag your sorry ass back here is because I just had a lively conversation with Chief Underhill. He's willing to drop *all* charges in exchange for your helping us to get some more evidence. I'll tell you more about it Tuesday. So go home and take your dog for a leak."

I did.

Chapter 39

"**G**IMME THREE RED, three gold, five pillows of lube, some chocolate."

I assembled the order. Andrew Miller had assigned me to keep Bobby, who sat in the hot seat beside him, supplied with candy and condoms. He stopped the geriatric Chevy Astro when people flagged it down, and Bobby rolled down the window and responded to a variety of desperate needs.

Late Monday morning Andrew had phoned to ask if I could possibly ride the van tonight with him and another volunteer. The scheduled third just reported that she'd be unable to fill her outreach shift. I jumped at his request, motivated more by a wanton impulse to see him again than by altruism. He advised me to dress warmly (the van's heating system was unreliable) and to bring no more than $10 with me. At Grayce's Space I helped them stock the van. Bobby, a kick-ass lesbian with a manner abrupt as her purple buzz cut, brought me up to speed on van protocol.

Patrolling the stroll spooked and depressed me. Cold and wet as it was, a constant cavalcade of johns, from a clutch of belligerents in university engineering jackets to a man driving a Land Rover with a baby seat in the back, inspected scantily-clad girls and women shivering in doorways and on the sidewalks. A sleazy nocturnal ghetto in the heart of Toronto the Good.

Andrew exuded a wholesome, good-natured warmth in his dealings with the people on the track — a counterpoint to Bobby's gruff but patient practicality. They worked well as a team, in spite of the tension I sensed between them, the cause of which wasn't at first clear to me. They listened carefully, exchanging sympathy, advice or light banter as appropriate, and didn't pressure people who refused their offer of condoms. Requests for money or excessive numbers of condoms met with polite explanations for their refusal.

An Asian transsexual with an unlikely mane of long blond hair reported that a cop had picked her up, driven her to a parking lot where he flashed his badge, showed her his gun, and demanded that she give him head without a condom or he would arrest her. They offered to help her report the incident. She settled for a copy of their legal rights handout.

It was a slow night, though, lots of time for us to chat. Curiosity — or sizing up the competition? — made me ask Andrew, "Has Rosemary had her pamphlet printed up yet?"

"The one she asked you to edit?"

"Yes. If you're wondering why I turned her down ... well, after visiting her Web site, I honestly felt that our perspectives on prostitution were not an ... appropriate match."

"Rosemary is extraordinarily zealous about her work. She sometimes goes a little over the top with her enthusiasm, but if you consider the terrible harm she's witnessed over the course of her career, you can easily understand her intensity about getting young women off the streets."

He seemed to understand my discomfort with his wife's fervour without taking offense or getting embarrassed on her behalf. Probably came from much practice.

"Intensity?" snapped Bobby. "Sounds more like fuckin' lunacy to me. At the rate she's ranting, she'll wind up executive director of a padded room." She shook her head in disgust. "Jesus saves. Right. Take a look around."

"Rosemary's just going through a bad patch. It'll get sorted out. I'm sure I can persuade her to moderate her views. That job is her life."

"Then she better chill or she's going to lose her life." Bobby was no diplomat.

Only his white-knuckled grip on the steering wheel betrayed his sudden anger. "PROS prides itself on its support for diversity." He threw her a mean glance. "You're obviously a beneficiary of that. Doesn't that support extend to Rosemary? After all she's done for PROS, you'd think the board and staff would be more tolerant."

He abruptly braked the van on Sherbourne, just south of Queen, effectively terminating their exchange. Bobby looked disinclined to pursue it anyway. He pulled alongside a strung-out young girl in a leather jacket and hot pink tiny skirt, her skin the colour of Wonder Bread. She teetered over to Andrew's window.

"Hi, handsome, whatcha got for me tonight?"

"Hi, Candace. How's it going?"

"Slow."

"What do you need?"

Her voice was high and shaky. "A fucking life. But you can give me a handful of reds."

I reached for the box of Trojan non-lubricated, good for blow jobs.

She stuffed the condoms in her jacket pocket and walked a few yards from the van before turning back. "Hey, handsome, didn't I see you in the van real late last week — along River Street? It was Sunday. Nah, maybe it was Tuesday. Anyways, I thought you stopped work at three."

"Must have been a different limo, Candace."

She shrugged and headed back to work.

Andrew glanced over his shoulder at me. "Poor kid smokes crack from a pop can. Can't get her facts any straighter than her life."

At the end of the shift, he dropped Bobby off at an after-hours club. He asked me to join him for coffee, but I pleaded my need for a few hours of restorative sleep before my meeting, now just six hours away. Not being a name-dropper, I didn't mention it was with the police chief.

As he drove me home, I complimented him on how effectively he communicated with prostitutes.

He blushed. "Communication's my job."

"Does your teaching kids have anything to do with your involvement with PROS?"

"You hit the nail on the head. When I first started teaching, the most average parents had to worry about was their kids getting drunk on prom night, using a bit of marijuana, staying out past curfew. Now it's hard drugs, STDs, HIV, weapons ... you do what you can, inside and outside the school."

"The van outreach strikes me as more geared to harm reduction. Rosemary's whole focus seems to be helping prostitutes who want to leave the trade."

He smiled, captivating as Paul Newman. "My classroom is a forum. I try to help my students make informed choices about their lives."

"How do you do that as an English teacher? I mean, I know subject areas have become pretty elastic, but isn't prostitution as literature a big stretch?"

"Occasionally I assign a good book on the subject. Last term we read Evelyn Lau's *Runaway: Diary of a Street Kid*.

Couldn't be more appropriate or inspirational — woman who went from teen hooker to best-selling writer. I've shown my senior classes a few documentaries and invited in some guest speakers. I'm always careful to choose materials that show the downside of drugs and the sex trade."

He pulled up outside my house. When I struggled to open the van door, he reached across to release the stubborn latch. In passing, his arm inadvertently rubbed my breasts. They perked up, the downside of vagrant hormones.

"Good night, Jane Yeats. And thanks so much for your help tonight." He smiled so sweetly I took no offense at the tiny kiss — surely of gratitude — that he planted on my cheek. No offense at all. I almost returned it.

Be still, my naughty bits. You don't do married men.

Chapter 40

TUESDAY MORNING I WOKE up feeling worse than Caesar on the Ides of March. I checked my e-mail. Even a missive from Rosemary Miller might have cheered me up. Alas, nothing. She must have scratched me off her dance card.

Reluctantly I pointed Harley to the station, where I was met by Ernie, warning me to watch my mouth — we were heading into a high-powered meeting with the Chief.

The man I used to call 'friend' introduced me to the man sitting at the head of the conference table. Chief Raymond Underhill nodded, thanked me for coming, then sternly warned me that everything I was about to hear was STRICTLY CONFIDENTIAL. Our meeting would not be recorded or videotaped. The department would deny that it had ever taken place — should I be so foolish as to pretend otherwise. Charming.

Underhill was a powerfully built man, with thick white hair and matching mustache. Clearly he relished the power of intimidation his rank bestowed. "We've prepared a list of charges you are currently facing. I'm asking you to go over them carefully so you'll be in a better position to appreciate our generosity." He handed me a single sheet of paper.

I speed-read my way through a list of alleged offences guaranteed to send me to the joint long enough to knit a turtleneck for the CN Tower.

Trying to keep my voice firm, I said, "Very daunting. Definitely I'm inclined to listen sympathetically — in exchange, of course, for your dropping every charge on this list."

"We are willing to do so if you agree to help us get the evidence to convict Mario Pepino. However, I must warn you that there will be an element of risk involved. We will take every possible precaution; however, we can not guarantee your safety." He was studying my face to gauge how well I was digesting his proposal.

"Why don't you just get Quasimodo to testify against Pepino?"

"Mr. Quasimodo will be spending the next few weeks in hospital recovering from his mishap and getting some counselling. The operation was not a success."

Ernie's snicker drew a disapproving glance from his boss.

"It's doubtful he'll be in any shape to help us out for quite some time. His mother has already hired a lawyer to keep him muzzled. In any case, it is our understanding that he'd sooner go to prison than testify against Pepino. Moreover, his credibility as a witness would get ripped to shreds in court: Quasimodo is a man of questionable integrity who makes his living as a drug dealer and part-time pimp. He stood to gain by Tina Paglia's death. At the very least, he's an accomplice to her murder. His testimony could be further discredited on the grounds that he offered it only to save his neck. The man is a very skilled liar who produces airtight alibis on demand. We do have some trace evidence — but all it proves is that Pepino, Paglia's landlord, and Quasimodo, her dealer, were in her apartment, probably on several occasions. But not necessarily the night of the murder. The case is so flimsy no sensible judge would commit Pepino to trial."

This was crushing news. "So if you can't nail Pepino for murder, why don't you search the store like you should have done two weeks ago and bust him for trafficking?"

Chief Underhill studied his manicured fingernails. "I have considered that option. For the past six months, we've been working with the RCMP and the OPP to dismantle a very well-organized network of drug traffickers operating in the Toronto region. Our suspects range from upper-level suppliers to street-level dealers. If what Quasimodo told you is true, Mario Pepino is a big player."

"Ohmygawd. I thought maybe Pepino was supplying a few small-time dealers like Quasimodo and delivering crack with the sandwiches. So how come Pepino escaped your net?"

"The operation began at the community level, targeting suppliers. When our enforcement team began to suspect that we were dealing with much bigger fish than we originally figured, we called in the RCMP. They set up a major Canada-wide and international investigation into large-scale trafficking of heroin and cocaine. Pepino probably gets his supply from an Italian-based crime group working through the airport here, with ties to suppliers in New York, Miami, Colombia and Peru. Many of the major players are owners and managers of valid business enterprises — like Pepino. We were getting very close to penetrating their network and our raids were significantly reducing the street supply."

He paused to contemplate a hangnail. "Something went terribly wrong in the past month."

It all fell into place. Failed raids. Underhill's apparent reluctance to "share" Quasimodo's information with his partner forces in the operation. The fact that no drug-enforcement officer was present at our meeting.

"You'll forgive my impertinence, Chief Underhill, but

I'm guessing that what's gone terribly wrong is an undercover officer leaking information ... to the bad guys."

The Chief cleared his throat. "Before I divulge anything more, I need to secure your co-operation. We are proposing that you wear a wire, confront Pepino with the 'fact' that you heard him murder Paglia, then witnessed him and Quasimodo dispose of her body. Sivcoski, backed up by homicide, will be positioned outside the sandwich shop. If you run into any trouble, they'll be all over him like flies on shit ... I'm sorry, in no time at all."

Ernie winked.

"If you can get Pepino to admit to Paglia's murder, we'll take him to court on first-degree. Whatever he gets convicted of is inconsequential as long as we get him permanently out of circulation."

"Pepino's going to want to know why I didn't phone you guys the second I realized what was going down."

"You had a better use for the information. Tell him you are going to lose your house to the bank if you don't get your hands on a lot of money fast. You're a writer. Be inventive. Now, may I have your answer?"

Reducing the street supply of cocaine is a noble aim, but I had other priorities. I would not fare well in the joint. Hell, my kindergarten teacher warned Etta that I had problems with authority. And with Pepino behind bars, my guilt over Tina would diminish. Perhaps I could even persuade Mario's successor at the sandwich shop to declare our patch of Little Italy a rat-free zone. Never again would I have to worry about being nailed like Jesus to the cross or made into meatballs. Call me motivated.

"I'll do it."

Underhill rose and extended his hand. "Thank you, Ms.

Yeats. I'll feed these charges into the shredder immediately after your meeting with Pepino. Now, let's swear you in as a police agent, then you and Sivcoski can work out how you're going to set it up."

I consented, and the deed was accomplished with fewer frills than a shotgun wedding. They didn't even lend me a badge.

"Isn't this ... unusual?" I asked my Chief.

"We get civilians involved only when there is no alternative. Often someone with a personal relationship with a suspect can get him talking. Occasionally civilians are very strongly inclined to help — ex-wives, for example. Did you follow the Thorpe case, Ms. Yeats?"

"The father charged with drowning his two kids in Lake Muskoka?"

"Precisely. His ex-girlfriend knew in her bones that he killed them. She called us with her suspicions and was wearing a wire when he admitted his guilt. When we played him the tapes, he immediately made a videotaped statement."

He made it all sound routine, omitting any possibility of something going horribly wrong — like the person on the end of the wire getting dead.

Underhill excused himself. In the hall, Ernie and I decided to plot our strategy at a nearby pub. Given that my cooperation had been so shamelessly coerced, he got to pay for the Smithwick's. I reminded him how bad it would look if newly-sworn Agent Yeats came to harm. He claimed his eyes would not remain entirely dry at my funeral.

Chapter 41

ERNIE ARRIVED thirty minutes before our planned sting, as I was lacing up my running shoes.

"You look like you've come for a late dinner," I said, glancing at his shirt and tie. He handed me a bouquet of flowers and set an LCBO bag on the dining-room table.

"Good. Mario might have noticed me coming to your door. The only damage my being here tonight might do is to your reputation." He checked out my jeans and Harley T-shirt. "That works. Pull on your leather jacket before you go. Give it your full NO-SHIT look."

"I hope the look puts me in the mood."

"You having second thoughts?"

"Those I had well before I left the station Tuesday morning. At the moment my only thoughts are burial or cremation."

He pulled a bottle of wine from the bag along with a body wire. "Fear is normal. Any cop who isn't afraid before a bust stands a big chance of getting hurt. That adrenaline rush focuses the mind. Let me tape this wire in place while I tell you about our backup."

His trembling hands and accelerated breathing whispered that Ernie hadn't been expecting Victoria's Secret under my T-shirt. Sexy lingerie rewards any man intrepid enough to get past my jeans. Heart of a biker, soul of a slut.

"You told me Pepino closes up Thursday nights on his

own. Puts out the garbage bags for early-morning pickup before he locks up. So here's the drill. While he's dragging out the bags, you enter the shop. When you're both inside, I'll slip out, join the guys in the van around the corner, and pull it up across from your house. We've got a couple of other officers hanging out on foot. First sign of Pepino even thinking about causing you grief — we're in there like the marines. But watch his body language. If he makes any threatening move, something the wire doesn't pick up, you scream. And try to stay in the front of the store, where we can see you."

I tugged my T-shirt back on. "Ernie, I don't have a script. Don't know what to say."

"Good. You'll sound more convincing if you improvise. Just play it by ear. You know the guy's temperament. Basically, follow the same line you used on Quasimodo. Scare him with what you know, tell him you're ready to deal. Insult the bugger. Trigger him into spilling something incriminating. He's not likely to attack you in a well-lit store with a huge window."

I must have looked unconvinced.

"You'll do fine," he assured me. "Your mouth is as provocative as your underwear."

"Think I could have a swig of that wine to steady my nerves?" I pulled on my jacket.

"When you get back." He glanced at his watch. "Five to twelve. Good luck, Jane."

"Thanks, Ernie. Bye, Max. Catch you later." I should have visited a lawyer to name Silver his official guardian.

Right on schedule, Pepino exited his front door, staggering with two green garbage bags in each hand. I walked briskly into the store. The food odours work better smothered under a blanket of melted mozzarella.

"What the fuck you want? You blind? I'm closing up."

Pepino lumbered past me graceless as a wounded hippo and planted his lab-coated frame behind the counter, his huge balled fists on its surface. To his right was an ancient cash register, beside it some bottled anchovies. Sneering elevated the upper hairs of his salt-and-nicotine mustache into his nostrils. Cyrano de Bergerac without the soul.

"Stupid woman, you cause me nothing but trouble. Make a fence on my property. Tell the health inspector you see rats in a store clean enough for the baby Jesus to get born in. Complain about my tenant, a lovely woman who's gone to heaven." He crossed himself. "So what you want now?"

I smiled sweetly. "I ran out of olives."

He jabbed a thick finger at me. "I'm an important man. Lotsa big business. You think I'm gonna waste my time making you a bag of olives this time of night?"

"Yeah, Mario. I do. And I don't just want any old olives." I glanced dismissively at four deep plastic trays nested under the glass-fronted counter. "I need your *special* olives. You know — come in a big yellow tin that says *Natural Greek olives. Very nutritive and healthy food for every age. The ideal complement for your table. Digestible, appetizing, aromatic.* I've developed a taste for those particular olives, Mario. They must be very addictive."

He looked at me through eyes suddenly gone wise. "You are a crazy *mangia* cake. Just to shut you up, get you outta my store, I give you fucking olives." He dipped a slotted spoon into one of the trays and offered me a sample. "Taste. You're the big expert. That's the olive you die for, *signora*."

To demonstrate my exquisite grace under the pressure of that thinly-veiled death threat, I nonchalantly tossed his glistening orb in the air and caught it in my mouth. Actually, it catapulted straight to my gullet, where it lodged. A violent hork cleared its passage to my stomach. "Mario, listen up. I have no plans to die — not for that olive or any of its cousins. In fact, the way I look at it, your olives are my salvation."

He stuffed a feast of olives into a Baggie, twist-tied it with excessive force and plunked it on the counter. "You shut up and go home, the olives are free," he said wearily.

Taken aback by his failure to rise to the olive challenge, my brain frantically scrounged for something to enrage him. I'd mistakenly been subtle, when he only understands crude.

"Tonight you are not getting off that easy, Mario. Tonight is going to cost you big-time. I know two things about you, both of which I am prepared to take to the police." I raised my right thumb as a visual aid. "One, I know what you *really* keep in those olive tins."

He rolled his eyes. "What? So you wanna salami, too? I see blackmail in your evil eyes." Offended he should assume I could be bought for a palmful of olives and a pound of flesh, I prepared to launch my major offensive. From under the counter he produced a meat cleaver of a provenance Chinese rather than Mediterranean. I anxiously watched him sharpen it with swift, practised strokes against a large emery stone. In one angry slash he halved a thick, metre-long salami. Probably the technique he used on Tina. I wondered if my wire would short when I peed myself.

He wagged in my face the aromatic hunk of purple gristle laced with sodium nitrites, desiccated beyond rehydration, and holding no more promise than Quasimodo's severed member. Pepino leered. "Also for free, I give you my recipe for how to get happy and don't make the neighbours crazy because you don't have a man in your bed. He mimicked, "One — eat your olives." Suggestively waggling the salami, "Two — fuck a salami."

That tore it. Etta's recent escapade with a dildo had exhausted my patience with sex toys. I reached across the counter, grabbed the meat from his fat hand and slammed it down so hard I cracked the plate glass.

"You murdered Tina Paglia. I heard you do it and I saw you dumping her body in my garden. I also know that this store is a cover for your drug dealings. I've got the evidence — a big bag of cocaine I stole from an olive tin in your basement. So stop farting around. You pay off my mortgage, I quit bothering you. It's a good deal, Mario. I don't lose my house to the bank and you don't die in jail."

Smacking his left palm against the side of his head, his entire body shook with maniacal laughter. His right hand closed around the handle of the cleaver.

Hastily I retrieved the salami, ready for battle.

Suddenly he stopped laughing. He banged the blunt end of the cleaver on the cracked counter top, his black eyes bulging with rage. "Now you listen to me, stupid woman. You violate my property with your fence, you shame me with rats, you slander my tenant. I say to myself, 'OK, don't do nothing, Mario. The poor woman's a crazy.'" Bang went the cleaver again. "But tonight, you go too far. Now I'm a big gangster man and a killer. *Signora*, maybe I gotta bad temper but I'm a respectable man. You wanna ruin my business, destroy my good name? I fix you."

Faster than Xena, Warrior Princess, I shielded my chest with my left arm, salami aloft. I also screamed.

Just as my frenzied brain registered that Mario had set down the cleaver and reached for the wall phone, Ernie burst through the door, gun drawn, five cops hard on his heels.

"DROP YOUR WEAPON," Ernie bellowed. Pepino dropped the phone. I held onto the salami.

Mario's face broke into a megawatt version of the welcoming smile he reserves for cops stalking a free veal. "Thank God you come. Me, I'm just phoning 911. You gotta arrest this crazy woman."

After Mario and I were escorted to the police station, a meeting convened with Chief Underhill. When Pepino persisted in demanding that charges be laid against the *mangia* cake and threatened me with a lawsuit guaranteed to ruin me, Underhill asked that I leave the room while they confronted him with my suspicions about his involvement in Tina's murder and drug trafficking.

Forty minutes later, Ernie offered to drive me home.

In the car, I asked, "So who got stung?"

"Shit. This has to be a first — a suspected perp calling 911 during an operation." His laughter was infectious. At my front door, the two of us still had tears streaming down our faces.

"Ernie, come on in. Let's kill that bottle of wine — if it's more than a prop."

Pepino's story of what happened the night of Tina's murder differed in certain particulars from Quasimodo's account. Like, he hadn't been anywhere near the crime scene.

Why, Pepino had screeched indignantly, would he have deserted his daughter's $50,000 wedding held that very night? "Not a beautiful girl, my Gina. Not young. And just a little bit pregnant. I keep my good name from being dragged into the dirt by a daughter with no respect for the Blessed Virgin and a bastard grandchild — so much money."

Pepino left the interrogation room uttering death threats against Quasimodo — he swore he was unaware that the dealer had been storing drugs in his basement. When Ernie had leaned on him about why Quasimodo had access to the basement, Pepino made a full confession.

As a cost-saving measure, he'd been buying cheap black-market, substandard olive oil and olives from Quasimodo, who had a key so he could make middle-of-the-night deliveries. Pepino fairly grovelled, begging the police to take pity on a man with so many daughters to marry, a good man with twenty years of donating sandwiches to beat cops. Pity they took: Pepino was sent home with a sharp warning to cease and desist his purchase of purloined products. No reference was made to free veals.

Ernie promised to keep me posted. After checking out Pepino's alibi, he planned to interview the still-hospitalized Quasimodo.

I couldn't resist. "Please tell the Chief I'll be happy to assist in any way I can."

"Don't give up your day job, Jane — whatever it is."

Hell will freeze over before I go to the cops with suspicions about anyone again.

Chapter 42

SATURDAY MORNING I COMBED through the PROS bad date sheets so finely a nit could not have escaped. The entries piled up so remorselessly I struggled to retain each one as a separate violation. The reports ran like this:

ASSAULT/KNIFE/ROBBERY: male, white, 6'1", 175 lbs., brown hair, blue eyes, over 40 years. French accent, said his name was André. Picked woman up on Dundas/Sherbourne and took her to the Belvedere. Paid her and she did date. He then drove her back. Before she got out of vehicle he pulled a knife, put it to her throat, and said he wanted money. He took all her cash. She got away without injury. He drove a small green Plymouth truck which he said was not his.

ASSAULT/KNIFE/REFUSES TO PRACTICE SAFE SEX: male, white, 6'2", blond hair, green eyes, full beard, 30 to 35 years. Picked up woman on Jarvis in a white Mazda, Ontario plate #YX3140. This man does not want to use a condom and carries a 7 to 8 inch blade that he threatens to use. Told woman he should stab her like he did a trannie last week and others. This man is extremely dangerous.

ASSAULT/CHOKING/ATTEMPTED RAPE: male, black, under 6', 190 lbs., black dreads, brown eyes, 25 to 30 years. Picked up woman from bar at Ford Hotel where he was staying in room 406. They went to room where he refused to pay her, grabbed her breasts, choked her, and tried to rape her. Woman finally got away.

Only after I'd absorbed the 461st (and final) report, did I admit that nothing I'd read jumped off the page to link Jessye's assault with any of the others. I'd tried to keep in mind Sandy's tagging a john's vehicle as the prime red flag for alerting pros to a freak — and me to a recurring reference that might signal a serial killer. But in the absence of a year's research, I couldn't imagine how I could complete the job.

Totally defeated, I began a list detailing what remained of my renovations. Despair drove me to begin a much shorter list of what didn't need doing. Being in no mood for home improvement, I tossed the second list in the bin.

Then I remembered the nursery catalogue that appeared in my mailbox yesterday — probably from a neighbour delicately hinting about the state of my yard. In the interest of community, I figured it wouldn't hurt to shake a few seed packets over the ground (come whatever month one does that sort of thing). I had just turned to "zero maintenance perennials" when the phone rang.

It was Ernie bearing glad tidings. "Jane, we've got a confession. Meet me for lunch at the Dundalk and I'll fill you in."

Hulking on the corner next to Mario's, the Dundalk Tavern is a grand architectural folly. A former bootlegging emporium during Prohibition, it is a hodgepodge of red-tiled roof, dirty mustard brick, dozens of shuttered windows, wrought iron grillwork, and peeling oak doors with ecclesiastical hardware. Nina Moretti tells me it began life as an Italian bank. A few years ago, a bomb exploded in the gents'.

I climbed the unlit staircase to the second floor, pausing at the bar to study the draft taps. Nothing imported, no microbrewery offerings. No chance of becoming my local.

Before I even sat down, Ernie asked what I was drinking. "Whatever you're having, Detective Sergeant."

He grinned. "Right. Jane Yeats, working-class hero, beer snob."

"A girl has to be particular about something. Beer and motorcycles work for me."

"I thought for real women it was their hair, shoes ..."

"For real women it's who they hang out with and ..." I glanced disparagingly about the tacky room, "... where."

"I don't suppose anyone ever called you a ball-crusher, Ms. Yeats?"

"No one who had any."

We clicked glasses. "Cheers, Ernie. And congratulations on tying up the Paglia case. So tell me."

"Quasimodo."

"Quasimodo? I'm surprised he was even willing to speak to you."

Ernie guffawed. "I'm in his hospital room, five minutes into trying to persuade him that it would be in his best interest to co-operate, when a priest shows up. Apparently Quasimodo's mother asked him to make a pastoral visit. She's worried about sonny boy's immortal soul. Quasimodo panics and launches into his confession."

"Lose your pecker and get religion?"

Ernie composed himself with difficulty. "Pretty much. It seems the hospital had him stoned on painkillers and tranks to help him cope with the grievous genital harm. The moment Quasimodo sets eyes on the priest, he assumes he's come to give the Last Rites. So he gets Tina's murder off his chest, along with a whole slew of other crimes."

"Poor Father Gregory."

Ernie almost doubled over. "Didn't miss a beat — just solemnly inquired, *would you like me to hear your confession, my son?*"

When our hilarity subsided, I got down to business. "Repeat's journal suggested he saw two people leaving the house."

"Right. Quasimodo got his girlfriend to help him remove the drugs and the body. She's another nasty piece of work. They're the Bernardo and Homolka of the coke scene. Anyway, we hauled her in, informed her that he'd ratted on her, and advised her to testify against him in exchange for a sweetheart deal — which she did. Good thing, given that his confession was made under very heavy medication and wouldn't have held up in court."

Ernie signalled the waiter for two more draft. "Feel up to checking out the menu, Jane?"

"You're joking." I began work on my second beer. "I have a very good bullshit detector, Ernie. While Quasimodo was giving me his version of the story, I was watching his face, observing his body language, listening as critically as you would. Nothing — not his demeanour, not his delivery — indicated he was lying. Nothing."

"Ninety percent of his account was true. As for the rest, just substitute Quasimodo for Mario — and put the girlfriend in his place as the accomplice."

"If he's that clever, why in hell did he return his coke stash to Pepino's basement? Wouldn't he assume you guys would finally conduct the thorough search you failed to do first time around?"

"Thank you for the learned critique," Ernie commented dryly. "He didn't return it to the basement. We seized what he says is the entire shipment elsewhere. The tin you opened had simply been overlooked in his haste to get away."

"It's an odd world, my friend. Tragedy ends in farce." I drained my Blue.

"Without your help, Paglia's murder probably wouldn't have an ending, Jane."

"Surely to God you're not referring to our sting?"

"No way. The Chief keeps reminding me that if Pepino hadn't been in the illicit olive trade, he could have sued the department."

"Well, piss on the Chief. The man has no sense of humour."

"I'll drink to that. But I was trying to acknowledge your part in the investigation. From the beginning, your guts told you Quasimodo was the perp. You found the drugs, tracked him down, confronted him. True, Benito is the real hero — if the guy still had his dick he wouldn't have gotten so demoralized he spilled his guts."

"Woof!"

"You, too, lady. But Quasimodo is dangerous — and smart. He offered to supply Pepino with the cheap olives and olive oil because he needed a stash for his latest drug shipment. We think he knew he was under surveillance. Last month one of our surveillance guys got his cover blown at the bar where Quasimodo made his contacts. But the little bastard never counted on Paglia snooping in Pepino's basement. He could have bought her silence with drugs — but any dealer knows crackheads are unreliable. So he cut her throat — figured that if her body got discovered we'd write it off to a serial killer, a copycat, or some crazy john. Even when he was forced to dump her in your yard — what the hell? She was just another crack whore. He didn't count on you taking her murder seriously."

"A month ago I wouldn't have counted on it either."

He nodded. "I just wish we'd posted a reward in the case."

"Are you joking? The Chief would donate it to Quasimodo's defence fund before he'd let me get my hands on it. Anyway, do I look like a woman who needs money?"

"Yes."

I returned home, trying to feel gratified that Quasimodo would no doubt be convicted for savagely murdering a woman whose greatest sin was not taking better care of herself. But there was none of the 'closure,' that too-tidy word that sits so well in grief-counselling manuals. Getting dead brings closure.

I stood in the kitchen, and wept for Tina. For Pete. For me.

Then I phoned Hammer. When I told him that Quasimodo had made a full confession, he got very happy. When I told him that Quasimodo's penis would remain forever at half-mast, even happier. Guys.

Chapter 43

MY TOLERANCE for being stood up is exceptionally low — maybe because I so rarely venture into socializing. I shivered outside the Royal Theatre for only ten minutes into the feature before practising on my new cell phone. I left "WHERE THE FUCK ARE YOU? I'M WORRIED. PAGE ME A.S.A.P." messages on Chelsea's voice mail and pager.

"Sure I'll come — never work on a Sunday — that's my day of rest," she chuckled when I'd called to see if she was free to catch *American Beauty* tonight. So she wouldn't have accepted a last-minute date with a john.

While I sulked in the Can over a lukewarm Blue, another half-hour leaked away. Time for action: Chelsea earns her living responding to calls and always promptly replies to incoming messages. And tough as it is for me to trust, Chelsea struck me as unlikely to bugger off without letting me know.

Something was afoot.

Five minutes later I vaulted off Harley in front of her apartment. Chelsea kept a spare key (and a very short list of those who could use it) with her landlady, an elderly retired hooker whose arthritis kept her at home. But inside Chelsea's second-floor apartment, I found no evidence of anything alarming.

Desperate for some clue to her whereabouts, I played the message before mine on her answering machine. "I've had to make a slight change to our plans, dear. I'll pick you up directly in front of the Red Lion on Jarvis at eight."

Distorted as it was by the machine's inferior speaker, the voice still retained the "Betty Boop-oop-a-doop" pitch that had grated my earholes to audio rind in Juice for Jesus. That — and the saccharine 'dear' — added up to Rosemary Miller.

So Chelsea could have had time to hook up with me for the nine o'clock feature. *What in hell could be so urgent about their meeting that she couldn't take a rain check? And, if not, why hadn't she told me about her change of plans?*

Jessye — the only possibility. Chelsea's single-minded search for Jessye. Maybe Miller had some information about Jessye's disappearance, maybe even a lead on her whereabouts. No less seductive a lure would send Chelsea haring off, mindless of all else.

My brain performed one of its rare leaps other people call 'intuition' and I call 'over-reaction.' *The Crazed Crusader — what if she's more than a harmless fanatic?* More than a religious nut who can recite long stretches of Scripture easier than the phone number for Pizza Pizza? Maybe the pressure of losing her job — and contacts — had accelerated her sense of urgency about sweeping whores off the streets. *Had her mission mushroomed into full-blown mania?*

Shit. What was that beatitude Miller recited on parting from me at Juice for Jesus — the one I reckoned she'd made up on the spot? My stomach migrated to my mouth as the words came back to me: "Blessed is the woman who cleanseth the earth by visiting a scourge upon the whores." Double shit.

Why, from the thousands of prostitutes in Toronto, would Miller target Chelsea? Because she was successful, didn't do drugs, was articulate — because God wasn't punishing her? Maybe, but there had to be more. Maybe her Web site alerted Miller ...

well, to what? Chelsea's efforts to locate her missing friend wouldn't make Miller fearful of discovery ... unless she killed Jessye.

Recalling that Rosemary's business card supplied only her phone and fax numbers, I scrambled about for a phone directory. Nowhere in sight, of course. Net-savvy residents of small spaces consign it to the recycling bin. We can get the same information online.

I booted up Chelsea's tangerine iMac and double-clicked Netscape Navigator, which swiftly surfed cyberspace to *Canada411.sympatico.ca*. I entered Miller's name, city and province. Within seconds I had a phone number that matched the one on Chelsea's Caller ID, an address and postal code. I didn't recognize the street name: 13 Haskins. Next I pulled up the City of Toronto's official Web site for their interactive map and pin-pointed my route to the house.

So little time it takes to kill someone. Even if traffic were light and I raced Harley well over the speed limit, the trip to suburban East York would consume at least fifteen life-and-death minutes.

I contemplated sending Miller a quick fax: DISTURB ONE HAIR OF HER HEAD AND THE CRUCIFIXION WILL LOOK LIKE A MERCY KILLING. Pity I couldn't alert the freak that I was on to her.

Get a grip.

I had no crime to report — except being stood up.

Suddenly I felt very foolish. Maybe in the course of her work, Miller had come across some information about Jessye's disappearance and merely intended to pass it on to Chelsea.

Still, circumstances were making me very anxious. Cursing the gun control laws in which I devoutly believe, I settled on a retractable knife Chelsea had tossed on the hall table, and tucked the slender threat down my left sock. Better I should be toting an Uzi. Hell, a .44 Magnum would do in a pinch.

As Harley roared into readiness, my Swatch glowed 10:16. More than enough time for Miller to hook up with Chelsea, drive back to her house ... and murder her.

Get a grip, girl. Common sense has fallen prey to hyperactive imagination. Besides, Miller could have taken her anywhere. She was meeting Chelsea outside the Red Lion. Why not inside? Certainly Chelsea knew to meet flakes in public places. Chelsea didn't own a car. Far easier for Miller to entice her to the boonies. Miller may be a bona fide fanatic, but that didn't make her stupid. She was also a control freak, more likely to draw Chelsea into her private domain. There she could orchestrate their rendezvous with no fear of interruption.

My reasoning wouldn't win a game of Clue, but '13 Haskins Street' was all I had to go on.

Speeding across the city on this moon-dim, freezing winter night, I felt utterly isolated. The landscape blurred as I raced through the dark tunnel of my intent, hell-bent on reaching Miller before she could ... *what?* Bore Chelsea to death with her piety?

Cursing the black-iced roads and the chill air that stung the strip of flesh my helmet wasn't protecting, I turned east off the Don Valley Parkway at Lawrence.

Once I veered onto a grass shoulder brittle with frost. I gunned my crotch rocket into its lifetime performance. Manipulating these five hundred pounds of metal with the finesse of a snowboarder normally pitches me into bike-orgasm. Tonight, conscious of how easily a bike can flip out on slippery surfaces, I focused on arriving in one piece.

At Brimley I slowed to the speed limit as I entered a web

of suburban streets dark and quiet, fifties architecture not even winning World War II could excuse. Red brick bungalows on lots four times the size of mine. In a world where small identities counted, our dwellings would be as distinctive as our DNA. Not this drab enclave.

On Haskins, I braked Harley on a dime in front of number 13, overly-exuberant seasonal decoration distinguishing this modest box from its neighbours. A Nativity crèche extended across the lawn to the property lines. A life-size Mary and Joseph, wise men, shepherds and critters ... the usual cast attended the baby Jesus. Above, having been unable to rent the Star of Bethlehem, someone had strung icicle lights tighter than a chastity belt along the eaves.

As I ran past the set for "O Holy Night," only the Canadian Tire stars were brightly shining. From the front porch the house looked 'nobody-home' dark. The picture window was obscured by a Venetian blind. Through a small circular window beside the solid front door, I saw a large silver crucifix fixed to the hall wall. Next to it, in an alcove a statue of the Blessed Virgin was eerily illuminated by an electric votive candle.

I crossed the lawn in front of the shrubs and turned the corner, hoping for an entry point invisible to a nosy curtain-twitcher. Near the end of a narrow driveway, a grey Ford Escort sat in the carport.

Thinking the rear basement windows might afford a discreet entry, I checked out the backyard. A twelve-foot-high cedar hedge ensured complete privacy. A deep U-shaped perennial border, defeated by frost, in this tiny perfect Eden.

Shit. Both basement windows were barred and blacked-out. Is this normal in the suburbs? I examined the entry door off the carport. Thank God for cheap locks. I gently turned the handle, putting my VISA card to better use than it had seen in months.

Muttered imprecations interspersed with heavy breathing muffled my progress.

Three steps and I was in the kitchen. Neat as a pin, of course. I crept along the carpetted floor of the dining room by the Madonna's dim light.

In the living room a body was slumped, legs apart, on the sofa, weirdly illuminated by the TV screen.

"What in the name of the Lord are you doing here?" Rosemary Miller's eyes met mine as she grabbed something from the coffee table and shoved it behind her back

On the TV, two tarts in nun drag were hotly engaged in oral sex.

"Give it up, Rosemary — whatever you've got stashed behind your lewd little butt."

Reverently I received the video sleeve. *Convent Capers.*

Chapter 44

"I NEED THEM TO RELAX," Rosemary whimpered. "My work really stresses me out. Actually, I've lost my job."

How the pious are fallen. I gloated no further. "Your video library doesn't interest me, lady. All I care about is finding my friend. Chelsea Walker.

"You met her outside the Red Lion" — I consulted my Swatch — "three hours ago. Tell me precisely where she is — or I tell the world the good news about your Solitary Vices."

She looked scared, then genuinely puzzled. "I wasn't with Chelsea for more than ten minutes. I asked her to speak to a group of students I'm making a presentation to next week. She'd be the perfect person to warn them about the perils of prostitution, what with her experience and losing her friend, Jessye, to the streets."

"So why was your meeting so short?"

"I insisted she emphasize the importance of a Higher Power during her talk. Young people desperately need to hear that message — it's key to any recovery program. But she didn't seem to get it ..." Her perplexed voice trailed off.

"So she turned you down?"

My perverse penitent nodded. "She wasn't too polite about it either."

"Life is full of disappointments, Rosemary. Where was

she headed after your sermon?"

"She muttered something about going to a movie — headed south on Jarvis."

I flashed *Convent Capers* in her face. "How do I know you're telling the truth?"

"Because telling the truth is my way of being in the world."

Soon she'd be claiming ownership of the Way and the Life, too. But God help me, I believed her, and left.

Not a single player in her Nativity scene took any notice of my bellowed curse as I started Harley. Not Mary. Not Joseph. Neither shepherd nor wise guy. Not even a frigging camel.

Where the hell do I speed off to now? Nowhere. I pointed Harley back home. The notion that maybe something else had delayed Chelsea warmed my cockles. There she probably was, scarfing popcorn in the Royal, watching the final scene of *American Beauty*. Maybe I could catch her coming out.

I was two minutes from the cinema when my jacket pocket took to vibrating — a very odd sensation. I pulled to a swift stop and reached for my alien cell.

The voice was whispered — quavery but still recognizable. "I'm in the old Atkinson building at the lake. Help me. Don't say anything. Just get here."

Those discreet little neck hairs I forget about until they jump to attention put me on high alert. So busy was I scrolling my brain for 'old Atkinson building' I almost broke the connection before it dawned on me that Chelsea was deliberately keeping the line open.

The old Atkinson building got saved from the wrecker's ball by a citizens' group — it was, after all, the site of Toronto's first newspaper. It was currently being rented out as studio space to starving artists, while a developer waited for City Hall to approve a loft conversion. Cell phone clamped tightly to my left ear under my helmet, I steered Harley's nose south to the lake. That I reached the building in one piece is no small miracle.

"Ten more minutes and I'll be done, bitch."

I could hear the sound of running water. *Had he forced her down to the lake?*

Chelsea didn't respond. *Was she drugged or concussed?*

I bounded the steps to the entrance. My fingers did the flying through the names beside the mailboxes to the only one I recognized. Studio 403.

"Can I help you?"

Startled, I turned to face a young woman encased like me in black leather, her hair a rooster's scarlet comb.

"For sure. I'm invited to a party. But I just discovered that his place is on the fourth floor. I've got a thing about freight elevators — you know, too much like a cage."

"Honey, can I relate to that." She patted my arm. "I always take the stairs — end of the hall."

I'd end up at his front door. What was I going to do — knock politely? My only chance was to catch the perv off-guard. "Is there any other way up to Studio 403?" I giggled in my best imitation of coy. "I kind of want to surprise him."

She winked. "Ah, party of one, eh? I hear you, girl. Sure, go round — top of the highest fire escape. The purple door gets you 403."

It was a tight squeeze getting to the fire escape past the blue Chevy Astro. From ground level the studio looked dark. Clinging to the iron railing for support, I slipped twice on the ice-glazed steps. The purple door was locked, but an ancient pane of glass in the tall rectangular window alongside it bore a promising crack. What I could see of the huge room looked deserted. Gloves on, cautiously I pushed the glass to the left of the crack far enough inward to secure the shard closest to the door between pinched fingers. It came away from the frame with very little pressure. I slipped my arm in and turned the door handle from the inside.

Either I had broken into the wrong studio or Chelsea's assailant had fled.

Then in the gloom I realized there was a room at the far end, partitioned off from the large space in which I stood, trembling.

I crept across the creaking oak planks. Ear to the door, I distinguished two sounds: a loud whirring and running water. *Saint Dympna, spare me Hannibal Lector.*

Softly turning the handle, I opened the door — and saw red. The safelight illumination revealed a classic darkroom layout. Dry bench with enlarger and easel, timer and guillotine on my left. Facing it across a five-foot aisle, wet bench with three near-full developing trays, sink with running water and print washer on top, chemical storage rack below. An old ventilator fan noisily laboured to extract the fumes.

One item not usually requisite to photography lay crumpled and bound against the rear wall. In the eerie red light I couldn't tell if Chelsea was conscious — or even alive. His back to me, a tall man placed a print in the dryer on the shelf above his prey.

But then Chelsea struggled weakly against her bonds — just enough commotion to distract the tall man for the moment it took me to grab the skull-and-crossboned plastic bottle behind the second developing tray.

This better be acetic acid.

I had the cap unscrewed as the tall man suddenly turned — and lunged.

Full in Andrew Miller's face I splashed the contents.

Howling a rapid passage three steps to the sink, he turned a flexible rubber hose onto his blistering face and hand.

Calculating maybe a ten-second window in which to release Chelsea, I switched on the overhead light, retrieved the knife I'd taken from her hall table, and slashed through the duct tape with which he'd trussed her tighter than Martha Stewart's Christmas turkey.

Her dilated pupils seemed to widen as Miller grabbed me from behind in a bear hug and thrust me against the dry bench. His right hand, its skin peeled back in one crispy curl, raised the blade of the guillotine. With the left he forced my fingers under its path.

His hard penis pressed into my butt as I glimpsed four bits of me topple off the edge of the cutting board.

Chapter 45

AS A NURSE CAREFULLY PEELED back the heavy bandages to check the plastic surgeon's handiwork, I averted my face. If my fingertips were turning black, necrosis was setting in. They'd have to be amputated for good.

Shortly after I'd been brought into Emergency, Dr. Newman had spent six hours performing four digital replants. It was Tuesday morning, almost twenty-eight hours post-op. The first forty-eight hours are crucial, he'd said. Even if the replantations were successful, I could be left with insensate, possibly non-functional fingers. Over the next year I might need revisionary surgery. He warned me about long-term problems with cold intolerance and joint stiffness. For months I could expect troublesome nightmares and flashbacks.

He refused to give me a prognosis. "You have a few things working in your favour, though. The paramedics got to you quickly, and I started work shortly after you arrived here. It was a sharp cut, the joints were intact. Your chances are quite good."

Since my severed digits had been remarried to their better halves, a doctor or nurse periodically checked my fingers' colour by eye and used a temperature monitor to measure blood circulation.

"Wonderful," this nurse finally remarked. "They're still a

nice healthy pink." I ventured a quick peek. For the first time in my life, pink looked good on me.

A few minutes later the phone rang, as I gave up trying to answer the question of the moment: *Who most needs the rejoined part(s) — me, my fingertips or Quasimodo, his penis?*

"Who is it?" I snapped. Hospitals make me cranky.

A baritone I remembered from a recent unfortunate conversation replied, "It's Frank Underhill, Jane. Are you feeling well enough to talk?"

Underhill? Underhill? Oh, that Underhill. What was I about to be threatened or charged with now? My imagination reached for a can of Smithwick's. I felt like Job at the end of a challenging day.

In my experience, cops have real issues around gratitude.

"Yes, I'm OK. Sorry for barking, Chief. I thought you were God."

He chuckled. "A breakthrough. I should tell you that Ernie wanted to make this call, but I pulled rank on him. Are you really feeling OK?"

"Yes, but the sadists who run this prison won't spring me."

"Well, I've got some news that might speed up your recovery. We have a full confession from Andrew Miller — and enough other evidence to build a powerful case against him. The body count currently stands at five ... and counting. But it may never go to court, despite him bleating all his crimes. Right now he's under psychiatric evaluation at the Clarke Institute."

I grimaced. "Surely if he's sane enough to teach school he's sane enough to stand trial ... or maybe not."

"Probably his only real hope is an insanity defence, but Miller refuses to allow his lawyer to go there. He figures he can persuade a jury of manslaughter, at most — because his killings were provoked and justified."

"Tell me he can't stage-manage his own sentencing."

"I stopped betting on case outcomes a long time ago." He paused. "To return to the reason for my call: as you recall, there was a reward for — "

Good grief, Charlie Brown. ONE HUNDRED THOUSAND DOLLARS. I took a celebratory chug of my imaginary beer.

"Of course, we can't release your cheque until the court determines the disposition of the case, but — "

Of course, I hadn't really earned the money. I tracked down Andrew Miller, only because Chelsea was clever enough to call me on her cell. I'd figured Rosemary Miller for the villain. Tina Paglia's murder turned out to be an unrelated, isolated incident. But what the hell? Why shouldn't I get a prize for lucky stumbling?

"Chief Underhill, thank you very much. But just knowing that beast is out of circulation is reward enough." Please don't take me at my word.

"My pleasure. You've made the force look better than we deserve. I'll send Ernie over to the hospital to do an informal debriefing. When you're well enough to come to the station, you can make a full statement."

"No problem. Tomorrow morning's good for me."

"Will do. I'll have him phone to confirm. And thanks again, Jane. "

What issues about gratitude?

Before the painkillers tugged me back into oblivion, I made a few phone calls. Decorum decreed that Etta be the first recipient of my good news. I had a dim memory of my mother hovering over me as I was wheeled into surgery, two rivulets of her purple mascara running onto my smock.

"Always knew you was a real tough one, Jane. Hell, you've survived me."

I knew she was crying at the end of the line. "Mom, I'm fine. Honest. My fingers are pinker than your favourite wig. I'll be out of here in no time. Actually, I'm better than fine — I'm rich." I told her about the reward.

"That comes to twenty-five grand a finger. I wouldn't say you was overpaid. Never mind, I'm gonna put on a big shindig at the bar to celebrate you still being alive. But it'll have to be after I get back from the cruise."

Mom was surprising Eddy, her 'Hoochie Coochie' man, with a trip to Florida over Christmas. Her travel agent was offering a special deal on casino ships. They just sail out of their home port each morning and afternoon. The gambling begins when they drop anchor outside the offshore boundary. But Etta says that's dandy — all she wants to do is play roulette and have sex with Eddy. 'Doing it' on board is as good as a waterbed, she claims.

"In the meantime, there's a song by Alabama featuring 'N Sync I want you to listen to real good." She held the phone against a CD speaker so I could enjoy "God Must Have Spent A Little More Time On You." That's the closest my mother will ever come to saying she loves me. It will do just fine.

"You should do something nice for yourself with that money, dear."

"I've always wanted one of those '50s fridges they retool to dispense draft beer."

"Take it from me — first a makeover, then a matchmaker."

My second call assured me that Max was thriving in Silver's custody. Knowing she couldn't visit me in hospital, I hadn't expected to see her. For months during her mother's slow death, she'd almost lived in intensive care. Avoided hospitals since then.

"If Max really gets to missing me, sit him down in front

of *Wheel of Fortune*. He's got a thing for Vanna White."

"So do I."

When I told her about the reward, she instantly devised a plan more seductive than Etta's. "Put out a contract on the premier after you get an agreement from the Arts Council to pay you ten percent of their cutbacks since he's been in office. And hire a Canadian."

My friend is a true patriot.

Late the following morning, Sandy Reeder unexpectedly dropped by to thank me on behalf of every sex worker in the city for bringing Andrew Miller's career to a halt. Before leaving she tucked six cans of Guinness under the bed.

I ordered in racks of ribs, home fries and onion rings from my local, Fast Eddy's. Normally they don't deliver to hospitals, but Eddy was overjoyed to make this exception. Apparently the neighbourhood grapevine was buzzing with misinformation about my recent exploits. That was nice — my initiation into the fraternity of the 'hood.

Ernie ate like he'd been on cabbage soup for a month while I rehashed what happened between my arrival at Rosemary's house and my departure from her husband's studio ninety long minutes later. Actually, I had to leave out the last bit. I remember nothing after the guillotine.

"It's a fucking miracle you two got out alive. I felt like I was sitting across from Jeffrey Dahmer in the interrogation room," Ernie remarked, liberating the last rib of its remaining strand of flesh. "Miller honestly believes he was called by God to exterminate the plague of whores infesting our streets."

"Don't talk to me about miracles and repentance. I'm a sick woman."

He quaffed his Guinness. "Miller's family background

fits the classic mould. His father was a vicious drunk who brought whores home. Screwed them in front of young Andrew and beat his wife when she complained. Andrew buried himself in his books and escaped to university on a scholarship. Marriage to Rosemary seems to have sent his rage and self-loathing underground. He worked overtime to become the perfect teacher and husband.

"Then something cracked his carefully manufactured respectability. Turns out Miller had a daughter, Susan, by his high-school sweetheart. Rosemary never knew the girl existed and was too self-absorbed to know why her husband was so supportive of her work with PROS."

"No doubt about her being self-absorbed — but to the extent that she remained in the dark about so much?" Hard to believe.

"Seems so. Maybe we'll get the bigger picture when … if she gets off the psych ward. Woman's a basket case, what with losing her job and then learning about her husband's real motivation for being such a New Age sensitive spouse."

"I never thought I'd feel sorry for her."

"Anyway, few years ago, Susan's mother died — ovarian cancer. The kid went bad, hit the streets, OD'd. Her death triggered Miller's ancient rage."

"C'mon, Ernie. Seriously dysfunctional households are common as fleas. Serial lust killers aren't."

He shrugged his overdeveloped shoulders.

"One thing's been really puzzling me. Most sex workers have really good street smarts. How did he con those five women into going off with him?"

"Easy. He cruised for his victims in a guise familiar to a lot of the street pros — as an outreach driver for PROS. Whenever one of the regulars phoned in sick, there was good old Andrew.

At the end of a shift he'd drop off the other volunteers, drive the van around the stroll for another hour or so, or check out the bus depot or train station. He lured them into the van with the promise of a drink and a pebble of crack."

"But it couldn't take the women long before realizing their mistake. Hell, two or three hookers get attacked every night in Toronto. Most know how to put up one helluva fight."

"Miller chose his prey very carefully. All the women he killed were junkies who worked the low-end strolls. So they weren't in any shape to defend themselves. In the van, he offered them a drink laced with Rohypnol — the 'date rape' drug. In no time they'd be stupefied. Twenty minutes later they'd lose consciousness."

"How does a middle-class man get his hands on a supply of roofies?"

"Over the Internet — from a supplier in Paris. Soon they'll be auctioning heroin on eBay."

I had to ask. "Ernie, was Daphne Murphy one of the victims?"

"We haven't released any names yet — still verifying identities and notifying family members." He paused, presumably to remind himself that I could be trusted to keep my mouth shut. "But I will be visiting a woman named Sally Murphy."

So will I visit to offer my condolences. Her sole hope, that her daughter's body be found, would be cold comfort. "Might you also be contacting the family of a missing woman named Jessye Brant in the very near future?"

He immediately looked like a cop again. "Did Miller boast to you about his kills?"

I looked down at my hand, which Ernie had avoided

since his arrival. "Funny, isn't it? I lose part of my hand to a guy I've only ever exchanged pleasantries with. We never spoke a word in that darkroom."

Suddenly Ernie slammed down his beer can so hard it crumpled. "We should bring back the death penalty for freaks like Miller. He should be fucking crucified on live TV."

I scowled.

"Think about it, for Christ's sake! That bastard stalked, abducted, terrorized and raped at least five young women. Then strangled them and dumped them wherever it was convenient. Sentencing is bullshit. I mean, Karla-fucking-Homolka will be buying her groceries at a store near you in a couple of years."

I couldn't blame him. Cops get to witness what the rest of us only read — or write — about. Silently, I hooked up with Dympna on the topic of justice:

Admirable St. Dympna, how just you were to all whom you encountered, and how careful you were to give every person his due, and more than he might desire or expect. By your power with God please come to assist us to be just to all we meet.

P.S. Except Andrew Miller. Wreak even more vengeance on the bastard than is his due. Amen.

Chapter 46

JOHN ARMSTRONG, a senior editor at *The Toronto Post*, phoned me bedside to offer me a five-part series detailing my investigation. Part five would be my experience in Miller's darkroom chamber of horrors. I unequivocally declined before he got his spiel out and suggested that he commission Sam Brewer to write the series, with me serving as ghost consultant. After all, I'd be called upon as a key witness. He accepted with alacrity.

I immediately phoned Sam, who lunged like a starving pike at my proposal. 'Retirement' fit him as badly as his clothes.

Hammer Hopkins slunk in for two minutes to thank me for nailing the dickhead what wasted Tina. He reached inside his nylon ski jacket to extract a bouquet of crushed irises, probably freshly liberated from the corner variety store. I almost said something about getting a life that wouldn't keep boomeranging him back into jail. But I can't imagine Hammer cheerily attending to backed-up toilets or mouse infestations. He's hooked on his edgy ways. Like me.

As soon as I get sprung, Max and I will take a slow walk through Trinity Bellwoods Park. Close to the site once occupied by Repeat's cardboard home, I'll tie a crystal to the branch of that huge oak tree.

A certain slant of light ...

I kept fretting more about Chelsea than the outcome of my surgery, and was relieved when she showed her face at my hospital room.

It began awkwardly — me, reluctant to relive that horrible night, Chelsea's characteristic ebullience muted by grief for Jessye.

Still, I needed to know what had happened post-guillotine.

"Not much. While he was busy hurting you I rallied enough to grab one mother of a wrench from under the sink — knocked him into the middle of next week. Dialled 911 before I fainted."

"What you're telling me in your low-keyed way is that you saved my life."

She smiled gently. "Call it two birds with one wrench — I did it for Jessye, too. If I hadn't fainted, he'd be dead. You know why he was delaying raping and killing me? So I could watch him develop the roll of film he took of Jessye."

After a long silence, she handed me a gift-wrapped box long enough for long-stemmed roses.

"Before I open this — how did Miller get you into the van? I thought he was working the patrol with three other volunteers."

"Apparently Rosemary mentioned she was going to meet me outside the Red Lion. He phoned Sandy at PROS to tell her that the van had broken down so she cancelled the patrol. Then he must have pulled it in close to the Red Lion and followed me after I left his stupid wife. When he offered me a lift I was trying to hail a cab at Carlton to get to the show. He said he had a few minutes to kill before he picked up the volunteers. I didn't think twice about getting in — hell, I must have bumped into him a dozen times on the stroll or at PROS. He seemed like such a nice guy. Totally normal."

"Like Ted Bundy — clean-cut, attractive and charming. Young women meeting him for the first time would climb right into the car. Jekyll and Hyde."

Her eyes strayed to my hand. "We were just chatting away about the bad weather, he predicted a white Christmas ... then he turned up St. George. Said the traffic would be a lot lighter along Harbord. He asked me to check the floor for his glove. When I bent over, he whacked me on the back of my neck. Next thing I remember, I was being dragged up the fire escape."

Enough of Mr. Hyde. I opened her present.

Inside nestled a pool cue. Not just any old cue, but a two-piece Brunswick with a leather grip.

"I did think of roses, but this seemed more appropriate. It's a gesture of faith in your fingertips."

"Hey, even if they fall off I'll have the steadiest bridge hand in town." My brave smile quickly dissolved into tears. A brutal wind sploshed polluted sleet against the window pane. Tina's corpse in my garden, Repeat's body in the park, Andrew Miller.

Chelsea sat beside me on the bed. Her lips softly brushed the back of my cue hand. "I'm right here."